Finding Redemption
Guardian Security Book Five

by

Desiree Holt

Finding Redemption

Contact Information: info@thewildrosepress.com

Cover Art by *Diana Loftin*

The Wild Rose Press, Inc.
PO Box 708
Adams Basin, NY 14410-0708

Visit us at www.thewilderroses.com

Publishing History
First Scarlet Rose Edition, 2019
Print ISBN 978-1-5092-2595-8
Digital ISBN 978-1-5092-2596-5

Published in the United States of America

Dedication

To Bill, the real Ethan Caine,
and all the Bills who work in the shadows

Dear Readers,

This book is a milestone for me. I published my first book with The Wild Rose Press in 2011. Getting that first book out there was scary indeed, but with each book it has gotten so much easier. Many grateful thanks to publisher Rhonda Penders for taking a chance on me, for giving me great editors, and for always giving me incredible support. Huge thanks to my dream editor in Diana Carlile. She gets me! And she has taught me so many things, like the perils of frontloading a backstory. This is a very happy marriage that will last forever.

Writing a book is a labor of love for me. My characters take over my life, and I work to make them come alive for all of you. But I could not do it without the help of key people in my life. First and foremost, my wonderful beta reader, Margie Hager, who has a super critical eye and finds all my mistakes. Then there is my incredible son, Steven Horwitz, who despite running a successful business of his own, manages the financial side of mine and is also a marketing guru. And last but way far from least, my wonderful Virtual Assistant, Maria Connor, who takes care of everything so I can devote myself to writing. I am truly blessed.

Thanks to my son, Steven, for suggesting I write a book about his friend, Bill, who has now left us and is watching over us from above. He made this story come alive and will always hold a special place in my heart.

And finally, to my readers, without whom there'd be no Desiree Holt. You enrich my life and inspire me.

I can be reached at authordesireeholt@gmail.com, and I invite you to join my reader group, where there's always something happening.

Looking forward to "seeing" you there.
Desiree

Prologue

Of course it was raining. How fitting that the weather should be miserable.

Lisa Taylor Mallory shifted on the folding chair provided by the cemetery, careful not to move out from under the umbrella held by the funeral home attendant. Next to her, four-year-old Jamie snuggled closer to her, needing the assurance of his mother's warmth.

Under his own umbrella, Pastor Howard Devol of Mangrove Baptist Church intoned passages from the Bible. He had already eulogized Charles Mallory to the point of sainthood. Lisa clenched her fists and swallowed the nausea that insisted on rising at the back of her throat as she listened to the words.

If you only knew. Just let this be over. Please, please, let us get this over with.

She let her gaze travel over the crowd of mourners. The abundance of black umbrellas nearly formed a canopy over the assemblage. Tampa society's A List as well as the giants of the financial world were gathered in their best funeral attire to mourn a man whose sins had been swept away in fire at the foot of a mountain.

"Keeping up the myth," Josh Taylor had told his sister.

This is for Jamie.

He was so frightened by the circus surrounding the death of his father. Lisa wanted him to have closure on what had become an outrageous situation. Despite the devil's trap her marriage had become, Charles Mallory had always been good to his son. So much so that Lisa had lived in constant fear Charles would one day disappear with him and leave her behind.

Sitting on her other side, Josh squeezed her arm, a signal that this farce would soon be over and everything would be okay. Not exactly the word she'd have chosen to describe the current state of her life. She clenched one gloved hand in her lap. No, okay wasn't even in the ball park.

At last, the interminable ceremony ended. Josh rose and nudged her to stand with Jamie. The pastor signaled her to come forward. With her brother's arm supporting her, she stepped over to the casket and took the white rose the pastor held out. She stared at the casket for a long moment, then dropped the rose on its mahogany surface.

In a voice so low only her brother heard it, she said, "Rot in hell, you son of a bitch."

Chapter One

Four years later

The day was typical February—gray, windy, the sky filled with thudding clouds, the cold insinuating itself into the house. Perfect, for the way she felt.

The air in the room was thick with the same tension that had wrapped itself around her and her brother, Josh, for months. Today was Jamie's birthday, and she was about to lose it altogether. She'd spent the morning hugging her favorite picture of him and crying until her throat was raw and she was sick to her stomach. She had barely survived a destructive marriage and the scandal that followed her husband's murder. After four devastating years, she'd finally gotten her life and her son's back on track. Now, it was all going to hell again. She wanted to scream, a combination of fear and frustation sitting like a lead ball in the pit of her stomach.

At the moment, she was pacing back and forth in her living room, hugging herself to ward off the chill that even the fire blazing in the hearth couldn't chase away. Even the warm peach and blue of the comfortable living room couldn't dispel the air of gloom hanging in the air.

Josh had just delivered the news that Guardian Security, in its search for Jamie, had come up empty. She was already teetering on the edge of nervous collapse, and the suggestion she'd made didn't help her state of mind.

"Please ask him again," she begged. "I thought Ethan Caine was such a good friend of yours. Best friends," she stressed.

"We are." Josh nodded. "He is."

"Then why did he turn you down when you asked him to find Jamie?"

The terror of Jamie's kidnapping three months ago, the shooting at the ransom drop, and not a word about Jamie since then had every nerve on her body on edge. She knew she was a mess. She'd lost weight, and it didn't help that Josh kept telling her it was something she could ill afford. When she looked at herself in the mirror, her skin was so pale it was almost translucent. Dark shadows under haunted eyes, like purple bruises, were a testament to her lack of sleep.

With the passing of each week and no news about her son, her degree of desperation rose. As first, the F.B.I. and then Guardian Security had come up empty-handed, and her defenses crumbled. Sometimes she could even smell the fear that clung to her. How much longer would it be until she snapped altogether?

Josh's voice broke into her thoughts. "I know this is a tough day for you, but you're making yourself sick. Come sit down. Please. Let's talk about this."

She stopped pacing, her too-thin body vibrating with unexploded rage. "I'm already sick, Josh, and have been since the day they took my baby. And the man you asked to help find him, the man you say is the best in the business, who is supposed to be your friend, flat out said no. What kind of friend is that?"

"I told you. He's in a terrible place right now. His

last op was such a disaster he walked away from everything, carrying a load of guilt that doesn't belong to him." Josh's jaw tightened. "I was really pushing it to go to him, but I thought…"

"That your friendship was stronger than it is?"

Josh shook his head. "That he could pull himself out of that dark place to help us. I apparently misjudged."

When Jamie was taken, Josh reached out to Ethan right away. The man was back in town, having left whatever he had been doing for the previous several months, but had locked himself away from the world in his house. Josh had been upset when Ethan turned down the request, but he just made excuses for him. His next call was to Guardian and the agency had jumped right on it but with no results. Now, Josh was planning to try Ethan again, and Lisa was terrified the man would refuse this time, also.

"Do you think he's better now?" Lisa twisted her hands together. "That he'll listen? Maybe I should go with you. I might—"

Josh shook his head. "No. I'm going to call in the big guns to help me. To make him see he's the right man—the only man—for this job."

"Tell me again why you think that." She tried to tamp down the desperation in her voice.

"Ethan Caine is a former Marine and veteran of Guardian Security, so expert at what he does that the government pulled him away from Guardian and tapped him to lead an off-the-books black ops group. He can reach out to people no one else can even get near. Dig into corners closed off to everyone else. No one else has the contacts or the dark skills he does. This time,

I'm not walking away until I make him see that."

She stood at the window, seeing nothing, thoughts tumbling around in her mind. The unusual friendship between the gruff warrior and the middle class icon still baffled her. On the surface, they had nothing in common. She wasn't even sure how they'd come together in the Marines—Ethan a noncommissioned officer, Josh a lieutenant. Still, somehow, an instant friendship had been forged, the kind people seldom found—solid and secure. When Josh finished his tour with the Marines and returned home, he had changed in subtle ways. He was tougher, harder, not the nerdy techie she'd grown up with. His muscles now had muscles, and he was a topnotch marksman, two things that still shocked her.

Both men left the Marines at the same time, Josh to come home to a job with a software company and Ethan to Guardian Security, whose roster of agents included former Special Forces—SEALs, Delta Force, Force Recon Marines.

The fact that Josh and Ethan lived in the Tampa area had been one more string tying them together, along with the fact they'd both lost their parents. Ethan's had left him a house out in the boonies, a place where he could disappear when he needed to. Josh would hang out with him there, sometimes persuading the man to catch a football game or go fishing. He even spent time on target practice with Ethan. Target practice! She still had trouble visualizing Josh as someone who had that kind of skillset.

But the friendship persevered. When Josh wanted to leave TechnoSoftware to open his own company, Ethan bankrolled the entire venture. With cash. Lisa still wondered what the source was of all that cash. He had also been the conduit for Josh's subsequent connection to Guardian. When the agency's computer system needed an overhaul, he recommended Josh who had delivered in spades. Now he and the Guardian partners had also become good friends.

Then, without warning, Ethan left the agency and disappeared off the radar. All Josh would tell her was the man had been tapped by the government to become part of some secret operation for years—the blackest of black ops—and even that much she wasn't supposed to know.

Until one day, he just came home and locked himself away in his house.

Lisa had never cared for him personally. He might be a man who served his country well, but the few of times she'd been in his company, she found herself turned off by his rough personality, the sloppy appearance he had adopted and his apparent lack of courtesy.

"You said you're calling in help to convince him. Are you talking about Guardian?"

Josh nodded. "They're really upset they failed in their attempt, and usually there isn't anything they can't handle. They're really pissed that they couldn't find a trace of Jamie or a clue as to who took him. But they said from the beginning I should get Ethan. They were stunned he turned me down. I called Nick this morning. He and Reno are flying out here to see him with me, hoping maybe that would help."

She raked her fingers through her hair, as if she could push the whole thing away. "When will they get here?"

Josh looked at his watch. "In about two hours. They'll call when they land, and we'll arrange to meet up."

Her lip trembled. "Do you think maybe Jamie really is dead?"

"Don't go there," Josh said. "He's not dead. Hang onto that."

Lisa was almost afraid to verbalize the other thought rolling around in her brain. "What if Ethan's not any good anymore? What if whatever sent him into hiding destroyed all his skills? If he's such a mess, would he even be able to function in such a situation that was likely to bring back bad memories?"

"He's been dealing with a situation," Josh told her in a quiet voice, "but he's still the best in the business."

"Maybe we shouldn't ask him at all. Maybe this is a mistake and he's just a big phony." Her stomach knotted at the thought that her last chance might be a big fake. "Who was he working for when he disappeared, anyway? The CIA? Or was it the NSA? Or maybe the DEA. Maybe he quit Guardian to become a mercenary. God! Maybe he was in prison and that other is just a story he concocted. Maybe he's even on drugs. Maybe that's the problem, and we're lucky he turned us down. Although where would we go next?"

"Stop it." Josh's voice was sharp. "That's absurd. None of that is the truth." He grabbed her hands and squeezed them. "We need him and his particular skill set."

"I know. I'm sorry. Right now I'd deal with the devil if it got Jamie back." She swallowed a hysterical giggle. "And I guess that's what we're trying to do."

"If you want to look at it that way, fine. Just

remember. We said from the beginning there's something weird about this whole kidnapping thing. You've heard nothing since the ransom was paid and no one's been able to find even the smallest trace of him."

"I know." Tears threatened again, but she took a deep breath to steady herself. "That's what I don't understand. And I refuse to believe he'd dead. I just can't, Josh. I can't."

"I think he's alive, too, kiddo. I'm pretty sure that's why they tried to kill you so you wouldn't be able to look for him. I'm not going to let up until Ethan accepts that, no matter his state of mind."

"Good. That's good. I just wish he was…" She threw up her hands in a helpless gesture.

"Was what? Like other people? If he was, he wouldn't be able to do the things he does." Josh gave her a hard stare. "And maybe that's what's needed in this situation. The fact that he isn't like everyone else is what makes him so valuable. He goes places and knows things no one else does." He sighed.

She swallowed and scrubbed her hands over her face, shoulders slumped in defeat.

"I hate him for turning us down before, but I want my son back more than I want to breathe. So yes. Please. Go to him and beg him. And I'm glad Nick and Reno are willing to help with this." She paused. "What if he's not sober? You said you worried he's been living in a bottle since he got home." She blinked as an unwanted thought stabbed her brain. "What if he got drunk on his last assignment and botched the whole thing? Maybe that's why he can't handle what happened."

Jamie might be alive, and Ethan Caine might do

something stupid that would get her son killed.

"I said maybe. Anyway, I'll never believe that. He always preached that whiskey and work didn't mix. He's wrestling with a lot of demons right now, but that doesn't mean he can't do the job. If you believe anything I tell you, believe that. Please."

She looked at the framed picture of Jamie she was still holding, and tears trickled down her cheeks. "Okay."

Josh pulled her into his arms, picture and all. She tried to let his belief in his friend reassure her.

"Whoever took our boy is way out of the mainstream or we wouldn't be having this conversation. Ethan is exactly the kind of person we need to look into this, and I won't stop until I make him understand that."

Lisa grabbed a tissue from the box that had taken up residence on the little side table and blew her nose. "Damn Charles, anyway. I know this has something to do with him."

Josh's mouth thinned at the mention of his late brother-in-law. "I know, kiddo."

Charles Mallory.

Lisa blew her nose again and cursed the day she'd ever met the man. Ten years ago, Aaron Burke, senior partner in one of Tampa's top law firms, where she was an up and coming associate, introduced her to his new client. The man with the financial golden touch and blinding good looks zeroed in on her like a long-range sniper and hit the mark.

Have lunch with me, Lisa. I've seldom met a woman with your mind.

Let's go to dinner, Lisa. In Paris. The plane is waiting.

Come to the Keys with me. I'll teach you to scuba dive.

God, Lisa, I never thought I'd meet a woman with your passion. Being inside you is like sliding into a flame.

I want you in my life, Lisa.

Marry me, and I'll give you the moon.

She'd been so uncharacteristically besotted with him she walked away from a growing reputation as a hotshot corporate lawyer to become a wife and mother because that's what Charles wanted her to do.

Plenty of time to practice law again later on, he told her.

Later on. She never knew exactly what that meant, and while she tried to figure it out, the nightmare began. Hell would have been a relief. Even Josh hadn't been able to help her.

"Let me get you out of this," Josh had begged over and over, whenever she was able to see him.

"I can't leave," she cried. "He'll take Jamie away from me. He swore it. Josh, he has the money and power to do it."

And then, like a cross-eyed blessing, Charles was killed. Was it any wonder she rejoiced at his death?

"Lisa." Josh's voice cut into her thoughts. "Are you listening to me?"

She shook herself out of her dark reverie. "What? What did you say?"

"I said, 'I wish the papers hadn't made such a big deal out of the ten million dollar life insurance policy. Or that it was left in trust for Jamie's welfare.' Coverage like that gives every nutcase ideas."

"When the policy surfaced, the police were just so

11

damn sure I'd killed Charles for the money," she reminded him. "If Aaron Burke hadn't produced the change of beneficiary form I'd still be sitting in jail."

"Burke." Josh said his name like it was a bad word. "It frosts my ass that Charles made him the trustee and not you." He made a rude noise. "That old bastard. I never trusted him, and I still don't."

Lisa stared at the pictures of her son again. "At least he turned over the money for the ransom without arguing." She fought back the tears that were ready to spill again. "And now someone's got both Jamie and the money."

She pulled in a deep, shuddering breath. She had to get hold of herself. Falling apart wasn't helping anything.

Josh put his hands on her shoulders and squeezed gently, his lifelong sign of reassurance. "We'll get him back, I promise."

"How will I pay him? Jamie and I…" She stopped and swallowed, fighting for control "I get along okay, you know that, but what if he wants some enormous fee? And you can't keep paying the freight. I could always sell the house, and—"

"Stop it. Would I balk at anything if it might get Jamie back?" he asked in a soft voice. "Anyway, he doesn't need the money. That's something he's got in abundance. And he won't take it any more than Guardian did. We're friends, Lisa. All of us. That counts for more than money. The minute Nick and Reno get here, we'll be on the job."

"So what will the three of you do? Go to Ethan's house and just walk in on him?"

"Maybe. We'll strategize and figure out the best

approach."

Her heart pinched at the thought of what might be happening to her son while they were doing this. Or might have already happened. She balled her hands into fists to control the rising tide of anguish.

"Can I ask you one more thing? About Ethan? Just so I can try to understand where he's coming from?"

Josh laughed. "Sure, but if you do, you'll be the first person who does. He really does have his reasons for, as you say, hiding out in the farmhouse."

"Like what?" she demanded. "You have to tell me, because I'm still struggling with the fact he turned you down before."

"Okay. I guess there's nothing for it but to tell you what I can, but don't jump to any conclusions." Josh shoved his hands into his pockets and stared off toward the window, although the look in his eyes was far away. "Ethan's last op went bad—very bad—because someone lied and someone else leaked details of their mission. They were betrayed, and innocent people were killed, as well as everyone on Ethan's team except him and one other person. It about destroyed him. He still blames himself. He walked away and has been hiding away ever since."

"An op went bad?" Her eyes widened. "And this is the man we think is our last best hope?"

"Did you hear me say it wasn't his fault? It won't happen this time. I promise you that. The people who betrayed him are not involved."

She chewed her bottom lip, a nervous habit she'd developed since she'd been shot. "You're right about one thing. If he gets Jamie back, that's all that counts."

"I'll hold you to that."

****

The ringing of the phone pierced Ethan's brain like a heated arrow. He pulled a pillow over his head and tried to bury himself under it. When the ringing stopped, he removed the pillow, but the abrasive sound began again almost at once.

"Damn it!" This time, he struck out with his hand at the offending instrument on the floor beside him, sending it skittering away from the bed. The ringing stopped, but then, in a second, it began again.

He depressed the Answer button. "Go away," he shouted at it. "I don't live here anymore."

"Ethan? Get your ass off what passes for your bed and pick up the phone."

The voice penetrated the blurry state of Caine's mind, and he blinked. He picked up the phone and held it to his ear, rubbing his eyes. "Reno?"

"Yeah, old man. It's me. Are you deaf?"

"If only." Caine rubbed his hand over his face, grimacing as he felt the tangling in his beard. When the hell had it gotten so long?

"Get up. We need to talk to you."

"Jesus, Reno. I look and smell like something the dog left on the porch, I don't even know what day it is, and you want to talk? And who the hell is we? You got a crowd out there?"

"Yeah. Ethan, this is serious." The teasing note left Reno's voice. "Your friend—" he stressed the word— "needs your help, and I can't believe you turned him down."

Caine lay back down on the mattress. He'd never gotten around to buying an actual bed for himself once he'd moved back into this shell of a house, and by now, he'd decided he didn't need one.

"I told him, I'm out of the business. Any business."

"God damn it, Ethan." There was no humor in Reno's voice now. "Get your head out of your ass. Nick and I just flew into Tampa, and we all need to meet with you. How about opening your front door? I'd ring the bell, but it might be booby-trapped."

"We all? What do you mean by all? You mean you and Nick? You're here? At my house?" Ethan rolled to his feet and went to look out the front window. Sure enough, there was a fucking car in his driveway. Shit, shit, shit.

"Go away," he growled.

"And Josh is with us. We're not leaving until you open the door."

Fuck, fuck, fuck.

He might as well give up and give in, because he knew none of the men out there would. He unlocked the front door then went to the kitchen to fix coffee.

"Got some of that for us?" Reno had come up behind him.

"Help yourselves. Cups are in the cupboard."

When they all had their coffee, they carried it out to the front porch, a much less depressing place to sit and talk.

"Okay," he told them, "make your pitch. But you might as well accept the fact that I've lost it. I'm not worth shit to anyone anymore. Last time…"

"I know what happened last time," Nick told him. "The blame isn't yours, and I wish you'd get that through your fucking stupid brain. It's not on you."

"This is really important, Ethan." Reno's voice was all business, something Ethan caught right away. "I mean damn important. I wouldn't ask you otherwise." Another pause, then, "Please."

Please? Reno never said please. It was always all business. When Ethan had worked combined missions with Guardian, the man gave the orders and the agents carried them out.

He groaned and looked at Reno, then Nick. "This must be damn important to get both of you here."

"It is," Nick agreed. "We're here to make sure you help the best friend you've ever had." There wasn't even a touch of humor in his voice.

Ethan turned his gaze to Josh. "And this must be some fucking bad trouble your sister is in."

"I told you. Her son's been kidnapped. The ransom was paid, but it's three months later and Jamie hasn't been returned."

He didn't want to tell them the first time around he'd hardly paid attention. He sipped his coffee. Was this Fate's way of telling him he had a chance to redeem himself? What if he failed? This was Josh he was talking about, his best friend in the entire world. Did he still have the balls to do it? Only one way to find out he supposed. This was his acid test.

"I want her to ask me."

"What?"

Josh stared at him. "You want what? Who?"

"I want your sister to ask me herself. If I'm going to put my ass on the line again—and I said if—I want to know who I'm really dealing with."

"You're dealing with me," Josh told him, then pointed to Reno and Nick. "Us. All of us."

"Is it your kid? No. I want a face-to-face with the kid's mother."

Josh started to say something, but Reno held up a hand.

"Fine. We'll set it up. Lunch tomorrow. The Club."

"The Club?" He ran his tongue over his teeth, wondering when he'd last brushed them. "Damn, Reno, I'm in no shape to go anywhere right now, let alone a fancy restaurant."

"Well, we're not bringing her out here," Nick told him. "We'll do anything but that, although she'd probably do it if we asked. She'll do anything to get her son back."

"The Club. Jesus Christ and all the angels." He sighed. "Okay, okay."

These three men had been good friends to him, over and above any business arrangement. They hadn't said no when he'd reached out to them for help. When one mission had nearly gone tits up, Reno and Nick had provided the additional support he needed. He, at least, owed them an hour for lunch. Not that he had anything else to do.

"Noon tomorrow," Reno said. "We'll make the arrangements."

Ethan stood on the porch and watched them get in the car and drive away. So Josh's nephew had been kidnapped. Whatever it was, he'd bet it had something to do with the asshole piece of shit his sister had married.

Hell. He hated situations like this. If he didn't like Josh so much, think of him as better than family, he wouldn't even be doing this. The few times he'd been around Lisa Mallory, she acted as if he wasn't even fit to wipe her shoes on. At least Reno and Nick would be there to run interference.

He stood up and looked around. He wasn't excited about lunch at The Club but better than bringing her here. The dilapidated state of the rambling farmhouse that had been in his mother's family for generations suited him just fine, but it wasn't meant for company.

The property matched both his physical condition and his state of mind. He cleaned—in a manner of speaking—only when he was in the mood. The weeds and native grasses growing wild in the ten acres that remained of the family property were constant reminders of the untended state of his life. And the nightmares that never seemed to go away. A state he'd become comfortable with.

In the bathroom, he stripped off the sweat pants he'd slept in, then turned on the shower full force. While the water heated, he stared at the face in the mirror over the sink and wondered who the hell he was anymore. He'd seen things that made Hell look like Heaven, and done things that robbed better men than he was of their sanity. His body was covered with the scars from his many battles. How he'd survived was still a mystery.

He thought again about that last op, the one that had turned to eighteen kinds of shit. It didn't matter how many people told him it wasn't his fault. He was still the one who'd been there with the dead and dying.

Sighing heavily, he stepped into the shower, wishing the hot water could wash away the blackness in his soul.

Chapter Two

The Club wasn't actually a private club but a restaurant designed to look like one. Located in the high rent district of South Tampa, it catered to the quietly elite and generational wealthy. High-backed booths, many small rooms rather than one large one, thick carpeting, dim lighting even in the middle of the day. The owners catered to people who came to have privacy with their meals.

"He won't show." Lisa huddled in the center of the large, curved booth, twisting her hands in front of her and wondering when she'd stopped being strong and started falling apart. Well, that was easy to answer. Exactly three months and three days ago.

"Yes, he will." Josh reached across the table and put his hand over hers.

"When Ethan says he'll do something," Reno added, "he always does it. Even if it's just lunch. Besides, if he changed his mind, he'd call. He wouldn't leave us hanging. Not after I told him how important this was. We've been through too much together."

"Reno's right," Josh told her. "Drink your wine and calm down. Please. We talked about this. Remember?"

"Yes, yes, yes. Don't worry. I'll do anything if it will get Jamie back." She blew out a breath. "And if he hasn't lost it all."

Nick Vanetta leaned forward. "I know Josh has told you this, probably more than once, but when Ethan was at the top of his game, there was no one in the world better. I don't think he's lost his edge. He's just been fighting demons. A mission like this is just what he needs."

Lisa took a deep breath, held it, and slowly let it out. "Okay. All right." She obediently picked up her wine goblet and sipped at the amber liquid.

Josh looked up. "See? Here he is now."

Lisa looked at the man the waiter was ushering to their booth. At once her body tensed, and she remembered a scene from a couple of years ago, when he threw a birthday party for Josh at Ruth's Chris Steak House. Only Ethan Caine would walk into an ultra-classy, very high-end restaurant in sweat pants, a dress shirt, and Nikes. With his money stuck in the waistband of his pants. And here he was again. Were they crazy for asking him this favor?

"I'm glad to see he dressed up for us. Which homeless shelter kicked him out?"

He had on a pair of sweat pants, worn Adidas gym shoes with no socks, and a T-shirt that hadn't seen the inside of a washer in at least a couple of weeks. She wondered if he had special privilege to violate the dress code for The Club.

"Cool it," Josh warned. He moved over in the booth to make room for Caine and held out his hand. "Thanks for coming, buddy."

"Sure. Can't turn down a free meal, right?" He slid in next to Josh and turned his eyes to Lisa. "Or the chance to hear what your sister has to say."

She didn't offer a hand to shake and neither did he

.They just nodded at each other.

This was the first time she'd sat in such an intimate situation with him, just a table's width away, and she took a moment to study him. She knew he was thirty-eight, but he looked at least ten years older. His thick black hair was peppered with gray and worn long enough that he tied it back with a leather thong. His beard looked more like the result of not shaving rather than a deliberate plan, and dissolution had added extra flesh around the jaw line and pouches under his eyes. His skin was an unhealthy, ruddy color, probably from the amount of alcohol she heard he drank with regularity. Although he carried a few extra pounds, she still remembered seeing him lean and mean.

And then a thought seared its way through her, shocking her. If this was, as the fairy tales said, once upon a time—before Charles had killed any interest she had in men and before Ethan Caine had destroyed himself—she could see herself being drawn to him. With a supreme effort, she suppressed the unexpected, unwanted spark of attraction for this ruined hulk of a man. She'd pull herself together and beg him for his help. Anything for Jamie.

But then she looked in his eyes and her breath froze at what she saw. Although they were alert, simultaneously studying everyone at the table and his surroundings, they were a bottomless black filled with so much pain it hurt to see them. That blown assignment must have been more than a disaster. More than anyone knew or realized. It was obvious he still carried the burden of so many deaths on his shoulders. Could she still trust him to find her son?

"Lisa?"

She shook herself at the sound of Josh's voice and pasted what had to be a grotesque mockery of a smile on her face. "I apologize. My mind tends to wander these days. Thank you very much for coming, Mr. Caine."

"Ethan. Don't thank me yet." His voice was deep but not smooth, more like the scraping sound of gravel falling on cement. "Right now we're just having lunch."

"That's true." She nodded, folding her hands in her lap and willing them to stop their incessant tremors.

"Before we get to the task," Reno said, "we just want everyone here to know that Guardian will be the backup on this. We'll provide anything needed, any kind of support." He looked at Josh. "But it's off the books. No money's changing hands on this, and we don't want a paper trail for the wrong eyes to see."

"Not that we don't trust our people," Nick added. "But when you hear the details, you'll understand why."

"Hey, wait a minute." Josh looked at each of the two partners in turn. "We can pay the freight on this."

Reno shook his head. "Remember when we had that glitch with our server that could have put us out of business and created big trouble for our clients? You spent three days of your own time fixing it and refused to send us a bill."

"And when Lindsey needed boutique software for drawing her plans," Nick added, "you barely charged us a thing for it."

"Right." Reno agreed. "So now it's our turn. End of discussion."

Josh started to say something, but then just nodded.

"So." Ethan cleared his throat. "Why don't we

order and then, Mrs. Mallory, you can tell me how you think I can help you."

Reno signaled the waiter who was hovering a discreet distance away. The men ordered the lunch steaks, Lisa ordered a salad, which she knew she wouldn't eat, and Caine added a double Jack Daniel's on the rocks along with a glass of iced tea. Lisa couldn't help the way her mouth twisted in distaste.

"Should I disapprove of the wine you're drinking, Mrs. Mallory?" His scorn for her was evident. "Don't worry. It would take a lot more than this to put me under the table. Anyway, a little hair of the dog that bit you helps the brain function better."

"If you say so."

When the waiter brought their orders, Caine immediately dug into his food.

Lisa frowned. "Shall we wait until you're finished before we discuss why we're here?"

"I can eat, talk, and listen at the same time," Caine told her, already chewing. "So let's have it. What's got you in such a bind you're willing to break bread with someone like me?" He looked at the two Guardian Security partners. "And drag these guys into it all the way from Texas."

"That was my idea," Josh told him. "In case you needed help convincing you to do this."

"Fine." He looked at Lisa again. "So convince me."

Lisa had been listening to the back and forth, doing her best to curb her impatience. Now she set her fork down on the table with precise care.

Be nice. You need this man.

"I'm in a desperate situation, Mr. Caine. Nick and Reno give you high marks, and my brother has a lot of faith in what he thinks you can do."

His piercing stare cut right into her. "Then why don't you give me the details and we'll see if everyone's belief is misplaced or not?"

"Here's the deal," Reno began.

Ethan held up his hand. "Are you the one with the problem? No? I didn't think so. Like I said yesterday, I want to hear it from the lady herself."

Lisa glared at him.

She wanted to pick up this steak knife and stick it in his throat. Instead, she took a long swallow of her wine, then put the glass down carefully. Remember Jamie. "I'm sure you're aware of everything that's happened in the past year. I'm referring to my husband's death and the subsequent scandal. The media had a field day."

"I know his little empire crumbled, he was in hock to his eyeballs, and somebody offed him. The cops tried to pin it on you, but they didn't have any evidence."

"That's because I didn't do it." Her tone was fierce, anger scraping her throat. "You can believe me on that."

"Hey." He waved his fork. "You say you didn't do it? Okay. Personally, I don't care one way or the other. I will say you had more than one damn good reason."

Not the ringing endorsement she'd hoped for, but better than a condemnation. "He left me in an incredible financial mess. I ended up selling everything, including my jewelry."

Caine drained his glass of iced tea and waved to the waiter for a refill. "Sorry about that."

She slapped a palm on the table, wishing instead she could slap the arrogant man across from her instead.

"I'm not asking for sympathy. The damned jewelry meant nothing to me. I'm just trying to give you some background."

He shrugged, drank half the glass of tea, and kept on eating. "Whatever."

Lisa cast an angry glance at Josh, then plunged ahead. "I had to rebuild a life for my son and myself. I was a practicing attorney when I met Charles. Corporate law. After the…well, afterward, I went back to work, but now I handle only family law. I have a small practice with two other people." She looked away. "Although I haven't been there much the last three months."

Caine sopped up the last of his steak sauce with a piece of French bread, then downed the rest of his Jack Daniel's. He raised an eyebrow at Josh, who motioned to the waiter. "Can we get to the main course here? I'm not much on appetizers."

Lisa curled her hands into fists to keep from actually striking him. Why didn't one of these men put Caine in his place? Or maybe this was his place, and she'd better get used to it.

"I need to do this in my own way if you don't mind."

Those soulless black eyes looked at her as if they could see into the very heart of her. "Whatever."

"Go on, Lisa." Nick gave her an encouraging smile.

"My son is my life, Mr. Caine." She was determined to keep things formal. "I live and breathe for him." When Caine opened his mouth, she surged on, "And I think I've had enough of your smart remarks." She took a careful swallow of her wine. "Three months ago Jamie was kidnapped. We paid the ransom, but we never got him back."

Caine picked up the fresh drink placed in front of him and looked at Lisa over the rim as he sipped from it. "Yeah, I guess all that coverage about the insurance money would be bait for anyone."

Josh leaned forward. "The ten million went into a trust to be used for Jamie's health and well-being."

Caine nodded. "Ransom would definitely fall into that category. So what happened? Did the Feds get into it?"

"Yes," Josh told him. "They coordinated everything."

"Even the drop?" The answering sudden silence spoke louder than words. "Okay, give."

Lisa sat up, her spine rigid, her hands so tightly wrapped around the stem of her wine glass she was afraid she'd shatter it. "The kidnappers told me to make the drop myself. No FBI, no cops, no anyone. Or I wouldn't get Jamie back."

"And of course you believed them."

"He's my son," she almost shouted. "I wasn't about to risk his life."

"Okay." Josh looked from his sister to Nick, then Reno and finally Ethan. "Let's everyone take a deep breath here and go on."

Caine took another drink of his whiskey, ignoring everyone but Lisa. "So what happened?"

"The FBI wanted to put people in place ahead of time and have a look-alike make the drop."

He watched her, expressionless, his eyes hooded. "And what did you do, Mrs. Mallory?"

"I'll tell you," Josh broke in. "She sneaked out of

the house and went to the drop site herself. They shot her, took the money, and we haven't seen Jamie since."

"Shot?" Caine raised his eyebrows. "Since when do kidnappers shoot the mark?"

"Exactly." Josh nodded. "We've talked about this, and there's something out of whack here."

Caine looked at Lisa. "Okay. Go on."

"Whoever took Jamie has disappeared off the face of the earth with him. The Feds tried to find him, we hired Guardian, the works, but no one can find a trace anywhere. And you know how easy it is to hide an eight-year-old boy in plain sight. He could be anywhere."

"That's why we asked Nick and Reno to get involved," Josh added, "and help us set up this meeting with you. Especially since you turned me down the first time. Besides, I wanted them to tell you that Guardian has already tried and failed. Only the kind of skills you have are going to work here. We're all convinced of it."

Lisa finished her wine and began shredding the tiny cocktail napkin. "We're... I'm asking you if you'll help us. Wait. No, not asking. Begging."

"Help you? Do what?" He drained his glass of iced tea.

Lisa watched him in amazement, a strange thought crossing her mind. She'd never met anyone who could drink such copious amounts of fluid and never have to go to the bathroom. And who mixed Jack Daniel's and iced tea?

"Next question," he went on. "Why all of a sudden today? I know what you think of me, Mrs. Mallory, so I'm damn sure you didn't wake up with my name on your lips this morning. And if you want my help, you might try cutting back on the sarcasm."

"She's just on edge," Josh cut in. "As you can well imagine. We've let the Feds have their shot and Guardian put their best men on it. But none of those men is you. That's it, plain and simple."

Ethan Caine barked a laugh. "That's a pretty sad state of affairs."

"I'm the one who suggested asking you again," Josh told him. "Today is Jamie's eighth birthday, and I think we've wasted enough time. You're the only person I know who can reach out to people we've never even heard of and ask questions. Nick and Reno agree."

"I'm asking you." Lisa looked across the table at him. "Please help me get my son back." Her throat tightened and her eyes burned. She clenched her fists in her lap. She would not cry. She would be strong for Jamie.

"So." He put his glass down. "You want me to step back into the muck and slime I'm still trying to wash away for a kid that's probably already dead?"

Lisa crushed the stem of her wine glass so hard it snapped, slicing into her skin.

"God, Lisa. Here. Give me your hand." Josh pulled out his handkerchief and wrapped it around her palm.

She stared at Ethan, then at Josh, her eyes burning with unshed tears, her heart racing with pain and anguish. How dare this man say such things?

"I told you all this was a waste of time. Let's get out of here." She started to slide out of the booth, the unwanted tears sliding down her cheeks. She had no idea where to turn next, but she'd find someone, somehow.

Ethan reached over and grabbed her arm. "Don't

you even want to hear my answer?"

"I think you've already given it," she snapped. "Josh, let's go."

"I want to hear what Ethan has to say."

"Then say it and be done." She cradled her injured hand in her other palm.

Ethan finished the last of his drink. "You and I are far from friends, Mrs. Mallory, but I know Josh. I trust him, and I owe him a lot. I was too wrapped up in my own pain the first time he asked me and never realized how strange the situation was. I'm sorry for that, although at that time, I'm sure I would have said no regardless."

Lisa looked at Josh, her eyebrows raised.

He shrugged but said nothing.

"So here's the deal," Caine continued. "This afternoon Josh is gonna come out to my house—a place, by the way, I'm sure you'd never set foot in—and we're gonna talk about this. I'll give him my answer. Reno, if Guardian will be providing all the backup on this, even though this is not exactly official, you or Nick should come with him."

"I'll be the one," Nick told him. "Everything at the agency will go through me."

"Fine." Ethan reached under his T-shirt to the waistband of his sweat pants, drew out a wad of cash as thick as his wrist, and dropped a handful of bills on the table. "Lunch is on me. See you in a little while, guys."

Lisa stared after him, the pain in her hand nearly forgotten in her shock at the abrupt termination of the conversation.

"That man is a pig," she told her brother.

Before Josh could answer, Nick Vanetta leaned

forward. "Lisa. Ethan Caine is what he is. He's also the only man who can help you. If this was my problem? He's the one person I'd want on it."

Reno nodded his agreement.

Lisa dropped the bloody napkin on the table, satisfied her hand had stopped bleeding. "If in fact he decides to grace us with his assistance."

"He didn't say no," Josh reminded her. "With Ethan that means we're halfway there."

Chapter Three

Caine parked his car in a garage that was in almost the same neglected condition as the rest of the property and trudged into the house. Tossing his keys on the kitchen table, he opened the refrigerator, pulled out a Coors, and drank half of it in two long swallows.

Fuck.

Lunch had been painful for a number of reasons. The most important was the resurgence in his mind of the images that constantly plagued him, the nightmares that made him drink to be able to sleep. And the weight of the guilt he carried despite the fact none of what happened had been his fault. Or so people told him.

But he knew better. His mantra was trust no one, and he'd been foolish enough to believe the people who held the future of the mission in their hands were honest, dedicated, patriotic people. What a load of shit that turned out to be. He'd gladly open the doors and let them out of prison if it brought back to life the good people and the innocent people who had died because of their greed and treachery.

He should have told Reno to bag it this morning and gone back to sleep, even if the man had flown all the way out from San Antonio. One look at Lisa Taylor Mallory and he knew he was about to do something that he'd hate himself for. The lady pissed him off with her mine-doesn't-stink attitude, but a long time had passed since he'd seen agony like that in someone's eyes.

How about yours, asshole?

Altogether, she looked like hell. The shadows under her eyes were a good indication of how little sleep she'd been getting. Her body looked like she'd been starved to death yet she ate almost nothing of her lunch. She twisted her fingers together constantly, a gesture of someone whose nerves were raw to the point of bleeding.

Damn Joshua anyway. And Reno and Nick. Ethan's one weak spot—his only weak spot—was his friends. He had very few, deliberately, but the ones he had he prized. He would do anything for them, and those three knew that. Reno and Nick had given him a home at Guardian when he desperately needed a direction for his weird collection of skills. Of course, he'd delivered on all his assignments, because that's who he was. Josh had been there for him when it all went to hell and he just wanted to crawl into a black hole.

Still…

Carrying the half-empty bottle of beer with him into his bedroom, he toed off his Adidas, pulled the wad of money from his waistband, and threw it on the dresser, then went to a battered roll-top desk in the corner of the room. Besides his car, there were two pieces of machinery Ethan kept in perfect shape—his high definition plasma television and his computer.

His computer was his contact with the world at large—how he communicated and how he read extensively about whatever spiked his curiosity on a given day. On nights when he couldn't sleep, it amused him to surf the web and see if he could find traces of people in his old line of work. The fact that he couldn't was reassuring. It meant that no one could find him, either.

Today he was using it to fill in the blanks.

Hitching his chair closer to the desk, he closed his eyes for a moment and, with an effort of will, banished the terrible images that haunted him. Being able to shut everything out and focus had always been one of his greatest skills. Today, he pulled it front and center. He took a long pull on the beer, set the bottle down, and typed 'Lisa Taylor Mallory' into the Google search box. He was only somewhat startled to discover there were more than a thousand sites that were in some way related to her. She had, after all, had more than her fifteen minutes of fame. Methodically, he began to scroll through them one at a time. At the end of an hour, he sat back, trying to wash away the distaste that had formed in his mouth with the last of the now lukewarm beer.

He had a pretty clear picture of Charles Mallory, and it turned his stomach. And of Lisa, a stunningly brilliant young attorney, unaware of the animal living behind Mallory's façade until it was too late.

He knew from Josh what his sister's life was like after her marriage. She'd been a virtual prisoner at the huge estate where they lived, guarded by men only a step above thugs, while the golden boy stayed away from home more and more. His absences became extended, his behavior at home increasingly erratic, and the velvet noose pulled even tighter.

No, she couldn't return to work. She was a wife and mother. No, she didn't need her own car. Carlos would drive her wherever she wanted to go. No, she didn't need outside activities. He provided everything she needed at the estate.

Mallory's obsession with her, his psychotic jealousy, his growing unpredictable behavior had worried Josh a lot, but he'd been powerless to do anything about it.

And when Charles Mallory's car went over an embankment, instead of finally being set free, Lisa was plunged into a greater nightmare. His death had opened a can of worms that turned into snakes.

The media covered almost every second of the widow's life from the minute her husband's car rolled down a mountainside. They hadn't even left her in peace as she struggled to get past the nightmare and create some kind of life for herself and Jamie.

Eventually, though, with no more tidbits to fan the flame, the media gave up and the stories ended. Lisa disappeared from the newspapers altogether.

Until the kidnapping.

He was well aware that every form of media—television, Internet, newspapers—had run the story, the reporters almost gleefully reporting on the further misfortunes of the tarnished widow. He'd hardly been able to avoid hearing or reading about it. It sickened Ethan that they would treat the kidnapping of a child this way. Jamie Mallory's face looked out at him from the computer screen, a typical eight-year-old, with curly hair and huge eyes.

He stopped reading there, preferring to hear any other details from Josh.

He was in the kitchen opening his second beer when he heard tires crunching on the gravel in front of the house, then footsteps on the porch.

"Ethan? It's Josh and Nick."

"Come on in. It's open."

The two men scanned the disheveled appearance of the room.

Josh shook his head. "I see the maid didn't make it in again."

"Since when did my living conditions become a matter of interest to you?" Ethan opened the door to the fridge again. "Beer?"

"None for me," Nick told him.

Josh shook his head. "Jesus, Ethan, I don't know how you aren't permanently pickled."

"If you two are through commenting on my lifestyle, let's go sit on the porch. We can talk there without my interior decorating bothering you."

Josh shook his head and followed the two men outside. They lowered themselves into three of the ancient rockers lined up. Caine took a swallow of his beer and looked at the two of them.

"Okay, who's giving me the details?"

"Josh is." Nick inclined his head. "I'm just here because, like I said earlier, this will be as invisible as we can make it but still run through me at the Guardian offices. Whatever you need, we'll supply."

"So." Ethan nodded at Josh. "You haven't had any word about or sign of the kid in three months?"

Josh shook his head. "Nada. Lisa's about to lose her mind. Jamie and I are all she has."

"Tell me about your sister." Caine began rocking slowly. "How did she end up with a piece of slime like Mallory in the first place?"

"Not a new story." Josh studied his hands. "She was the bright light at Rivas, Burke, and Doyle.

Youngest ever to be fast-tracked for partnership. She ate opposing counsel for breakfast."

"And?" Ethan prodded when Josh stopped.

"And one day Aaron Burke brought in his hot new client, the wizard of the financial world."

"Charles Mallory." He couldn't disguise the contempt in his voice.

"He had Lisa squarely in his sights. She looked to be unattainable, and Mallory always wanted what he didn't think he could get."

Caine raised an eyebrow. "Yeah, but what did Lisa see in him?"

"Come on, Ethan. She was twenty-eight years old." He flung out his hands in a gesture of frustration. "For all her unbelievable knowledge of the law, she'd spent most of her life buried in it and was far less sophisticated than people thought. Charles offered her the moon and happily ever after, and she bought it."

"It must have come as quite a shock to her when the Feds swooped in and she found out where his money came from."

"No kidding. Shock is a mild term. The mess Charles left threatened to strangle her, especially when she was arrested for his murder."

"Ugly picture. She's got guts to come through all of this." Ethan finished his beer. "Want a Coke?"

Josh chuckled. "I didn't think anything nonalcoholic was allowed here."

"I keep it for my clean-cut friends like you. Nick? One for you?"

"Sure. I'll take one."

"Be right back."

In the kitchen, Ethan leaned against the refrigerator

door, the Coke in one hand and another beer in the other. He could feel himself being sucked into the whole Lisa situation, and it fried his ass to realize it. Shit, shit, shit.

He walked back out to the porch, still cursing silently. "Okay." He handed out the Cokes. "What happened after the trial that never was?"

Josh popped the top on his can and took a swallow before answering. "The financial mess was like quicksand. Lisa was being hounded by everyone except Santa Claus." He rotated the can in his hands. "Shortly before the accident, Charles mortgaged the estate to the hilt and got a fat bundle of cash out of it."

Ethan frowned. "What the hell did he do that for? He couldn't have needed the bucks. Not with the money flowing from his drug empire."

Josh shrugged. "Charles was a middle man for the cartels. The only things the Feds and I could figure out is he spent money he owed and needed some quick cash to get them off his back. He sure didn't stint when it came to his lifestyle."

"Too bad he didn't do himself in before that. What happened to the property?"

"The IRS appropriated it to satisfy the tax debt."

"And all the other creditors? I can't believe they just said so sad, too bad, have a nice life."

Josh twisted his lips into an evil grin. "The only good thing Charles did was make sure everything was in his name alone. Even the bank accounts. Lisa couldn't be touched because she wasn't personally liable for most of the stuff. She packed her suitcases and Jamie's and walked away clean."

"If she was left with nothing, how did she take care

of herself and the kid?" Ethan shook his head. "She managed to buy a place to live in, or did you front that for her?"

"I'm a lot less trusting than Lisa." Josh took a swallow of the cold soda. "Before she married Mallory, I talked her into putting all her investments and cash into a joint account with me. An account Charles couldn't touch. Just as protection." He shook his head. "She gave me a hard time about it but finally did it. That and the sale of her jewelry gave her enough to support herself and Jamie and buy a small house for the two of them."

Caine rocked for a long time, letting his mind absorb the information. "How did the snatch happen?"

Josh unfolded himself from the rocker and leaned against the porch railing, staring ahead at the unkempt landscape. "Jamie and Lisa were having lunch at Monkeyshines, near the Lowry Park Zoo. It's one of Jamie's favorite places. He went to the men's room and never came back."

Not a new story. "She didn't go with him?"

"He was almost eight years old, for Christ sake. Old enough to pee by himself."

"Apparently not." He watched Josh's nervous pacing. "How did they get him away without him yelling for her, anyway?"

Josh twirled his drink slowly in his hand. "The restrooms are in a short hallway you can't see from the tables. There's an exit door at the end of the hall. We figured someone was waiting, got him alone, gave him something to knock him out, and whipped him out the door."

"I checked the place out," Nick said. "It's very

easy for a snatch and grab."

"Rough." Ethan studied his beer. "And Aaron Burke gave her no trouble about the money?"

"Nope. Just handed it over."

Ethan drained the last of his beer. "So what happened when she made the drop?"

Josh gave him chapter and verse—Lisa leaving the duffel with the cash at the drop site late at night, going on her own because she believed they would kill Jamie if she didn't. And how, as she walked away, she was shot with a long-range rifle. The bullet hit a rib and splintered.

Josh blew out a slow breath. "It was touch and go for a while. I don't know how she survived."

"Why kill her if she left the money?" Ethan frowned. "Something's not right there."

Nick agreed. "Unless killing her was part of the original plan." He shook his head. "Otherwise, it just doesn't make much sense."

Josh nodded. "I know. I keep coming back to the same thing. But that doesn't make sense, either." He stopped speaking, his face tight with emotion, and ran his fingers through his hair in a gesture of frustration. "How does an eight-year-old boy get taken and just disappear off the face of the earth?"

"We tried all the child-selling schemes," Nick added. "The cults, live auctions, you name it. Not a smell."

Ethan said nothing and silence draped itself around them. He could visualize the payoff, the mother fearing for her son, desperate to believe he'd be returned. Walking away, even though consumed by fear and anguish. The rifle shot.

A long time ago, when he could still feel things and when his emotions weren't locked in a subterranean vault, a woman like Lisa Mallory would have captured his heart and soul, but he no longer had either. Yet, in spite of all that, a knife-like stab of pain pierced him. He wondered if he was diving into the deep end of a pool here, one that he'd never be able to swim out of.

Josh began to pace again, sliding glances at Ethan from the corner of his eye.

"Damn it, sit down, will you?" Ethan snapped. Jesus. Would they just let him absorb all of this? "I can't think with you dancing around in front of me."

Josh dropped into the empty rocker, nervously rotating the Coke can with his fingers.

Ethan stared straight ahead, letting his mind sort through what he'd learned about Lisa Mallory on the web and piece it together with what Josh told him. And again, seeing the utter pain and fear on her face. If nothing had turned up in three months, there was a wrinkle here no one had found yet. That being so, his experience told him the Taylor family had bigger trouble than they thought.

Shit, hell, and damnation.

Could he really go down that road again? What if things got fucked up again? What if—

He slammed the door on those thoughts, leaned back in the rocker, and stretched his legs out to rest his feet on the porch railing. "We don't even have a starting point here. And I'm way out of touch these days."

Ethan looked over at Nick, sitting quietly, watching him process everything the way he used to. Then at Josh, whose face was carefully expressionless, although his eyes were filled with an emotion Ethan wished he could ignore.

"Ethan, I—" his friend began.

"If it was anyone but you," Ethan said, cutting him off, "I wouldn't even be listening to this story. You know that. Let me think this through, and then I'll want to talk to your sister again."

Josh just studied him for a long moment. Ethan met his stare unblinking, hoping he'd managed to mask the pain that was never far away, that thoughts of a new mission kicked to the surface. Then he stood up.

"All right. When can I expect to hear from you?"

"Soon. Now get out of here, both of you. I have stuff to do."

Ethan watched them climb into Nick's car and disappear down the long driveway. Then he turned and went back into the house, stripping off his clothes as he went. The beer and whiskey were great and dulled a lot of open sores, but right now, he needed his head as clear as possible. If he found a smell of this kid and thought he could go after him, alcohol was the last thing he'd need.

He didn't want to think about what might be ahead of him. Didn't want to picture what he'd face if he let his friendship with Josh push him into this. No matter how he'd distanced himself from things in the past, how hard he worked to bury horrific images in his mind, they were always there, hovering like birds of death. Cries of pain, screams of agony, scenes of unbelievable cruelty.

And the memories of treachery, especially that last op. They were all still nightmares that lived in his head. He'd sworn never to go back to that life. He struggled daily for peace, trying not to release his tenuous hold on it. But giving it up might offer the only path to finding Jamie Mallory.

And then, of course, there was Lisa. A complicated woman on the verge of a nervous breakdown, and who could blame her? The few contacts he'd had with her, despite her habit of looking down her nose at him, always left an impression of great intelligence and banked fires. Again, he was struck by the thought that before he'd let life destroy him, Lisa Mallory was a woman he could easily have been attracted to. More than attracted.

He made a noise of disgust. Forget that. Bad news. Her life was ruined as much as his was. Why the hell had she ever married that shithead Mallory anyway?

He stood under the hot shower until the water ran cold, then let the icy drops beat on him. At last, he stepped out and toweled himself off. Wearing the towel wrapped around his hips, he padded to the kitchen and put on a pot of coffee. While it was brewing, he dug through his desk for a small ragged notebook. He foresaw a long night ahead of him.

But first, he sat down at the kitchen table, rested his head on his forearms, and did something he hadn't allowed himself to do since the big shitstorm had all but destroyed him.

He cried.

****

Lisa paced as she waited for Josh, something she'd become quite good at. The time had crawled since he dropped her off, moving slower than honey dripping off a basting brush. She checked every clock in the house and even called the number for the correct time to make sure they were all set right.

Every day was gray since Jamie had been taken. Even when the sun was out, like today, she felt its warmth everywhere except on her. She practically hugged the aura of depression to herself, as if happiness and sunshine were forbidden until she got Jamie back.

Asshole! Asshole! Asshole!

In eight years, her gutter vocabulary in reference to Charles had increased exponentially. She found herself using words she hadn't even known existed before. The only regret she had about his death was she hadn't had the pleasure of killing him herself. When the awful truth about Charles was laid bare—drug use, orgies, gambling—only Jamie's need for her kept her centered. Now it was her need to find him that drove her.

Her hand throbbed, and she pressed it against her side. Josh had bandaged it before he left, telling her she didn't need stitches, but reminding her to keep antibiotic ointment on it.

She still had the picture in her mind, frozen like a snapshot, of Jamie the last time she saw him. His blue eyes were bright with the anticipation of their visit to the zoo, his cheeks flushed with excitement. He'd barely been able to eat his hot dog or drink the Coke Float he loved.

"I have to go to the bathroom, Mommy," he'd told her, sliding from the booth.

He'd hurried off in his jeans and Tampa Bay Buccaneers T-shirt, waving as he rushed off to the hallway where the restrooms were. She didn't dare tell Josh how many times she'd gone back to Monkeyshines, sitting at the table right by the hallway, staring at the men's room door as if willing her son to reappear. Her brother already thought she was losing her mind, and he probably wasn't far from wrong.

Seeking something to distract her and ignoring the pain in her hand, she dusted every photo of Jamie displayed in the living room, rearranging them, then returning them to their original places. But that was no diversion. All it did was enhance the misery that gripped her since the day her son disappeared.

Charles, what have you brought down on us now? If you weren't already dead, I'd kill you myself.

A dozen times, she hurried to the window, sure she heard a car in the driveway.

The image of Ethan Caine still danced in her brain—arrogant, hard, a ruined survivor. Yet, as much as she hated to admit it, there was an electricity about him that penetrated her shell. God, she was really losing her mind if she was fantasizing about that man. Talk about desperation.

By the time Josh pulled into the driveway, she was ready to jump out of her skin. She was on him the minute he walked into the house, grabbing his arm with a grip like a steel claw, almost shaking him.

"What did he say? Tell me right now."

"Hey, hey, hey. Come on, Lisa, take a breath." He took her hand and led her to the couch, making her sit down. Then he dropped into the chair opposite her.

"He said no, didn't he? I knew it." She twisted her hands together to still their shaking. "God, he is the most unpleasant man I've met in a long time. I can't imagine how you're friends with him."

Josh leaned forward, taking her hands in his. "Stop. Focus. Listen to me. He didn't say no."

"He didn't?" She was almost afraid to hope.

"No. He did what Ethan always does. He asked a lot of questions and processed everything through his mind. Then he said he'd call later. But Lisa? This is just his way. I know he'll do it."

"Really?" She grabbed her hands away from him. "And exactly how do you know that?" She rubbed her forehead. "God, we're crazy to depend on a man who's let himself go to rot the way Ethan Caine has."

"Lisa—"

"This is Jamie we're talking about. How do you even know what that crazy man will do?" She sat forward, hands clasped tightly together, her heart clattering against her ribs, and drew in a shuddering breath. "So what exactly did he say?"

"I told you. He said he'd call me, but I think—" Josh began.

"He'll call you?" Her voice rose in pitch. "He'll call you? Josh, we're running out of time. Doesn't he know how desperate I am?"

Josh gave a short laugh. "I'm sure he knows you wouldn't ask for his help otherwise."

"So how long are we supposed to wait for him?" Her head began to throb, a signal that the headache she'd been fighting all day was about to kick in. She forced herself to take deep, slow breaths to ease the tension that constantly gripped her.

Relax, Lisa. Breathe.

"I know you're close to the edge, honey, and I promise you, Ethan knows it, too. He won't take forever to get back to us. But he won't agree to do it unless he thinks he has a chance of success. Right now I'm willing to bet he's doing some quiet digging around to see if his contacts are still active."

Lisa hugged herself again, sure she'd be cold for the rest of her life. "How do you know everything about his black ops career is even true? You keep telling me that's stuff you can't talk about, so maybe it's not even real. Maybe the whole thing is a big fat lie to make himself out to be some mysterious character. Whip up his ego."

Josh held up a hand. "His career with Guardian is no lie. Let me tell you a little story. One night, a few months after he left Guardian, he was home for a couple of weeks, called me out of the blue, and we got together for dinner. We were sitting there having a drink and he got a call on his cell phone. He said very little other than yes, okay, and I got it. After he hung up, he asked me to drive him to a parking lot at an abandoned factory."

In spite of herself, Lisa was curious. "So did you?"

"Yup. As soon as we got there, the biggest, blackest helicopter I've ever seen touched down, the door slid open, some guy all in black shook Ethan's hand, and then they were gone. It sure didn't come from Rent-A-Copter."

"But—"

He held up his hand to stop her again. "He knows plenty of people you wouldn't invite to your house, but whatever he did before it all came crashing down, honed him into the perfect person for this. I know he drinks like a fish, but he holds his liquor. He does not use drugs of any kind except an occasional aspirin, despite the rumors. And, as he is fond of saying, the statute of limitations has run out on anything he may have ever done." He gave her a faint smile. "At least in this country."

Lisa couldn't quite see Ethan Caine as the dark hero Josh painted, but she was at the point where she'd join forces with the devil himself if it would get Jamie back.

"Damn it, Josh. I know I sound like a broken record, but it would help a lot if we just had some idea who would do this, and why we haven't heard anything." Her voice shook with repressed fear, and she gnawed on a fingernail.

"Lisa," he began.

A tear carved a track on one cheek. "I don't believe he's dead, Josh. I just know I'd feel it if he were."

"Honey, we have to be prepared for anything. You know that." He pushed himself out of the chair. "But I'm with you. I have this odd feeling Jamie's still alive. Now. How about a cup of tea?"

"How about a glass of wine?" she countered. At the look on his face, she added, "Don't worry. I'm not turning into an alcoholic." She forced a smile. "One glass, all right?"

"Okay. But just one." He found an open bottle of chardonnay in the refrigerator, snagged two glasses from the cupboard, and filled them with the golden liquid. He handed one to Lisa and grinned. "Try not to break this one."

She sipped at it, watching him focus on her. "What?"

"You ate almost nothing at lunch," he pointed out. "Why don't I fix us some steaks for dinner, with baked potatoes?"

She waved his suggestion away. "I can hardly choke food down. I keep wondering if Jamie's getting enough to eat. How he's being treated. If he thinks we've forgotten about him."

Josh put down his wine, took Lisa's glass, set it on the counter, and put his hands on her shoulders. "You won't do Jamie any good if you make yourself sick. When we find him—when, not if—he'll need you, and you'll have to be in good shape."

She shrugged off his touch. "I know I sound like a broken record, but I'm convinced we're missing something. This has to do with Charles in some way. I'm sure of it. I just don't know what. Damn that man to hell, anyway. And damn me for being so stupid as to marry him."

"If you hadn't, you wouldn't have Jamie," Josh pointed out.

Jamie. The only clean thing to come out of the abomination that her life as Mrs. Charles Mallory had turned into.

She saw the worry lines etched into Josh's face. He'd been her rock and strength through all of this. If trying to eat would ease his mind, it was a small enough thing to do.

"Okay. Steak it is." She gave him a tight smile. "But your precious Ethan Caine better not be yanking my chain. It doesn't have many links left."

Chapter Four

The commuter flight from Tampa to Key West took ninety minutes, flying in what Ethan described as a flying paper towel tube. The small plane shimmied and shuddered as it droned through the air, and the cramped condition of the cabin did nothing to increase anyone's comfort.

His phony credentials had been perfect enough to get him through security at Tampa International Airport. With his history both at Guardian and in black ops, if he flew as Ethan Caine, the shooters would be lining up. He managed to get a window seat and hunched himself into the small space allotted. With a battered straw Panama tipped down to cover his face, he closed his eyes and let his mind ramble.

He'd taken the time to contact both Josh and Nick before he left. Both calls had been brief. "I'll be gone for a week."

"What?" Josh raised his voice. "You're going away now? Are you kidding me?"

"When I come back, I'll tell you if I can help or not."

"What am I supposed to tell Lisa? She's already at the edge of every nerve."

"Whatever you need to." He'd hung up on Josh's angry voice.

It couldn't be helped. He needed some answers,

and if he couldn't get them, he couldn't do what was being asked of him. He might have been out of the black ops game for a while, but you never forgot how to prepare. Considering the disaster his last mission had been, the clusterfuck of all time, he wanted every base covered this time. And he knew only one place to get what he needed.

"I'm going to assume this trip is necessary," Nick Vanetta told him. "We're running out of time here."

"So everyone keeps reminding me. If it wasn't, I wouldn't be doing it. There's a man I've known since I left Guardian. We were part of the same, uh, team for a long while. He has access to every black area in the universe, and he's too smart to answer questions over the phone. He makes his home in the Keys so that's where I'm going."

Ethan had spent a long night thinking about his own past, questioning his abilities after that last disaster and whether he could pull himself together enough to do what was being asked of him. But if this visit didn't pan out, he had nothing to offer Lisa Mallory.

He hadn't seen Dino Brancuzzi since he'd turned his back on black ops. They had worked some missions together, nasty little jobs that were crucial to the country's safety and security but for which the government needed plausible deniability, and become good friends. Ethan might have removed himself completely from the world he'd lived in for so long, but Dino still kept his fingers in the pie. He still ran the same deep water fishing charter service out of Key West, but he still did contract work for the government as well as some multinational corporations.

So Blackwater Charters—a chuckle, since

Blackwater was the code name for the first job they'd done together—mixed covert ops with fishing for marlin. Others he'd worked with in some of his ops also carried their particular skills and training into civilian life, with businesses like a helicopter service, a gun club, and deepwater salvage. Like Dino, they often did off-the-book jobs for Uncle Sam.

Ethan could have reached out to any of them, but he and Dino had always been the closest. They'd been together the longest and more than the others, Dino had contacts in every dark corner of the world. If it happened, he either knew about it or could find out about it. Whatever he needed, if Dino could do it, he would.

The thought of dipping his toes in that water again made Ethan's stomach clench. He still wrestled with too many nightmares. Still saw the faces of the dead too often. But Josh was a good friend, and Ethan always took care of his friends. And no matter what he thought of Josh's sister, with her son missing now for three months, she had to be caught in a living hell. If anyone could find out what he needed to know, Dino would be the one.

The sun blazed white fire when the plane landed in Key West. Ethan pulled his sunglasses from the pocket of his rumpled shirt and slid them on before stepping out onto the tarmac, protecting his eyes from the glare. The heavy, humid air made his shirt stick to his body in just the few minutes it took to walk to the terminal. Well, what did he expect at the southernmost tip of the United States? Polar bears?

A few years back, the terminal building had undergone some renovations and now was more eye-catching for the tourists. Ethan, however, missed the chipped floors and cracks in the glass doors before the city council decided to spruce the place up.

He pushed through the tiny mobs of people with pale skin and Technicolor outfits. In the curve of the driveway outside the building, jaded taxi drivers waited outside their vehicles, laughing and joking, for the next wave of passengers.

The driver at the head of the line was leaning his arms on the roof of his car, watching the doors with an avaricious gaze. When he spotted Ethan, his Chamber of Commerce smile broke out, showing gleaming white teeth. "Where you goin'? I'm the best ride on the island."

"As long as you don't kill me getting there. You know Pelican Marina?"

"Oh, sure, oh, sure." He bobbed his head. "You fishin'?"

"You could say that." Ethan threw his carryall into the cab and folded himself into the back seat. "Let's do it."

He hadn't been in Key West in years, but the old-fashioned cottages, brightly colored flowers, and turquoise water of the Atlantic Ocean brought back every memory. Real estate titles dated back to the King of Spain, and the price of a tiny patch of land was indeed a king's ransom. Fishing, water sports, and the legend of Ernest Hemingway, as well as the infamous Duval Crawl—a pub-crawl down the main street—drew tourists by the thousands. The abundance of tourists had always provided good cover for his activities, allowing him to blend invisibly into the crowd.

And the Keys were an ideal jumping off spot to

head out into the Atlantic or the Gulf of Mexico if you had work to do that didn't bear media attention. The confluence of the two bodies of water had long provided access for drug smugglers and later on for terrorists.

That, however, was a long time ago for him. Except the kidnapping of Jamie Mallory, which poked at him like a hot iron, might just thrust him right back into the life he'd turned his back on.

As he drove, the driver kept up a running commentary of activities and events. Ethan pulled his hat down again and wished the man would shut up with the travelogue. He wasn't here for a vacation, and he sure didn't expect to enjoy himself.

The cab stopped in a gravel parking lot next to an arched sign held up by two metal pelicans. A long wooden dock stretched out into the water with colorful boats of all types bobbing in their slips on either side. Ethan's nose caught the familiar tangy scent of salt water, his ears the discordant symphony of the seagulls and pelicans wheeling and screeching overhead.

He hauled himself and his bag out of the back seat and thrust several bills at the driver.

"Have a good time, man." The driver grinned.

"That'll be a miracle," Ethan muttered and trudged through the archway toward a small wooden building on the right. The faded sign over the door said Blackwater Charters. An innocuous name for a not-so-innocent business.

He opened the door and stepped into a small office full of artic air. Sitting in a worn leather chair, feet up on the desk, a telephone to his ear was a man tanned to a deep olive with his salt-and-pepper hair tied back in a ponytail and a gold stud gleaming in one ear. He took one look at Ethan and sat up, dropping his feet from the desk.

"I'll have to call you back," he said into the phone and hung up. "Damnation! Ethan Caine in the flesh."

"I think that's the 'too, too, too solid flesh'," Caine quoted, "although I'm not sure how solid mine is anymore. How the fucking hell are you, Dino?"

Brancuzzi stood and took the hand Ethan held out. "Shocked to see a walking ghost is how I am." He studied Ethan. "How are you doing?"

Dino knew every detail of his last op and what had happened. Ethan had come here to hide when he'd walked away and spent a week drunk at Dino's house.

"Same as ever."

"I was hoping you'd say better than ever."

"One thing at a time."

Barely moving his eyes, Ethan took in each familiar detail of the office. A cracked leather couch and two plastic chairs were the only pieces of furniture other than the desk and chair. It looked like the typical, slightly shop-worn charter office, a place where people on a budget could hire a boat and fish among the rich and beautiful. But the desk held a sophisticated computer setup and a fancy array of communications equipment. Ethan suspected if his friend ran no legitimate charters at all, he'd still have no money worries. His boat went out and came back every day, he blended in with the locals, and no one paid attention.

Ethan dropped his bag on the floor and sat in one of the plastic chairs. He frowned when it rocked slightly. "Nice furniture you've got."

Dino shrugged. "My clients don't require special

interior decoration." He sat back down, propped his feet on the desk, and stared at the man in front of him. "I never thought I'd see your ugly face again."

"Yeah, well, I didn't think you would either. But here I am." Ethan fought a grin. He knew the casual pose his friend affected was so much camouflage.

There wasn't a casual bone in Dino Brancuzzi's body. Every nerve would be on alert, every muscle tightly coiled should sudden movement be necessary. The grin on his face didn't quite reach his watchful, wary eyes.

"I won't ask what you've been doing, because I know the answer's nothing." Dino narrowed his eyes. "Not a whisper about you in all this time."

"Good. I'm tired of being whispered about. But I can't say the same for you, Slick."

"Don't believe everything you hear. You should know that." Dino studied Ethan's face. "So what brings you to sunny Key West?"

Ethan narrowed his gaze at Dino. "I think I need your help."

And that was no lie. If anyone was plugged into every whisper or source in the underbelly of the world, it was Dino Brancuzzi. More than anyone else, he could find where Jamie was and hopefully still alive.

Dino's eyebrows climbed up through his hairline, but he said nothing, just waited for Ethan to continue.

"Let me tell you a story." Shifting in the uncomfortable chair, Ethan gave him every detail of the Lisa Mallory situation, from her marriage to the kidnapping of her son.

Dino made no comment until the narrative was finished, then he leaned forward on the desk. "You're going to find the son." A statement, not a question.

Ethan heaved a sigh. "Yeah, well, Mrs. Mallory and I will never be social chums, but you know how I feel about kids. And it's damned interesting that, since the snatch, there hasn't been even one hint of what happened to him."

Dino nodded. "Kidnappers either return the goods or dump the body. If the package is dead, they can't get rid of it fast enough. So we assume the kid's alive?"

"Yeah. At least we hope he is."

"And you want me to sniff around," Dino guessed.

"What I want—need—is help with things I can't get my hands on any longer, but I figure you can." A corner of his mouth turned up. "Maybe from some of your fishing buddies."

"Poke into some corners, you mean."

"Only if you're comfortable with this." Ethan lifted his hat and raked his fingers through his hair. "Truth to tell, my friend, there's no one else I would trust in this situation."

Dino nodded. "I hear you. What's your gut telling you?"

"That this still has something to do with the husband. A primo asshole."

Dino nodded. "I agree. This didn't just come out of nowhere. And if it was an enemy getting revenge, against who? The wife? For money? They got it. If they don't return the kid, there's usually a body. This time you have nothing. So. A puzzle." He began rolling a pencil between his fingers. "You said the IRS yanked all his records?"

"Uh huh." Ethan leaned forward. "I could file an Open Records Request with them, but I know you and

Uncle have a little, shall we say, ongoing relationship, so I'd say you have a better chance of getting the stuff ASAP. Besides, I want info Uncle can't get his hands on. The stuff Mallory hid about his real business."

"Gotcha." Dino nodded. "I'll make a call. See if I can get some of what you need emailed to me, maybe even today. Depends on where it comes from."

"One other thing. Guardian is helping me with this, keeping it off the books, of course. Nick Vanetta is my point man. I'd like it if you and he could put the details together. You each bring different things to the table."

Dino hiked a brow but nodded. "Of course. We'll make it work."

"Okay." Ethan levered himself out of the rickety chair and picked up his bag. "I'll go find a room someplace and let you know where I am."

"The town is packed with conventions," Dino protested. "You can't get a room at any price. I've got an extra bed at my place you can use. Nothing fancy," he added, "but at least it's clean and you can make yourself invisible if you want."

"Thanks. I appreciate that."

"Come on. Today's quiet, so let me run you over to the house. Then I'll come back here and see what I can dig up."

****

"He did what?" Lisa Mallory stood in front of her brother, hands fisted on her hips, fighting the rage gathering inside her.

"He left a message that he'd be gone for a week and he'd call when he got back."

"I knew it. I just knew it." Lisa paced back and forth. "The man is just an ass. I'm sorry, Josh. I know he's your friend, but I'm in the biggest crisis of my life and he takes off someplace? Why did I expect anything else?"

Josh held out his hands in front of him, palms outward. "Hold on. I didn't say that." He blew out a breath. "My guess is he's gone to make contact with some people from his...previous occupation. See what he can find out."

"Then why didn't he say so?" She pounded a fist against her thigh. "Doesn't he know I'm losing it here? What kind of man just takes off like that and leaves me twisting in the wind?"

"Lisa, hold onto this thought. If he was going to turn you down or walk away, he would have done so already."

She clenched her fists, trying to still the anger that bubbled through her system, the only emotion keeping her fear in check. Ethan Caine just stuck in her craw, a man whose disdain for her had been evident at their uncomfortable lunch. She didn't trust him the way Josh did, but she had no place else to turn. He knew it, and that left her at his mercy. She hated it.

"Every day we waste is another day Jamie's slipping away from me." She chewed on a thumbnail, a bad habit she'd picked up over the past few months.

"Sit." Josh put his hands on her shoulders and gently forced her into the chair behind her. "Just...sit. Let me get you some tea. No wine," he added when she opened her mouth to speak. "You need to lay off the wine before you become an alcoholic. Tea."

"Do you really think he's trying to find out something?" In her marriage to Charles, she'd felt like such a victim. She was determined not to be at anyone's mercy again, including the unpredictable Ethan Caine's.

"Yes. I do. He said one week, and I guarantee it won't be longer than that. Maybe less. Lisa, Ethan knows what he's doing. How to research an op and plan it. He won't do anything until he's gathered all the information he can."

"Everything's just taking so damn long." Lisa swiped her hair away from her face and tucked it behind her ears. "I've racked my brain again and again to see if I've missed anything, but I haven't. The police said drug dealers would have let me know that's what this was about. They'd want their so-called honor back. But who else could do this and make a little boy disappear so completely?"

"You don't know what other enemies Charles had," Josh reminded her. "Here." He set a mug of hot tea on the little table beside her. "Drink this. It'll settle your nerves."

"I can't handle any more of this, Josh." Her eyes burned with tears she forcibly held back. "I can't sleep because I have nightmares about Jamie. I can hardly focus on one thing at a time. A nervous breakdown would be almost a welcome relief."

Josh knelt before her and took her hands. "Lisa, you've managed to hold it together this long, though God alone knows how. Please try to hold on a little longer. I know in my gut Ethan will do this, and he'll find Jamie. Alive. He can reach into any black hole necessary. Anywhere. Can you just trust me on this?"

"All right." She gripped the hands holding hers. "But he'd better have some good news for us when he returns."

Chapter Five

"Help yourself to whatever you find." Dino waved his hand around the small house. "The extra bedroom's not much, but the bed has a good mattress. And there's beer in the fridge. I'll head back to the office and make some calls. Be back around seven, and we can catch some dinner."

Ethan hoped his friend didn't mean that literally. Fishing had never been an activity that appealed to him. He'd spent so much of his professional life sitting absolutely still in one place, when he was on his own time, he wanted to be able to move and make noise if the urge struck him.

Alone, he changed from the clothes he'd worn on the plane to shorts and a T-shirt that had seen far better days and slipped his feet into tattered Nikes.

"Buy yourself some decent clothes, for God's sake," Josh always ragged at him.

But he had no need for anything except what he had, and shopping was an experience more stressful than he needed.

"If my manner of dress offends people, they can just shove it up their collective asses," he always said.

Now, in his ragtag clothes, he looked around the compact bungalow Dino called home. Tile floors picked up the tropical theme of the islands, and a huge window in the living room look out to the end of the street and the beach beyond. Even on this side street, tourists in every manner of garish dress were bumping along on the sidewalk, laughing and shrieking, carrying colorful bags from the island's overpriced shops.

He opened the fridge and reached for a beer, thinking to plant himself on the front porch rocker, drinking and watching the world go by while he waited. But before he could snag a bottle, he slammed the door shut. He'd taken a good look at himself in the bathroom that morning, an action that brought home some painful truths. He was way out of shape. If he was required to do anything to get Jamie Mallory back more strenuous than using a cell phone, he had some serious work to do. And he needed to start now.

Locking the front door and pocketing the key Dino had left with him, he walked to the end of the block and onto the beach. In years past he'd run five miles every morning on beaches like this, or similar places. Now he was having trouble with an old man's stroll.

Swallowing a sigh, he made his way to the hard-packed sand at the water's edge and eased himself into a slow jog. By the time he'd covered a mile, he was sure he'd have a heart attack. He was leaning over, hands on his thighs, dragging air into his lungs, when a group of teenagers flew by him, waving and hooting.

"Damnation."

He straightened, waited another minute for his pulse to slow a little more, then began the jog back. By the time he reached the bungalow, he was ready to call an ambulance, but he dragged himself up onto the porch and collapsed in the rocker.

He was still sitting there when Dino pulled into the narrow driveway just before seven. His friend took a look at him and laughed.

"Did someone leave a dead body on my porch, or are you still breathing?"

Ethan flapped a hand at him. "Ha ha. That's a great sense of humor you've got."

Dino punched him lightly on the arm, then leaned a hip against the porch rail, studying his friend. "What did you do to yourself? I only left you a few hours ago. I didn't think you'd get into trouble so quickly."

"It's the new Ethan Caine Self-Improvement Program."

"Put on a T-shirt that doesn't stink quite so much, and we'll get some food. I have things to tell you."

****

Dino had brought printouts of two emails with him. Each contained pages of records that he and Ethan spread out on his kitchen table, a record of Charles Mallory's life for the five years prior to his murder.

For hours, they sorted through copies of phone records, credit card receipts, travel records, client lists. By the end of the evening, a pattern had begun to emerge.

"Mexico." Dino tapped his pen on the pad where he'd been making notes.

"Yeah, I'd say so," Ethan agreed.

He'd drawn a big circle on the paper in front of him and made tick marks for phone calls to the same numbers, receipts for travel to the same places, clients with related addresses. The grouping of marks formed three clusters within the circle, all of them overlapping.

"Cancun," Dino continued. "And Playa del Carmen. He shows money transfers for businesses in and out of there, businesses that I know are fronts for drug cartels. And don't ask me how, okay?"

"So what now?"

"Remember how we used to do this, amigo?" Dino grinned, but there was no humor in it. He drew ten squares on a clean sheet of paper. "First we figure out who's operating in the area, who the most likely people are Charles might have been doing business with—and you can bet that's what took him there. Nobody takes that many vacations, and besides, it's a perfect spot for drug dealing and money laundering."

He plugged in his laptop and booted it up, his fingers dancing over the keys.

"Don't tell me you can now Google drug cartels and guerilla groups." Ethan's tone was dry.

Dino nodded. "In a manner of speaking." He turned the computer so both men could see the screen. "You'd be surprised what the government lists on its web sites these days. Especially if you say the secret word."

Ethan looked. "I've kept an eye on it, believe it or not. Just out of idle curiosity."

"Uh huh." Dino tapped the screen. "Well then, just bear with me. So here we have Uncle's list of known groups operating in the general area we're interested in. You can eliminate these six." He indicated them with a finger. "They'd never be involved in something like this." He highlighted them and hit the delete key.

"And you know that because?" Ethan raised an eyebrow.

"Because in ten years we've gotten a pretty good sense of who'll commit what crimes and what's on the agenda of each group."

"Nice of these guys to have a code of conduct."

Ethan helped himself to another bottle of water from the refrigerator, twisted off the cap and took a long swallow.

Dino looked at him, eyebrows raised. "Another part of the Caine Self-Improvement Program?"

"Don't ask."

"Okay." Dino turned back to the laptop. "The guerillas are the kidnappers of choice just about everywhere. This is their business. They fund their activities with ransom money so we look at them first."

Ethan rubbed his forehead. "But how would they be connected to Charles? Isn't it a stretch from cartels to out and out nut cases?"

Dino shrugged. "Yet to be determined. But there's too many things here connecting to each other to ignore them. There's a link here somewhere." He shut down the computer. "Tomorrow I can tap into some other sources that I've run a few...fishing charters for. Pick up some more info."

Four more days passed while Dino did his thing, hunting information through his hidden contacts. Each morning, Ethan pulled himself out of bed and began his routine—jogging, swimming, more jogging, pushing himself until he was exhausted at the end of each day. He hadn't had alcohol of any kind since he stepped off the plane, instead drinking huge amounts of water and Gatorade.

Dino chuckled when they ate that night, Ethan refusing anything but lean meat, broiled fish, and salads.

"You're really serious about this, aren't you?"

"Let's say the kid's still alive and I have to get him out. I can't afford to die halfway there."

By the fifth day, Dino had scraped all the information from his sources he could. "These are some badass people your lady's gotten herself hooked up with," he told Ethan.

Ethan made a face. "She's not my lady, and she's not hooked up. I doubt if she even knows these people exist."

Dino opened the folder he was carrying and began spreading papers out on the table. "So much the worse. She'll have no idea what she's up against."

What he gave Ethan had more questions than answers. Through his sources, he'd been able to pinpoint one group as the most likely kidnappers. Their home base was in Cancun, although they sometimes operated out of Playa del Carmen.

"They call themselves *Las Tormentas*. The Storms. They say they sweep everything clean. People are afraid of them and say they are like a storm of devastation, leveling everything in their path. Shortly after Jamie was snatched, they got a new infusion of funds."

Ethan memorized everything, then burned the papers they'd been working with and flushed the ashes down the toilet. When he came back into the living room, he had his carry bag with him. "I took a chance earlier that we'd be finished tonight. Made a reservation on the late flight to Tampa. But information isn't the only thing I'll need."

"Equipment, you mean."

"Yup. Hardware. Firepower. Night goggles. Stuff like that."

Dino nodded. "I figured. I don't know what you're getting from Guardian and what you need from me.

Some of their stuff may be too, uh, open for this."

Ethan actually chuckled. "You mean too traceable. You're right. We'll get Nick on the phone, and you and he can figure it out."

"I'll work out a pickup with him for the stuff you can't take on the plane. They can send their fancy helo for it."

"Works for me. Let's get to it."

Ethan got Nick on the phone, introduced Dino, and they went over all the details. They discussed extraction, hopefully assuming they'd have Jamie with them. Nick had a team he was using, but Dino offered two of his men who knew the area.

By the time they finished the call, all the arrangements had been made. Tomorrow Nick would send the helo to gather whatever equipment of Dino's that would be used and he'd put it together with the stuff from Guardian. For the first time since that last op had gone to fucking hell, Ethan felt a surge of emotion. Some friendships never died.

They made one traditional stop on the way to the airport, a last drink—rum and Coke for Dino, plain Coke for Ethan—at the Dolphin Bar at the pier where the Straits of Florida and the Gulf of Mexico meet.

"Can you believe people come here every evening just to celebrate the sun going down?" Ethan asked.

"Key West, my friend. It's a ritual." Dino tilted up his glass.

They both stared at the blending of the two bodies of water, knowing how many people had crossed that blurred line for reasons that would never come to light. Or how many were yet to come, including, very possibly, Ethan himself.

Dino finished his drink and gave Ethan a long look before he stood up. "Remember these aren't people who want to play nice. *Dios de protégé*, my friend."

God protect you.

****

Lisa slept fitfully, tormented by disturbing dreams. Somewhere a bell was ringing, and she couldn't make it stop. She sat up abruptly, suddenly aware that it was not in her dream. It was her cell phone, and it was ringing insistently.

"H-Hello?" She pushed her hair from her face and tried to untangle the sheet from her body.

"Lisa? Hey. Wake up."

"Josh?" She squinted at her alarm clock. Six a.m. "Has something happened? Oh, god, is it bad news about Jamie?"

"No, it's good news. Get up. Ethan's back, and he wants to talk to us." His voice was controlled, but he couldn't hide the edge of excitement.

He doesn't want to get my hopes up.

Her breath caught. "Did he say anything?"

"No, but if he didn't have anything to tell us, he wouldn't have asked to see us, especially at this ungodly hour."

"I'm getting up right now." She kicked off the covers and headed for the bathroom. "Where does he want to meet?"

"Manny's Diner. It's a dive not far from downtown, but he feels comfortable there. I'll pick you up in twenty minutes. And Nick flew in late night. I'm guessing Ethan called him from the Keys."

"He's certainly racking up the frequent flyer miles for a job he's not making money on. Couldn't he have

67

joined us by cell phone?"

"They can afford it, and he didn't want to trust it to electronics. Go on, now. Get ready."

She was waiting in the driveway, shifting impatiently from one foot to the other, long before Josh pulled up exactly twenty minutes later. She'd passed on makeup, only grabbing the jeans and sweatshirt she'd thrown on her chair the night before and tugging a ball cap over her pony-tailed hair.

"If the fashionistas could only see the famous Lisa Mallory now," Josh chuckled, then looked at his sister's face. "You have to ease up a little, sis. If Jamie's alive, you've gotta keep it together."

"I know, I know." But the tension wouldn't let go of her body. Throughout the short drive, she jiggled one leg and chewed her thumbnail.

Josh reached over and pressed a hand on her rapidly moving thigh, and she shoved it away.

"Lisa, if you don't settle down, you'll implode."

"What if Jamie's dead?" Her voice cracked. "What if that's what Ethan wants to tell us?" She rubbed her hands nervously on her thighs.

Josh reached over and grabbed one of her hands, giving it a squeeze that said don't panic yet. "Even Ethan Caine isn't that insensitive. He'd handle that differently."

"So you say. I'm not convinced."

Josh wheeled the car into a gravel parking lot surrounding an old railroad dining car painted black. A chipped sign over the door read Manny's and under it Come On In.

"What is this place?" Lisa frowned. "It's a far cry from The Club."

"Ethan feels comfortable here," he told her. "I have a sneaking suspicion he owns it."

Lisa grunted. "He should invest a little in decorating."

A rundown restaurant for a rundown man.

Nick Vanetta pulled up in his rental just as they exited their car, and the three of them entered the restaurant.

Inside, one end was blocked off for the kitchen and bathroom. The rest of the interior was jammed with a row of cracked vinyl booths and a scarred counter.

Ethan was sitting in the end booth at the back, facing the door. His gaze met hers as she came toward him, but his face gave nothing away.

Her eyes widened as she took in his appearance. He'd shaved his beard, trimmed inches off his dark hair, and his face sported a hot-looking shade of red, thanks to a sunburn. The fleshiness around his chin and eyes had shrunk, and his eyes seemed sharper, clearer, although the traces of anguish were still visible. The plate in front of him held scrambled eggs and tomato slices, with a mug of black coffee on the side.

"Jesus." Josh's voice was hushed. "Where is Ethan Caine and what have you done with him?"

Ethan grunted. "That's some comedy act. Maybe you should take it on the road."

Nick sat down beside Ethan while she and Josh settled themselves opposite them. A heavyset man in jeans, a T-shirt, and a not-so-spotless white apron approached with four glasses of water, four mugs, and a carafe of coffee.

"Menu's up on the wall," he told them, filling the mugs.

Nick accepted a full mug while Josh and Lisa both shook their heads.

The man shrugged. "Suit yourselves." He set the carafe on the table and walked away.

"What's with the new diet?" Josh squinted at the plate. "Where's the truckload of food you usually eat?"

"You should try it some time. Eating right is eating healthy."

Josh burst out laughing. "Ethan Caine concerned about his diet and…"

"Stop." Lisa curled her hands around her water glass. "We aren't here to discuss eating habits. Or menus. Or make jokes." She turned a glare toward Ethan. "Where have you been? I knew this was a mistake."

Nick cleared his throat. "Mrs. Mallory, I—"

"Lisa, please. I think we're past formalities here."

"Okay, Lisa. I know how desperate you are for news of your son. I have one, too, and I know how I'd feel if this happened to him. But let me assure you of this. If I was in your shoes, if this were my son, I'd want Ethan Caine to be the man heading the search. That's about the strongest recommendation I can give."

She shifted her gaze to the man in question. "So what made you decide to do this?"

He shrugged. "Maybe I'm a sucker for kids. Doesn't matter. I said I'd do it and I will."

"Why did you run off to the Keys?" she demanded.

He took a swallow of his coffee, his eyes glued to her face. "I went to see a friend. Someone who could help me figure this out."

"And?" She'd kill him if he didn't tell her something soon. "No bullshit, Mr. Caine. Is Jamie alive or dead?"

Ethan took so long answering Lisa wanted to leap across the table and yank the words from his mouth.

He took another sip of coffee and set his mug down with a precise movement before looking up at her. "I don't know for sure, but I'm guessing he's still alive."

"Guessing?" she cried, then swallowed and forced a calmness she didn't feel. "What do you mean guessing?"

"Lisa," Josh warned. "How about letting the man talk."

"Here's what I learned." Ethan's words were slow and heavy as he related everything he and Dino had discovered—the records of Charles's activities for five years prior to his death, narrowing the circle of possible kidnappers and zeroing in on a location.

"But that tells us nothing," Lisa protested.

"No, it tells us a lot. It tells us Charles spent a lot of time in the Yucatan and not just getting a tan. It's a hotbed of cartel traffic. And there's a group down there that makes its living kidnapping people. If that's who kidnapped Jamie and didn't return him, there's something here we don't know." He forked a bite of egg into his mouth and chased it with coffee.

"But what could it be?" Tears of frustration pricked at her eyes.

"How much do you know about the Quintana Roo jungle in Mexico? Ever heard of it?"

Lisa frowned. "A little bit. Why? What does that have to do with Jamie?"

"Quintana Roo is a state on the Yucatan Peninsula. Ecotourism is the hot new market, it seems, and the Roo is cashing in on it." He made a face. "Playa del

Carmen, just south of Cancun, is the jumping off place for tours into the interior. But more than one third of the state of Quintana Roo is a tropical forest—more like a jungle—with vast undeveloped areas that are difficult to reach."

"And?" She leaned forward, the tension in her body stretching her like a guy-wire.

"I think one of those groups snatched Jamie and someone has him in the Roo. I don't know why, but Charles had too many visits there for this all to be just so coincidental. If someone is hiding Jamie, what better place could they find than a plantation hidden away from civilization?"

"My God." Lisa whispered the words. "That means…there's still a good chance he's alive. Jamie could be alive."

"Don't get too excited, Mrs. Mallory." His voice was flat. "We don't know anything for sure. Yet."

Her stomach tightened again and bile rose up in her throat. "Someone could have him locked up all this time? Who? Why? Why not give him back?"

Ethan's eyes never left her face. "Could be someone wanted a child and decided yours fit the bill. If that's the case, they could have taken any child and not gotten involved with a messy ransom demand." He rubbed his jaw. "I felt from the beginning there's something here that's not quite right, and I want to find out what it is."

No one said anything for a few moments. Then Ethan shook his head, reached for the carafe and refilled his mug. "Well, drink up. I have more preparations to make before I can get there and check it out."

"What do you mean?" Lisa scowled at him. "What kind of preparations? Why can't you just get on a plane and go?"

Ethan Caine watched her with his hooded eyes.

Josh's hand closed over hers, giving it a gentle squeeze, and she forced herself to take a deep breath. "All right. I'm sorry. What is it you have to do?"

He spoke to her as one might explain something to a child, his tone a mixture of frustration and forced patience. "The Quintana Roo is a very unfriendly place. And these thugs I'm looking for don't play nice in the sandbox. I know you want me to head for the airport now. But I've got to take a week to fix what I've done to myself since…since the last time I was out. If I'm out of shape, it won't do anyone any good. And after all this time, a few more days won't really matter."

She stared at him. "Let me get this straight. You can't go because you're a wreck?"

A muscle jumped in his cheek. "I have other arrangements to make, too."

"And after your week at a gym?" Her voice was filled with venom.

"I go to Mexico. Find the place where *Las Tormentas* hang out. Identify their leader and a foot soldier I can turn for information. Once I know for sure they're the ones who took him, I can squeeze for answers."

Lisa began drumming her fingers on the table. Why were they just sitting here talking instead of going to get Jamie? "So when do you start?"

Ethan pushed his coffee cup away and let his eyes rake over her face. "The minute I leave here."

Lisa took another sip of water. "What if they kill

him before you can get there? Wait." A chill raced over her. "What if they've already killed him, but no one has found the body? Oh, my god." She swallowed hard against the nausea bubbling up in her throat.

"If they were going to kill him, they'd have already done it," Nick interjected. "A week won't make a difference. I also don't believe he's already dead. Guerillas tend to brag about kills, reminding people what they can do if they are crossed in any way."

"But I gave them the money," she cried.

"Exactly why we're sure he's still alive. It would be bad for business if they killed off hostages after the payoff. No one would hire them."

Josh put his hand on her arm again and looked at Ethan. "What's the plan?"

He poured more coffee into his mug from the carafe on the table and added three packets of sweetener. "Fly into Cancun and scope out what cantina these thugs hang out in. Figure out which one to pay off for information so I can pinpoint Jamie's location."

"The right group?" Oh, god. She felt lightheaded. "You mean—"

"He means," Nick said in an even voice, "the kidnappers could be someone Charles met there but aren't from the area. Or a dealer in Switzerland who does jobs for the cartel there. Or someone who works for the cartel and doesn't like Charles."

She looked at Ethan. "Is that true? Are you chasing a ghost here?"

His face was devoid of expression, but irritation flamed in his eyes. "Anything is possible, but every source I tapped into said this is the group and this is where it happened. And believe me, those sources were checked six ways from Sunday."

"There's a slimmer than slim chance any of those other possibilities exist," Nick assured her. "This was too well-planned for it to be carried out by someone who just showed up to do business. And if it was a group that wanted to express their hatred for Charles, they would not be silent about it. The body would already have been found, setting an example."

Lisa relaxed a fraction. Everything Nick said made sense. She'd just have to hold on to that.

"So." Ethan patted his mouth with a napkin. "Once I get what I need, I'll head for Playa del Carmen and start to work."

Lisa stopped drumming her fingers and curled her hands into tight fists. "I'm going with you."

All three men stared at her.

"Are you nuts?" Ethan was the first to speak, his voice like a sharp knife cutting the air. "Out of the question."

She glared at him. "He's my son. I'm going with you. That's the end of it."

"Or what?" He raised an eyebrow. "You'll tell me to peddle my papers elsewhere?"

Lisa felt as if every nerve and muscle in her body was stretched to the breaking point. Gritting her teeth, she leaned forward. "Jamie is my son. I can't just sit on my hands and wait to see what happens. I'm going, with or without you, so it might as well be with."

"Lisa…" Josh's voice had a warning note that said, *Don't argue with this man.*

"This is a very dangerous undertaking," Nick pointed out. "And you've had no training."

"Ethan can train me. I'm a fast learner." She

looked around at everyone, stopping at Ethan. "What's your…what do you call it…cover? Who will you be?"

"A gringo tourist bum looking for some night life." His lips curled in a mock smile. "I fit the part, don't you think?"

She took a deep breath and plunged ahead. "Wouldn't it look less suspicious if you're part of a couple?" She gave a short laugh. "Maybe honeymooners?"

"She's got a point there," Josh admitted with reluctance.

"Please," she begged. Then, to her utter humiliation, tears leaked from her eyes and flooded down her cheeks.

Josh tightened his arm around her, and she leaned into him until the storm subsided. She grabbed napkins from the holder on the table and wiped her face.

"I apologize." She took a long drink from the water glass in front of her. "I don't usually fall apart like this in front of strangers."

"No problem." But Ethan's eyes looked at her as if she were a lab experiment. "But that's a good enough reason for you not to go. The jungle is rough, these people are rougher, and there's no place for emotion. Stay home where you belong."

"No!" She slammed her hand on the table. She was so ready to jump out of her skin she was shaking. "I belong on this trip. I'll do whatever you tell me, but I have to go with you." She drew in a deep, shuddering breath and let it out. "Don't let the tears put you off, Ethan Caine. I'm a lot tougher than I look. I had to be to survive all those years with Charles Mallory. I can think on my feet, I'm good in a crisis, and I'm a crack shot."

Ethan's eyebrows rose, and he looked at Josh.

Josh nodded. "She's telling the truth. I'd say she's a natural with a weapon."

"I bought a gun the day after Charles was killed," she told him. "I went to a range and learned how to use it."

Ethan turned his gaze back to her. After a moment he sighed, a sound of resignation. "All right. I know in my bones I'll regret this, but we'll go as the loving couple."

"I hate to admit she's right about the cover," Nick interjected. "Couples are always less conspicuous. Less threatening."

"Thank you—"

"Don't thank me yet," Ethan growled. "There are ground rules, and they're not negotiable. I won't have either the time or inclination to be your babysitter."

She nodded. "Whatever you say."

"That's the first one. Whatever I say goes. No arguing. I mean it. This is my playground, not yours. There's no room for amateur mistakes."

"Agreed."

Ethan looked at Nick. "You're the point man, right?"

He nodded. "This will all be on the down-low. Along with everything else, I'll get burner phones to you. Don't use any of them more than once. And you'll have a sat phone. Cells don't work in the jungle."

"I'll need aerial and topographical maps of Quintana Roo," he reminded Nick. "A list of contacts in the area and someone to meet me with the required equipment."

"Consider it done."

Ethan turned his head to look at Lisa. "Like I said, I'll be leaving in a week. I have to get in shape, and if you're going, so do you."

"W—what do you mean?" She frowned. "What kind of shape?"

He grimaced. "Mexico is hotter than hell. We might be hacking our way through a jungle, maybe sleeping under a tree. Doing God knows how much walking. Not to mention evading plenty of guys who would cut your throat like nothing. So that gives me one week to teach you the basics of survival. Self-defense. And despite what Josh says, make sure you know how to shoot a gun without killing yourself."

"Like he said, I can shoot."

"We'll see." Ethan fiddled with his mug, then gave her his penetrating stare again. "Last thing. If we plan to accomplish all this in such a short period of time, you have to move into my house."

At that, Josh burst out laughing. "You want her to come live at your house? You really are crazy. It's barely habitable for you."

"Yeah." Nick managed a grin. "I second that."

Ethan glared at him. "This isn't a social visit. Like I said, we don't have much time. She's gotta be there twenty four/seven to make this work."

"Ethan's right," Nick told them. "I'd be against you going, too, Lisa. But if you're determined, Ethan has to call the shots."

"Fine. I'll do it." The fierce determination in her voice startled them. "When do we start? No, Josh." She held up her hand as she saw him about to object. "This is my son and my decision. So forget whatever else you were going to say."

Ethan shrugged. "No time like the present to get started. Let's go by your house so you can pick up whatever you need. And remember, we'll be traveling light."

"I'll need my car, too."

"No. You won't be leaving my house until we head for the airport. Leave it in your garage."

Lisa took a deep breath and let it out, steadying herself. So be it. She'd wade through hell with the devil himself if it meant getting Jamie back. And maybe that was exactly what she'd be doing.

"Fine. Let's get going."

They all slid out of the booth, and she watched Ethan dump some money on the table. He waved to Manny as they filed out the doors, Lisa first and Nick bringing up the rear.

As Lisa turned to ask Josh a question, a sharp crack split the damp morning air and she heard the sound of glass splintering.

Chapter Six

Lisa suddenly felt herself slammed to the ground, gravel digging into her face, a heavy body on top of hers as she heard shots—one, two, three. She lay against the rough ground of the parking lot, barely able to breathe with Ethan's heavy weight pressing her down. She tried to push herself up, only to find steel arms wrapped around her.

"Shut up and don't try to move until I tell you to," Ethan's harsh voice commanded, his mouth close to her ear.

Keeping her in a tight grip, he rolled them until they were under the steps leading into the diner. The gravel scraped her face and stones pricked at her, even through her clothing. He maneuvered one hand under her head to cushion it, but she still felt as if someone was jack hammering her into the ground.

They lay in the shelter of the stairs for what seemed an interminable amount of time. With his big body holding her to the ground, her lungs were compressed until she was sure she'd never be able to draw a breath again.

Finally, she heard Nick ask, "Everyone okay? Josh? Lisa?"

"Yeah," Ethan replied. "Fine. We're clear, but we better get the hell out of here."

"Everyone got their gun?" Nick called.

"Right here." Josh came out from behind the dumpster at one side of the lot in a crouch and hurried over to where they were lying, a pistol gripped in his right hand.

Lisa's jaw dropped. "Joshua. You carry a gun? What the hell for?"

"Protection. Questions later, please." He hunched into the opening with Lisa and Ethan. "You saw it? I spotted it the same time you did."

Nick was at the side of the diner, looking in all directions, his gun still at his side.

"Spotted what?" Lisa spit pebbles from her mouth, brushing her lips with her fingers. "Those were gunshots I heard, right?"

Ethan rolled off her and held out a hand to help her up. "Right on the first try. If I was one second slower, at least one of us would be dead. Thank god for Nick."

Tremors shook her body, and she dug her nails into her palms to steady herself. "Who would be shooting at us?"

Nick rose from his crouch. "Good question."

She followed his gaze to the diner door. Cracks radiated from a hole in the top pane of glass. "My God."

Ethan's jaw tightened. "Damn. We need to get the hell out of here. Josh, get her in my car. I'll be right there."

He took a key ring from the pocket of his jacket and tossed it at Josh. Then he pulled a wad of bills from the waistband of his sweatpants and disappeared back into the diner.

Nick was still scoping out the area, his weapon firm in his hand.

Lisa was grateful for Josh's strong arm around her as he hurried her to the big Expedition and pressed the key to pop the locks. She leaned into his body, forcing her wobbly legs to support her.

"Someone shot at us," she told him, shock still gripping her.

"Uh huh. Thank God, Ethan's reflexes are still good. And Nick's."

"My God," she repeated. For a moment, she remembered the shooting at the ransom drop, the kick in her side, and the searing, breath-stealing pain. Panic balled in her stomach like a lead stone.

Josh opened the door of the SUV, guided her into the passenger seat, and hunkered down beside her. He searched her face with worried eyes. "Let me go get you some coffee. You look like you're about to pass out."

"No." She nearly shouted the word. She wasn't sure she could hold a cup steady enough to drink. "I mean, I'm fine."

I'm not fine. Far from it. But I can't pass out. If I show I'm scared, Ethan won't let me go with him. And I have to go.

"You don't look fine to me."

Then Ethan was back, carrying a large plastic cup, which he held out to Lisa.

"No, thank you." She could hardly make her mouth work.

His face was like a granite mask, but something fiery flickered in his eyes. "Coffee. Black. Drink it. Helps counteract the shock." He pressed the cup into her hands.

Josh nodded. "Like I said, you need it. Drink.

Please."

"Fine." It occurred to her that coffee seemed to be her life-giving fluid at all the times of crisis in her life. She forced a steadiness in her hands as she popped off the lid and blew on the hot liquid before sipping it, welcoming the burn as it slid down her throat. She didn't want to think what would have happened if Ethan hadn't thrown them both to the ground. Or Nick hadn't fired at the fleeing vehicle. "How did you know they were going to shoot?"

"Too many years doing too many things." His eyes shifted, a look of anguish darkening them. "Noticing things."

"It becomes second nature," Nick added, still on high alert.

Josh remained crouched against the open passenger door. "He and Nick saw the same thing I did, Lisa. Black car, black windows, trolling the street. Then the window rolling down just enough for a muzzle to poke out. Only it didn't register with me the way it did with Ethan."

She swallowed more coffee. Ethan was right. The shot of caffeine was helping her system settle down. "Who do you think they were shooting at?"

"Could have been you," Nick answered. "They tried to get rid of you once and failed."

Her eyes widened, and she felt the blood drain from her face. She took a large gulp of the hot liquid to steady herself, knowing again, if Ethan sensed her fear, he'd never take her with him.

"But they could have come after me any time during the past few weeks." She gripped her hands around the coffee so tight she was afraid she'd crack the plastic cup. She could almost smell the fear on herself.

"They could be watching you," Nick pointed out. "Waiting for the right moment. They see any activity that puts them on alert...well...they have a lot at stake."

Ethan shrugged. "Could have been me, too. I made a lot of enemies over the years. Lately, I've made myself a little more visible. And I've been poking into some uncomfortable places the past few days. When you put yourself out in the open, the wolves begin to hunt." He glanced over at her. "Or like I said, they could have been aiming at you."

"But why now, after all this time?"

Again, it was Nick who answered, "To throw a scare into you. Keep you from looking for your son. They see more activity on your part, and they want to stop it. Something stinks here. I can smell it." He took one more glance around before holstering his weapon. "We'd all better get the hell out of here. Looks like we're already running out of time. And I don't want to hang around and give them another chance at us. That could have been just a warning. Or not."

"Josh?" Lisa looked at her brother. "Will you be okay? I don't want you getting shot over this."

"I'll be fine. I don't think anyone's after me, but I'll lay low, anyway." He closed the passenger door and tapped it twice. "If you want to call me, use one of Ethan's cell phones."

"Okay." She started to ask him about the gun, but they were already pulling out of the parking lot.

Ethan was his usual silent self as he drove, and Lisa was glad for the quiet. She was still shaken by the shooting and needed to get herself under control. Any sign of fear and she knew he would take off without her.

On the drive to her house, they followed a meandering, convoluted route.

"Where are you going?" she asked. "Do you need directions?"

"I need to make sure whoever shot at us—or their friends—aren't on my ass." His voice was a low growl. "They probably know where you live, but I don't want to give them any extra advantage."

When it seemed he was satisfied they were clear, he turned onto her street and pulled into her driveway.

"Take only the bare essentials," he ordered. "We won't be heavy in the luggage department. You'll have to do without your fancy duds."

She glared at him. "You're a reverse snob, Mr. Caine. I wasn't born with a silver spoon in my mouth, and money's no good if it destroys your life. I don't need anything but my son."

She started to climb out of the SUV, but he stopped her. "Give me your keys. I want to check the house first."

Her eyes widened. "You think someone might be here?"

He shrugged. "I've learned not to take chances. Lock these doors until I come out. If I yell go, start this thing and get the hell out of here."

He moved away silently, leaving her alone in the car.

Lisa fought back the panic that surged forward and chewed on her thumbnail until at last he came out onto the porch and motioned for her.

"Looks clear, but I'll wait for you in the living room just to be on the safe side."

Packing took only a few minutes.

"All set," she told him, hauling her suitcase into the living room.

They locked up the house and were on their way.

Again, he drove in an apparently aimless manner until he was satisfied they were clear, then headed out of town. He said nothing, a silent presence, and Lisa occupied herself thinking of every curse word she knew to vilify Charles. Even in death, the bastard was still destroying her life.

She leaned back against the headrest, remembering the awful trip to the morgue. The police insisted there wasn't enough of the body left to identify except through dental records, and Josh had tried hard to talk her out of it. She wanted to see for herself. She couldn't rest until she convinced herself the lump of flesh they'd pulled from the burned car was Charles

The coffee Ethan had handed her earlier triggered a memory still branded in her brain.

****

Four years earlier

"Mrs. Mallory." The detective who had come to the house to notify her stood next to her. "This isn't a pleasant sight. Identifying a body is a horrible experience under normal circumstances, and this is anything but. Are you sure you want to put yourself through this?"

Lisa nodded. "Yes. Yes, I do. I'm fine. I'll be all right." She had to make sure he was dead.

He made another attempt. "His car rolled off an embankment and the gas tank exploded. I don't—"

"Please. I need to be able to put closure to this. For myself and my son." In addition, to make sure that bastard can't come back and hurt us again.

The detective shrugged. "All right. Just be aware the body is badly burned. I'll have them set it up in the viewing window.

"No." She almost shouted the word. "I don't want to see him through a glass or in a photograph. Take me into the morgue." She looked up at the man. "You can do that, right?"

"Lisa." Josh touched her arm. He had been at her house when the police arrived and insisted on driving her here himself.

She shook it off. "Can we stop arguing and get this over with?"

The morgue was ice cold, the air filled with the chemicals of death. She was sure all the perfume in the world couldn't disguise the pervasive odor that hovered over everything. Two members of the medical examiner's staff, gowned and gloved, stood by stainless steel tables, the remains on them hastily covered with canvas so her eyes wouldn't be offended.

She stood at the autopsy table, flanked by Josh and the detective. A canvas similar to the others covered what lay on it. A stainless steel pan was attached at the side, and a scale hung from a pole hooked to one corner. For organs, she thought, remembering all the television shows she'd seen. If there were any to remove, that was. Alternatively, to weigh.

She thought she was prepared for what she would see, that her hatred would shield her against the horror, but the reality was even worse than she imagined. What was stretched out on the autopsy table wasn't even the remnant of a human being.

Almost all the flesh had been burned away, but

charred bits of it still clung to what was left of the bones, reminding her of spare ribs that had been expertly gnawed. The skull was a grinning monstrosity, the teeth like chipped enamel plugs protruding from what was left of the jaw. The skeleton wasn't even complete. Many of the bones had been partially destroyed by the fire.

"Compare it to a crematorium," the detective answered her unspoken question. "When the fire heats to a certain temperature, it disintegrates bone, leaving only a residue of ash."

Bile rushed up into her throat, and she swallowed hard against it. She forced herself to stare at what remained of Golden Boy Charles Mallory, the devil who had taken her to hell. Whatever she had expected to get from this wasn't there. This was just a charred, stinking lump of flesh and bone fragments. And maybe that's all he'd ever been under that golden exterior.

She needed this to be him, needed the man to be dead, so she could, finally and forever, have peace. And somewhere deep inside her, she knew the gruesome remains on that table were what was left of Charles.

She nodded once. "Yes. That's him." She turned and almost ran from the refrigerated environment. Josh caught up with her in the hallway.

"Lisa." He pulled her into his arms.

She was shaking so hard her teeth chattered.

"Here, Mrs. Mallory. This might help." The detective handed her a cup of coffee he'd procured from somewhere.

Josh took it and held it to her lips.

Lisa forced herself to take a sip, the liquid spreading its heat through her body. Too bad it couldn't reach her soul. She was sure she'd be cold there forever. But Charles was dead.

"At least the nightmare is over." She leaned against Josh. "Thank God."

****

"Mrs. Mallory?"

"Huh? What?" She shook herself from the ghastly reverie and realized they'd stopped moving.

"We're here."

She blinked. "Sorry. Exactly where are we?"

"Just east of Tampa. This is probably one of the few remaining rural homesteads in the area. It's good for me. Nobody bothers me about homeowner rules and shit like that."

She looked out the window at the rambling farmhouse showing visible signs of neglect, surrounded by weeds and shrubbery gone wild. Her distaste must have been evident in her face.

Ethan sat unmoving in his seat, car keys dangling from his fingers. "You can change your mind any time you want. I'll just take you back to your house and get on with what I have to do."

"No. I don't care if you live in a hovel. Which, by the way, isn't so far from what this is. Let's just do what we have to do and get Jamie." She opened the door and got out.

She realized the house was an extension of the man—a once proud warrior now falling to seed and uncared-for. Life had been hard on both of them.

He flipped open a panel on the wall in the entry hall and punched in a code. Instantly, four green lights came on. He unlocked what looked to Lisa like a closet door. Instead, it was a small room filled with more electronic equipment than she'd ever seen in one place. She watched, fascinated, as he flipped switches, typed commands into computer keyboards, and a bank of monitors on the wall came to life.

"But this is unbelievable," she said, her eyes wide. "This place…it's like a fortress."

Ethan nodded. "Of necessity. Especially now after that shooting. I have cameras and electronic sensors all over the property. That way no one sneaks up and surprises us."

"Oh." She shivered at the thought.

He led the way down a short hall. "There's a bedroom that's fairly clean and it's got its own bath." Opening a door, he walked across the room and raised the windows. At once, a breeze blew in and stirred the musty odor. "I'll just air it out a little."

Lisa looked around the room. A king-sized bed, a dresser, a nightstand, and two doors. Dusty but not as bad as she expected. Unused for a long time.

Ethan pointed. "Closet. Bathroom. I'll get you sheets and blankets from the linen closet. The room hasn't been used in years, so I didn't see much sense in keeping the bed made up."

"This will be just fine." She started to say something else but was interrupted by the doorbell. "Are you expecting company?"

Surely not. And what about the fancy security?

Ethan was already moving out of the room. "Not to worry. I know who it is."

Still, a gun had appeared in his hand. He held it against his thigh as he moved to the front hall.

She followed him, stunned by the sight of a huge delivery truck in the driveway. What could he possibly have ordered? At the end of an hour, she was even more amazed. Another bedroom, devoid of furniture, was filled with a treadmill, free weights, and what she'd seen on television advertised as a home gym. What surprised her most were handholds on one of the walls that she recognized as a training wall for rock climbing.

"Are we starting a physical fitness program?" she asked. "Do we really have time for this?"

"We don't have time not to do it." He was busy arranging free weights on their stand. "We've got one week for both of us to get in shape for whatever happens in Mexico. I spent the past week trying to undo the damage I foisted on my body for the last ten years. But that's just a start."

"And what's with the wall?" She waved a hand at it. "Will we be mountain climbing?"

"You never know what you'll have to climb. That thing is left over from years ago. But I checked all the pegs and they're still sturdy. I wish we had a month to get ready."

"A month!" Lisa raked her hair from her face. She couldn't imagine waiting another month to find Jamie.

"Yeah, but we don't have that luxury. Without at least some conditioning, I won't be much help rescuing Jamie. Neither will you. The Quintana Roo isn't for the weak." He straightened up and looked at her. "Go put on whatever you'll be comfortable in and come right back here. We start in five minutes."

Chapter Seven

Lisa was convinced it would be a true miracle if she didn't drop dead by the end of the day. Every muscle in her body was on fire and even her bones hurt. The only thing that kept her going was the sure knowledge that if she quit, Ethan would never take her to Mexico with him. She could still go by herself, but she was smart enough to realize how ridiculous it was for her to run off to a foreign country with no resources, looking for a needle in a haystack.

So she sweated over stretches and the treadmill, gritting her teeth as much against the pain as to keep from swearing at the man pushing her, pushing her.

"Keep moving," Ethan ordered while he worked out with free weights. "We'll be doing a lot of walking. Gotta strengthen those legs."

Those legs were trembling by the time he switched off the treadmill.

"Break time." Ethan tossed her a towel.

"Thanks." She mopped the sweat on her face and neck, then sat carefully on the weight bench, not wanting to let him see how shaky she was.

He disappeared for a moment, returning with two bottles of water and handing her one. "You need to drink a lot of fluid when you exercise. If your body gets dehydrated, you can't keep up with the program."

"Don't worry." Her tone was flat. "I'll have no

problem keeping up with it. No matter what you throw at me."

When they quit at the end of the day, however, she was afraid she'd have to eat her words. Only the image of Jamie constantly in her brain kept her going.

"I stopped at an all-night market last night. Steak and salad for dinner. Thirty minutes. Then we study." He turned to leave the room.

Study? Study what?

Lisa draped her towel over the handles of the treadmill and headed for her room. A long, hot shower helped ease the soreness of her aching muscles. She pulled on jeans and a tank top, gathered her hair into a ponytail, and swallowed two Ibuprofen tablets. She was sure tonight she'd have no trouble sleeping.

"Shake it, Mrs. Mallory." Ethan's voice boomed down the hallway. "Food's ready."

Ethan was already at the table. In front of each of them, he'd placed a huge T-bone steak and a large salad.

"Eat." He poked a piece of steak in his mouth. "You'll need the protein."

Lisa slid into her chair. "How about we kill the formality for the duration. Anyway, I'd like to forget I was ever Mrs. Mallory. Except for Jamie," she amended quickly.

"Okay. Fine. Eat your steak, Lisa."

With his sharp eyes watching her, she forced down every bite of food. Her stomach, ill-fed for so long, rebelled at first, but she managed to fight the spasms.

"That where you got shot?" He pointed to a puckered scar high up on her left arm.

"Yes. I was lucky. It tore some muscle, and that's

all." She glared at him. "And it's fully rehabbed, as I'm sure you could tell today."

"You've got grit, I'll give you that. And luck, because a couple inches to the left and we wouldn't be here having this conversation."

"Yes. Josh pointed out to me how stupid I was to handle the drop myself and how lucky that whoever fired at me is a very bad shot." She pushed away her empty plate and sat back in her chair.

He nodded once in approval. "Good."

"Not much of a conversationalist, are you?"

"Nothing to talk about." He scraped the plates and put them in the dishwasher, then filled two mugs with coffee and brought them to the table. "Decaf. Drink up."

"Why are you doing this?" She pushed the cup away, her face pinched as she caught his gaze. All the anxiety and uncertainty she'd felt since the first meeting with this man, her distaste for him, her anxiety over Jamie sat in her chest like a solid ball of steel. "It's obvious you don't like me. Why didn't you just say no again?"

"My reasons."

Well, this was getting nowhere fast.

"This is my son we're talking about. I think I deserve to know why you're willing to go after him." She eyed him with speculation. "Josh says you're a good friend. Nick and Reno highly recommend you. What am I missing here? Is it me?"

He ignored her, instead pouring four packets of sweetener in his coffee and stirring it with slow, methodical sweeps of the spoon. At least the table wasn't covered with flying residue the way it had been at their lunch. And his table manners had improved.

"It's just the two of us here. Are we not even going to have polite conversation?"

"You don't think I'm polite, remember?"

Ethan's eyes pinned hers, and she saw again that same sharp pain, that same anguish, that she'd seen since their meeting the other day. The load of guilt Ethan Caine carried had not diminished one bit. For the first time, she actually felt sorry for him. What a terrible thing he lived with.

And then, there it was again, that hot flash of attraction that lasted a millimeter of time but too long as far as she was concerned. Think of something unrelated.

"Do you really think the shooting today had something to do with the kidnapping?"

"Don't know for sure." He got up and refilled his mug.

"But…"

He looked over at her. "Up until this week, a lot of people weren't even sure I was still alive. Now I've poked the hornet's nest. The shooter could be any one of dozens of people. I didn't win any popularity contests."

"Aren't you even concerned?"

"I'd be a fool if I weren't. But people have tried to take me out for years. Whoever this is better be a real professional or he's dead meat." He lifted his coffee mug. "Okay. We're done with Twenty Questions."

Lisa couldn't help but let her gaze roam over the man sitting across from her. What an enigma. She'd never met anyone like him. And whatever he'd been doing to himself since she last saw him was having a major effect.

His tall frame had more muscle definition, the skin was tighter, and she could better see the strong, powerful body. The T-shirt stretched to fit broad shoulders, and the sweatpants he was wearing rode low on lean hips. His hair was longer, but with the beard gone, she could better see the planes and angles of his face.

Ethan Caine was a damned good-looking man in a rugged way. She bet he had been hell on wheels with women before he decided to hide from life. She didn't know what to do with all the conflicting emotions colliding inside her. Part of her detested him, repulsed at what he'd become.

At the same time, part of her reacted to the absolute maleness of him. Strange, since she hadn't reacted to a man since the second year of her marriage. After the nightmare with Charles, she'd been sure she'd never be interested in any man again. Now she and Ethan Caine were going to be joined at the hip for the next several days. She'd better get a clamp on her unexpectedly active hormones or she'd be in real trouble.

"Homework time."

His voice jarred her back to reality. He sat down in his chair, opened a folder, and began spreading the papers on the table.

"What's this?" She frowned. "What kind of homework?"

"Before we set foot out of this house, we have to memorize everything about these people we're looking for. And about the geographic area, especially the jungle." He refilled her mug and returned the carafe to the counter. "We won't be carrying a briefcase with us.

And these aren't the kind of questions you ask at the tourist bureau. So. Let's get started."

Tired as she was, she was having trouble blending this Ethan with the one in her mind. She knew he and Josh had been friends for some time, but her years with Charles pretty much kept her in isolation. She and Josh had to plan carefully for their time together and for him to see his nephew. It had been a miracle he'd been with her the night Charles was killed.

She'd had little contact with Ethan when he worked for Guardian, of course. Why would she? The rare occasions she'd spent in his presence, he'd been just off an undercover assignment and looked much as he did during the past year. This, today, was an unfamiliar and unexpected Ethan. Sharp, focused, knowledgeable. He changed before her eyes from the disreputable hermit into a warrior preparing for a mission. She had a hard time reconciling the two. Maybe the rumors about him had been true after all.

"Think of this as a lecture that you'll be tested on," he told her. "It helps organize the facts in your mind."

In clear, concise sentences, he fed her the information on *Las Tormentas*, pointing out what they'd be looking for and how they'd go about it. Then he pulled out two maps and gave her a geography lesson. About the time her head began to buzz, Ethan shuffled all the papers together and slid them back into the folder.

"That's enough for tonight. You'd better get to bed. You'll need your rest."

Lisa didn't move, just sat watching him. Finally, she said, "You still haven't given me a real answer to my question."

"Oh?" He cocked an eyebrow. "And what question was that?"

"Why you're doing this."

He stared at her with his hooded gaze for a long time. "Let's just say I owe Josh a great deal. There isn't much I wouldn't do for him."

"But I mean nothing to you. Nor does Jamie. And this is not just a walk to the corner drug store."

"No, it isn't. My reasons are my own." He emptied the rest of the coffee and rinsed out the carafe. "But you can count on the fact that if Jamie's alive, I'm the one who can get him out." He paused. "And that's all the answer you'll get. Good night, Lisa."

He was gone before she could say another word.

As she made her way to her room, she caught glimpses of him checking doors and windows as well as the monitors in what she called the electronics closet. Some people might call the way he lived paranoia, but Lisa was damned glad for it. For anything that kept them safe.

Breakfast the next morning was even more silent than dinner had been.

"Before we start today's training," Ethan told her, "we have some housekeeping things to take care of."

She frowned. "Like what?"

"Hold on." Ethan left the room and returned with a small gym bag. Reaching in, he pulled out a wig and held it out to her. "There's an almost hundred percent chance the kidnappers will recognize you, so we have to counteract that."

She took the wig, staring at it. "You want me to put this on now?"

"Uh huh." He reached into the bag and handed her

a zippered pouch. "Lily Cameron's makeup. Go fix yourself up and come back here. I need to take your picture."

"For?"

"Passport picture. Can we just do this, please?"

Lisa swallowed her exasperation and took everything into the bathroom. With her blonde hair tucked up into the wig, her entire appearance changed. The new hair was long and dark and very curly. She decided to go to town on the makeup, wondering if Ethan would tell her to use some common sense. When she walked out of the bathroom, curls surrounded her face and her eyes were made up with dark eyeliner, heavy smoky gray shadow and heavy eyebrow pencil.

Ethan looked at her and grinned. It was the first time she'd seen any sign of humor on his face.

"Perfect! Exactly what I wanted. Not even your brother would recognize you."

She snorted. "No kidding."

"Okay. Picture time." He snapped four shots of her with his phone. Then sent them off, probably to Nick. "Good. Back to your real self. We have work to do."

They settled back into what would become their routine. Treadmill. Weights. Self-defense. Lunch. Start over again. On the fourth day, he asked to see her gun. Lisa dug the little Ruger 9mm out of her purse and gave it to him.

"Not bad." He released the magazine, checked the gun, then slammed the magazine back in and racked the slide. "Let's see what you can do with it."

Off to the side in the backyard was an old barn that looked like a strong wind would collapse it. Two targets were pinned to the outside wall. Boxes of bullets were stacked on an old wooden table.

Ethan walked Lisa up to within ten feet of the targets and stopped. "All right, hot shot. Let's see if your talent matches your mouth."

If I didn't need him, I'd shoot him instead.

She took her stance, sited, drew in a breath, partially let it out as she'd been taught, and squeezed off six shots, counting them in her head. When she was finished, she lowered her hand and ejected the empty clip.

He walked up to the target, traced her hits with a finger, and shook his head.

She knew she'd burned a circle dead center. "Maybe you could help me focus a little better," she said with heavy sarcasm.

He turned to walk back to her. "Smartass. Let's see how you do from farther away. The bad guys don't always oblige you by getting close."

Lisa pressed her lips together to keep any more smart remarks from slipping out, moved back five feet, and repeated the sequence. Again, she hit all six dead center. He had her shoot all the way back to thirty feet, moving in five-foot increments. Then he had her do staggered rapid-fire.

He was relentless, changing her stance, changing the angle of the shot, changing the pacing. By the time they'd used up two boxes of bullets, her shoulders ached and her arms were ready to drop. She was beginning to long for the torture chamber of the gym.

"Okay. Enough." He took the gun from her and placed it on the table. "Rest. It's my turn."

She dropped into a wooden chair next to the table, massaging her hand, and watched Ethan go through his paces. It was like watching a machine. Smooth, functioning effortlessly. He was a dead shot from any distance and any angle. Watching him, a slight shiver skittered along her spine. Ethan Caine was a killing machine. His body showed no tension, no hesitation, as he emptied magazine after magazine into the target.

In the week she'd been at his house, she'd seen the emergence of the man Josh said he once had been. He was tougher, more focused, deadlier. Here was the image of the man who had led the blackest of black ops. And wasn't that what she wanted? Needed? A man with no fear, who'd be deterred by nothing?

When he turned and headed back to the table for the last time, his face held absolutely no expression. She could easily see him in any dangerous scenario doing things most men would be afraid to discuss.

She avoided looking directly into his eyes. She didn't want to feel any empathy for this man. What had happened to him was soul damaging and her heart went out to him, but she couldn't afford to let it affect her. She needed to fuel her anger at his arrogance and her residual distaste for him. It was her only ammunition against a growing, unwanted sexual attraction.

Why, oh, why was she always attracted to the wrong kind of man?

She was just grateful he had agreed to do this, and that's what she had to remember. She didn't have to like him to be grateful, and she certainly didn't have to show her gratitude in a way she'd regret.

Still, for the first time since the day Jamie disappeared, Lisa felt a small spark of hope stirring within her.

Chapter Eight

As Lisa headed to the kitchen Friday morning, she ran into Ethan standing in the front hall with a man she'd never seen. Neither of them was smiling, but their posture indicated business rather than antagonism. They spoke briefly in quiet tones. Then the man handed Ethan a thick envelope, they shook hands, and the man left.

"A friend?" she asked.

"In a manner of speaking. From Guardian with some stuff for me. Nick had an agent they work with here deliver it to me." His face was as blank as solid stone, hinting at nothing. "Let's eat breakfast."

He served them both bacon and eggs and mugs of coffee. His folder and a pad of yellow paper were on the table next to his place.

"Studying again?" She motioned to the papers.

"Checking facts again. We leave tomorrow."

"Tomorrow?" Her eyes popped open. "It's hard to believe we've been doing this for a week."

A week unlike any other she'd spent. From daylight to dark, they trained. With the equipment. On the mats. In the yard with the guns. By now, she was sure she could take almost anyone hands down and shoot from any position and any angle. The whole thing had a surreal quality. She was going into a strange country with a man she hardly knew, armed to the teeth to rescue her son. Whatever happened to her nice, sane existence?

She met Charles Mallory, and nothing had been normal since.

"I wish we had a month, but this will have to do." He looked down at the pad in front of him. "Our flight leaves from Tampa International—"

"I'm ready." She tried to sound more confident than she felt. Now that they were actually going to do this, her stomach twisted in knots and a sliver of fear raced through her.

"I'm glad one of us is." He gestured toward the envelope with a forkful of food. "We're Ed and Lily Cameron. Welcome to the honeymoon."

She raised her eyebrows at his comment. She hadn't given a thought to different identities. "We need fake names?"

"Do you know how many people would be waiting for us with heavy hardware if the name Ethan Caine appeared on a passenger manifest?"

"B—but what do you do when you normally fly?"

"I don't. Let's just leave it at that. We leave on the ten a.m. Continental flight, change planes in Houston, and get into Cancun about two. Our reservations on the flight and at the hotel are for the Camerons."

"No direct flight?" Lisa bit off a tiny piece of toast, wondering why they were complicating the trip with a layover.

"Not for the hours I want." He stirred sweetener into his coffee. "Besides, this way I can tell if anyone's keeping an eye on us. It's hard to be invisible in a bunch of places."

She almost choked on her toast. "You think the

people who shot at us will be following us?"

"Maybe. It's a good bet they've got eyes out looking for me. Eyes that might have nothing to do with you. Except they could screw up our trip if we're not careful."

"Then isn't it just adding to the danger if we don't take a direct flight?"

"No." His lips thinned. "Like I said, it gives me more opportunities to see if we have a tail." He swallowed some coffee. "Besides, I don't think anyone will be looking for a loving couple."

"I hope you're right." She picked up her own coffee mug.

"I have all the ID we'll need in this envelope except for your passport," Ethan went on. "We'll have that tomorrow. After supper tonight, give me everything in your purse except cosmetics. I'll lock it up in the safe."

"All right."

"Your gun, too."

"My gun? What will I use?"

The look he gave her was part irritation, part impatience. "Don't you read the papers? You try to get on the plane with a gun, you won't see daylight for months."

Of course. How stupid. Now he'd think her a dumbass for sure.

Ethan swallowed a mouthful of food. "I have stuff being delivered to us after we land. Including a duplicate of your Ruger. I don't think you can handle anything larger."

Lisa watched him eating, cutting his food, and chewing it carefully. Again, when he sweetened his coffee it was without the careless disregard he'd displayed at The Club. All week, she'd seen a totally different side of this man than he'd ever exposed.

"You fake it, don't you?" she asked without preamble.

He looked up, startled. "Excuse me?"

"You're a fraud, Ethan Caine. You've created an offensive persona to make sure the world doesn't ever see what's underneath. What are you afraid of?"

The mask snapped into place again. "You're nuts, you know that? What you see is what you get."

"But it depends on what you let people see. Doesn't it?"

He didn't answer, and at last, she went back to her plate of food. Who is he, really? Before the disaster that led to his "retirement," who had he been? Now he was just a figment of his own imagination, dealing with disaster and hiding behind a wall of pain and guilt. Josh had told her no matter how many times people tried to convince him it hadn't been his fault, he brushed them all away. He led the mission; he was responsible. And it was a burden that was slowly destroying him.

They spent the day refining the self-defense moves he had taught her. After dinner, he shut everything down and brought her a zippered canvas tote. "Wear one tourist outfit. Take jeans, shorts, and one T-shirt."

"I won't be a very well-dressed honeymooner. Won't they be suspicious?"

His grin held little humor. "We eloped. We're buying what we need in Mexico. Anyway, as a new husband, I won't want my bride wearing too many clothes."

The thought of being naked with Ethan Caine sent

a sudden rush of heat through her system.

In a pig's eye.

But she couldn't get the images out of her mind. The flex of his muscles as they exercised. The now-leaner body in jeans and T-shirt at the firing range, every move smooth and fluid. The thick pelt of hair on his hard-muscled chest that lay like a shadow beneath a white shirt.

The feel of his hands on her body as he moved and guided her, like a living flame heating her skin wherever he touched her.

I'm going to be in big trouble if I don't get my mind back on the business at hand. Don't be stupid, Lisa. Ethan Caine is the last man in the world to have fantasies about. As if fantasies ever came true, anyway.

She dumped the contents of her purse into a plastic baggie and handed it to Ethan along with her gun. After he locked everything in the safe, he handed her the new identification.

"I think we can treat ourselves to one beer. We've earned it. Okay with you?"

"Yes." She almost smiled. "That would be nice."

They sat on the ancient rockers on the front porch, each holding a cold bottle of Coors, watching the sun bathe the landscape with its last rays of the day. Neither of them said a word. She had learned during the past week that Ethan Caine wasn't much for small talk, so she sat in silence.

Finally, he broke the silence. "You did good." Each word sounded as if someone dragged it out of him.

She laughed for the first time in weeks. "Thanks for the vote of confidence. I'm sure you were waiting for me to hang it up."

"Matter of fact, I was. You surprised me." He tipped the bottled back and drank two healthy swallows.

Lisa watched the movement of the muscles in his neck as he drank, then shook herself. Holy mother of god. What was with her? She was smack in the middle of the biggest crisis of her life—even bigger than trying to deal with her marriage—and her hormones decided to do a wild tarantella. She was getting entirely too fascinated by Ethan Caine and his body. A man, by the way, she was pretty sure she didn't even like.

Must be years of abstinence. Or the misery that described sex with Charles. I didn't think I'd ever have an honest urge again in my life. And sex is last thing I need to think about right now. Especially with Ethan Caine. I must be losing my mind.

"Well." He drained his bottle. "Time to hit the sack. We're outta here at eight a.m. Josh is taking us to the airport."

"Oh!" She'd just assumed they'd drive themselves.

"I'd rather not leave the beast in the parking garage. Don't know exactly how long we'll be gone. Anyway, we won't be coming back through TIA."

When they rose at the same time, Lisa found herself so close to Ethan that a sheet of paper would barely have fit between them. She couldn't move. Her feet were frozen to the porch. Heat rolled off his body, wrapping itself around her. Something halfway between passion and lust flashed in his eyes. Then it was gone.

He sidestepped, breaking the invisible thread holding them in place. "Good night. I'll wake you in the morning."

The screen door slammed behind him.

Lisa stared after him, mouth open. What the hell just happened? Nothing she wanted to deal with, that was for sure. She shook herself and went into the house, careful to lock the door behind her.

I'm losing my mind. That's what it is.

But her dreams that night were filled with images of a hard-looking man with no life in his eyes, except one flash of heat.

****

Damn. Hell and damn.

Ethan slammed the door to his room and dropped onto his mattress. Raking his hands over his face, he muttered every curse he'd ever learned in every language he knew. This was not happening. This was just not happening.

Lisa Mallory had asked him early on the reason he was going into the jungles of Mexico to find her child. How could he tell her? If he could successfully return Jamie Mallory to his mother, he'd feel as if some part of his dark, damaged soul had been redeemed.

And now there was this other wrinkle, one he certainly didn't need. He couldn't remember the last time he'd actually been attracted to a woman. Not that he hadn't had sex, although he seemed to need it less and less as he buried himself in the agony of his nightmares. But the women he'd been with were merely vessels, as crude as that sounded. He couldn't even remember what they looked like.

And now here was this woman, skin and bones and the worst case of nerves he'd seen in a long time. Mouthy. Irritating. Carrying a load of shit with her. The last kind of woman he'd ever want to be with. So why was he sitting here with an erection so hard he couldn't bend over?

If he hadn't trained himself in rigid self-discipline, after that moment on the porch, Mrs. Lisa Mallory would right now be underneath him on this mattress. Naked. Engaged in some very hot, sweaty sex.

Against his better judgment, he was about to take her into a danger zone on a mission that no amount of training could fully prepare her for. In the humid tropics where danger upped the flow of adrenaline. Where anything could happen. And he was supposed to keep his mind on business while he pegged the bad guys, located her son, and extracted him.

Shit. Hell and damnation.

****

When Josh arrived the next morning, Lisa noticed two things at once. The first was the gun tucked in the small of his back. It was covered by the loose shirt he wore, but when he turned to Ethan, the fabric shifted and there it was. Josh with a gun? It still shocked her.

"You think someone is going to attack us again?" she asked.

"No, but better safe than sorry. Here." He handed the envelope he held to Ethan.

Lisa could see Ethan was still pissed at himself. It was evident in the rigid set of his shoulders and the tightness of the muscles in his face.

He passed the envelope over to Lisa. "Put this in your purse and keep it easily accessible."

She tried to control her shock when she opened the passport and saw her picture.

"Auditioning for a job in a strip club?" Josh joked.

"I was—"

He held up a hand. "Just kidding. It's a perfect

disguise." He grinned at Ethan. "Nick took care of the passport through Guardian. He overnighted it to me because he wasn't sure if you got mail out here."

"Ha ha." He was monosyllabic once they climbed into Josh's car. His silence didn't help Lisa's nerves, her body rigid, her hands pleating and unpleating the material of her skirt.

"Nice to have such pleasant companions," Josh said, trying to lighten the atmosphere.

Ethan grunted while Lisa stayed silent, chewing her thumbnail and looking out the passenger window.

"Well." Josh cleared his throat. "I'm happy to see you two got along so well. This should be a pleasant trip for you. Especially since it's your honeymoon." He glanced at Ethan. "Mr. and Mrs. Cameron."

Ethan drew in a breath and exhaled. "Just drive, Josh. Okay?"

Josh frowned, sliding a glance at his friend. "Someone want to tell me what's going on? Otherwise, no one's going anywhere. Especially the airport."

"Everything's fine." Lisa tried to make her voice even. "I think Ethan and I are just a little tired from intense preparation and uptight about what we're going into."

"I still wish you'd change your mind." The smile couldn't hide Josh's worry. "I don't care how much Ethan trained you. You shouldn't be in the middle of this."

"Either take me to TIA or I'll take myself. But I'm going."

"Fine. Fine." Josh shook his head. "Whatever."

They drove the same kind of aimless route Ethan had used the other day. Up and down side streets, doubling back on themselves, heading one way on the Interstate then back the other way.

She looked at Ethan, frowning.

"Josh is just making sure we don't have a tail." Ethan's gruff voice was like splintering wood.

She had to force herself not to look out the rear window. "You still think someone's found us? Could follow us? Maybe the people from yesterday?"

"I think anything's possible. That shooting wasn't just idle target practice." He turned and looked into the back seat where she was sitting. "I've stayed under the radar for years. Hardly anyone even knows where my house is. Now I'm out there where people can take potshots at me. We'll have enough trouble selling ourselves as honeymooners. I don't want anyone blowing that cover too soon."

"Oh." It hadn't occurred to her that he'd be putting himself at this kind of risk by agreeing to help her find her son. She quickly tamped down any feeling of regret. Jamie was the only important thing. She'd worry about everything else when he was safely home.

At last, they reached the airport and pulled up to the departure entrance for Continental. Josh climbed out of the car, ignoring the airport guard trying to wave him on. He shook hands with Ethan, and Lisa saw some silent message pass between them. Then he turned to her and enveloped her in a tight hug.

"I hope you know what you're doing." His voice was gruff with emotion.

"I know I'm going to find Jamie." Her own voice was tight with unshed tears. "I feel it."

Josh visibly forced himself to let go of her and stepped back. "Have a nice honeymoon, Ed and Lily."

But Ethan already had a grip on Lisa's arm, hurrying her into the terminal.

Riding the electric tram that carried them from the main terminal to airside where all the gates were located, he sat with his arm draped casually across her shoulders. At first, she started to draw away, but his hand tightened on her and he leaned over to whisper in her ear.

"Honeymooners, remember? If you can't play the part, tell me now."

She gritted her teeth, turned her face to his, and gave him a simpering smile. "I can do what I have to," she whispered back.

If only the damn wig didn't itch so much.

They passed through security without a hitch, and Ethan stopped at a Starbucks to buy coffee for them.

"Would you like something to eat, sweetheart?"

The words sounded like they were being dragged from his throat, and Lisa had to smother a grin. "No thanks, honey. I'm too excited to eat. And you know flying always makes me nervous."

Ethan handed her the coffee. He still had his sunglasses on so his eyes were impossible to see, but his face was a hard mask.

Some honeymoon. She pasted a smile on her face, hitched the straps of her purse and her tote onto her shoulder and took a sip. "Ooh, just right," she cooed. "Thanks, sweetie."

She linked her arm through his, nearly knocking his coffee out of his hand, and tugged him along the concourse, hips swaying.

"Aren't you going a little overboard?" Ethan spoke through clenched teeth.

"Just getting into the act." *And I can do it as well as you can. Asshole.*

When they sat down in the waiting area Ethan played his part of the typical newlywed husband. Hugging her. Kissing her cheek. Stroking her arm. But underneath it all, she could still feel the tension humming in his body. She glanced at him once or twice and wondered if everyone else could tell they were playacting. Performing. Staging.

Then, as if a switch had flipped, another problem sprang up. Whatever had flashed between them last night was still sharp in her mind, and every time he touched her, she was reminded of it. Her skin tingled, her nipples hardened, and she squeezed her thighs together to still the unexpected throbbing that vibrated through her body.

God! She hadn't had sex in longer than she could remember. Now, of all times, her stupid body decided it was ready? And with a man who was the antithesis of everything she liked?

Get yourself under control, Lisa. You won't be any good to Jamie and the mission if you're thinking about sex, and with Ethan Caine of all people. God, how had she let this happen?

She sensed Ethan was affected, too. The way the muscles in his arm tightened as he placed it loosely across the back of her chair or around her shoulders. Or the rigidity of his body whenever he leaned over to give her a stage kiss.

What would their situation be like when they got to Mexico?

She forced her mind to focus on Jamie, calling up the scene in the restaurant when he'd disappeared, the panic, the terrible night of the failed ransom drop. She dredged up every pain-filled night since then. By the time they boarded the plane, her thoughts were on Jamie only, her reaction to Ethan locked away in her mind. She could do this. No problem, as long as she concentrated on her son.

In spite of his big show as the new husband, Lisa sensed Ethan's eyes never stopped moving. His body, next to hers, was coiled like a steel band. He gave new meaning to the word hyper-alert. She wondered if anyone besides her thought it strange he kept his sunglasses on.

****

Ethan silently cursed his physical reaction to Lisa Mallory. Why the fuck did his body choose now to wake up? For perhaps the one hundredth time, he reminded himself what a crazy idea it was to accept this mission, especially with her along. More than just the insanity of going back into the field again, this situation was like a bomb set to go off.

Since his last assignment had gone to hell and back, all but destroying his life, he'd been very careful to form no attachments to women. Anyone, really, except Josh, but specifically women. Who wanted someone with a soul as black as his? The ones he used for sex knew it was merely a physical release and expected nothing from him. That was what he wanted. No, needed. Every emotion was buried as deep as he could hide it. He was sure there wasn't a female alive who could accept what his past had been and what it had done to him. Or one he wanted to share it with.

Now here was this female, giving him an erection he constantly had to work to conceal. No matter how many silent orders he gave to his cock, the stubborn thing wouldn't go to sleep. Shit! He couldn't afford to let anything distract him, or they could all end up dead—he, Lisa Mallory, and worst of all, young Jamie. What the fuck was it about her, anyway?

His eyes carefully catalogued each face they passed over, seeking one hint of familiarity. Of danger. He kept his sunglasses on to hide the constant movement of his eyes, hoping people would think he was hung over from his wedding. Or just hung over, period. A useless bum not worth a second look.

So far, so good.

When they were called for boarding, he tightened his grip on Lisa's shoulder, signaling her to sit tight until he felt they should move. Finally, when the line was almost at an end, he urged them forward and onto the plane.

"We're on our honeymoon," he told the flight attendant at the cabin door. "Are there two seats left in the back?"

"Newlyweds, huh?" She winked at them. "Lucky for you we have our little two-seat row empty. Usually no one wants to sit there because we stow a lot of junk opposite it."

"Suits us fine." Ethan kissed her cheek. "Right, sweet thing?"

Lisa nodded, and the smile she managed was closer to genuine than he expected.

He still wore his sunglasses that as they moved through the plane's cabin so he could memorize each face. Thank god, some skills never disappeared.

At last, they were at the end of the aisle, squeezing themselves into the two seats. He tucked her tote and his duffle bag underneath them and settled in. He said very little during the flight to Houston, although he kept his arm around her and every so often leaned over and nuzzled her cheek.

"Play it up good," he told her in a soft voice. "I want everyone to remember the Camerons as a loving couple."

"Why did we board so late," she whispered, "and ask for seats in the back?"

"So I could check out the passengers. And back here I can watch everyone else get off and see if someone looks a little off center."

"Do you always live like this? Suspicious of everyone?"

"Goes with the territory. It's how I stayed alive all those years." He took her hand and kissed it, whispering against her knuckles, "Just concentrate on playing your part."

And he'd play his, ruthlessly suffocating the unwanted responses to her that were more than acting.

With less than an hour for the Houston layover, Ethan steered them into a tiny open snack bar where, he explained, he could watch everyone go by. Her body nearly vibrated with nerves, but he had to give her credit. She was playing her part to the hilt and not bombarding him with stupid questions. He was happy to board the plane again, repeating the same routine as before.

The flight attendant handed out tourist cards for everyone to complete. Lisa copied her information from Ethan's, then put it in her purse.

"Don't lose that," he warned. "It could end up being your Get Out of Jail Free card."

Chapter Nine

Finally, they landed in Cancun and walked out into one of the busiest airports in the Caribbean. Concourse shops displayed colorful Mexican clothing and artifacts. Mariachis played in one corner as people strolled by. Tourists jostled each other as they hurried to security and the departure gates. And Lisa was glad to be on the ground. One step closer to finding Jamie.

A representative of Continental handed them a general information packet and herded them through immigration.

"Just act like it's no big deal for the honeymooning Camerons," Ethan murmured. "Hand them your passport and you'll be fine."

She waited while the official examined it.

When he asked the nature of their visit, Ethan said, "Honeymoon," and hugged Lisa to his side.

"Newlyweds?" He smiled and handed their passports back to them. "Your wife is *mucho linda, Senor* Cameron. *Bienvenido a Mexico*. Enjoy your stay."

"What did he say about me?" she asked.

"He said my wife was very beautiful."

She snorted. "Shows you how much he knows. I look like shit."

"If you packed about twenty pounds back on that skinny frame of yours, you'd be a knockout. I'd have a hard time not stripping your clothes off and fucking your brains out."

Lisa stopped and stared at him, open-mouthed.

Ethan pulled on her arm. "Don't let it go to your head. Come on. We have to get out of here."

He hustled her toward one of the rental car desks, where he signed and paid for Ed Cameron's reserved rental, a Toyota Camry.

"Do you need a map, *senor*?" the reservations clerk asked.

"Yeah, that would be great. And directions to the Holiday Inn Express." He planted what had to be the tenth kiss on Lisa's cheek. "Can't wait to get my sweetie in our room." He winked at the girl.

She laughed and handed him his papers. "Someone will bring your car to that exit over there." She pointed at the end of the baggage claim area.

"*Gracias*." He took Lisa's arm and hustled her toward the exit. As they came through the doors, a gray Toyota Camry pulled up and a thin man in slacks and a shirt with a wild print got out. He nodded briefly to Ethan, their eyes exchanging a silent message, then jogged down the sidewalk area.

Minutes later, they were out of the airport and on the highway into town.

"That didn't look like the regular rental car pickup," Lisa commented. "We were the only one receiving a vehicle."

"It isn't, and we were."

"So let me guess. More of your secret stuff. You arranged for someone to bring our car to that spot when they called down from the rental desk." She shook her head. "Forget I even asked."

She decided asking questions got her nowhere so she just stared out the window at the scenery, absorbing it, remembering its geography from the map.

"Cancun is actually a barrier island," Ethan explained as he drove. "It's connected to the Mexican mainland by two bridges, one at the north end and one at the south." He honked at a van that cut in front of him. "Kukulcan Road, the only main thoroughfare, runs directly down the middle of the city."

"I've certainly seen enough advertising about this place," she commented, staring out the window.

"The Hotel Zone takes up most of the island," he went on, "not just with hotels but restaurants and shops, too, that cater to the constant stream of tourists. Downtown Cancun, or Cancun Centro, is where the locals live and play, shop and eat. Less expensive."

"Is that where the Camerons are staying?"

"Nope. We're at the Holiday Inn Express. I spare no expense for my little honey."

Lisa didn't know whether to laugh or smack him.

"We'd be expected to stay there," he clarified. "But the cantina I have to scope out is downtown. I'm hoping there are some other tourists so we won't stick out like sore thumbs. No matter how I play it, a situation like this is always risky."

He was silent on the rest of the drive. Lisa took in the scenery as it flashed past, fascinated by the lush tropical foliage everywhere, the adobe houses with Spanish tile roofs and the bright sun that lit everything up like a Technicolor movie.

The Holiday Inn Express bordered a residential section at the edge of downtown Cancun. Ethan pulled into a side street before entering the hotel parking lot, reached under his seat, and retrieved a package.

Lisa watched in amazement as he broke the tape and pulled out two guns, two boxes of bullets, and an envelope he tucked into his jacket pocket.

He glanced up and caught her stare. "What? I told you someone would take care of the fire power."

"So that man who brought the car really—"

"Doesn't work for the car rental place."

Lisa wanted to ask for more explanation, but that was all he would say. And she wasn't about to push it.

He loaded both guns and leaned forward to stick one in his waistband at the small of his back. The other he gave to her.

"Put this in your purse. Now. And don't leave it anywhere."

She complied with hands that shook only slightly.

In the hotel parking lot, he locked the car and towed her into the lobby.

"Reservations for Ed and Lily Cameron," he told the clerk and grinned as he handed over a credit card. "We're on our honeymoon so tell the maid I might be leavin' the Do Not Disturb sign on the door now and then."

"*Si, senor.*" The clerk smiled at him and handed over the plastic key cards.

Up in their room, Ethan pulled the drapes shut, then spent fifteen minutes checking out every inch of the room, including lampshades and furniture.

"Looking for gold?" Lisa asked.

He put his fingers to his lips and mouthed, "Making sure we aren't bugged."

She felt the blood leave her face but stood silently while he finished his examination.

At last, he nodded his head. "We're clear."

She swallowed. "But—but no one knew we were coming except the people you talked to. And who'd bug Lily and Ed Cameron's room?"

"I'll remind you again someone shot at us. I don't know if they were after me or you, but I don't plan on it happening again. People like this can find out anything they want to know if something alerts them. And you never know what that could be. If it's you, then it definitely has to do with Jamie and someone is going to a lot of trouble to make sure we don't get any answers."

Her breath caught in her throat. "Do you think that means he's alive?"

"I think it means there's a possibility, so we have to be more than careful. I managed to stay alive all these years by doing that. I don't intend to stop now."

Lisa sat down in one of the big armchairs, her legs suddenly weak. She kept forgetting just what kind of life Ethan Caine had lived and how dangerous the mission they were on could prove to be. For both of them.

Looking around the room, she realized it had only one bed. A king. She swallowed again.

Ethan caught her glance, and a rough laugh rumbled out of his throat.

"We're on our honeymoon, remember, Lily? It might have looked a bit suspicious if I asked for two rooms or even two beds."

"But—"

He held up his hand. "We'll figure it out later. Meanwhile, we have shit to do. I want to check out the cantina myself where *Las Tormentas* hangs out before I drag you into it. Besides, I need to home in on the weak link in that group. Someone who can be bribed or pressured to confirm that *Las Tormentas* actually did the deed and tell me where they took Jamie."

She got up from the chair. "I'm going with you."

In a blink, he was crowding her space. "Did you hear me? Have you forgotten our arrangement already? I call the shots."

"But—"

"Uh uh." He made a sound of disgust. "There you go with the buts again, Lisa." His voice was hard and firm. "I've done this a hundred times before. Here and elsewhere. I know what I'm doing, and now I'm wasting valuable time arguing with you." He reached into the packet from the car and pulled out a map. "Here. I have an assignment for you."

"Assignment?" She raised an eyebrow.

"This is more detailed than the ones we looked at. I need to know every road on here that leads into the Roo. Some of them are just little spider trails. There's a marker in the packet. Mark every one out of Playa del Carmen that will take us into the jungle. I don't know yet which one we'll use."

"I think I can manage." But her sarcasm was wasted on him.

He turned toward the door. "Lock the deadbolt, and don't open it for anyone but me. No matter what."

"Wait." She reached out a hand to his arm. "If anyone's watching us, won't they think it's strange you going off like this when we're on our honeymoon?"

"Why, honey," he drawled, back in his newlywed mode, "I'll just make sure they know you need a nap because I tired you out so much last night. And I'm off to buy you a trinket in appreciation." He turned back at the door. "Put the deadbolt on as soon as this door closes. Do not open it unless it's me on the other side. No matter what."

He slapped his battered Panama hat on his head and was gone.

Lisa stared after him at the closed door, a tense thrill of excitement keying her nerves. She was trying not to get her hopes up too much, but this was the closest they'd come in months to finding some kind of an answer. Could Ethan do it? Could he put aside the nightmare he was living with to see this through? She had to believe the answer was yes. He was, after all, her one last hope in this tragedy.

She looked at the map on the table, glad she'd have something to occupy her mind while she waited. The first thing she did, however, was take off the wig. God, that thing was hot. And itchy. She set it on the counter and ran her fingers through her hair. She hoped she'd have time for a shampoo before she had to put the beastly thing on tomorrow. She left the makeup on, however. Too much trouble to redo it as heavy as it was. Then she sat down at the table, map spread out, and picked up one of the markers. She automatically looked at her watch, wondering how long he'd be gone, leaving her to her nerves and anxiety.

Hurry, Ethan.

****

La Mama's was exactly like a million other bars and cantinas Ethan had spent time in over the course of what he euphemistically called his career. Dark, an extreme contrast to the bright tropical sun outside. A long bar on one side, tables filling the rest of the ell-shaped space. Not clean, not dirty. Dingy. Shopworn.

The backwater of life.

This was the place Dino had told him *Las Tormentas* spent their recreational time. Ethan made it a point to wander the area aimlessly, stopping in several cantinas along the way, spending a few minutes in each one before finally entering La Mama's. He took a deep breath to settle himself and kicked his brain into gear. Time to put his demons in the closet and do what he was supposed to. What he'd been trained for. What he'd committed to. Maybe if he succeeded at this, he could reclaim a little bit of his soul.

He ambled into the cool darkness wearing a slightly befuddled expression, blinked against the sudden absence of light, and finally sat down at a table in the far corner. In his wrinkled khakis and outrageously designed shirt, he could have been any tourist come to town. Hat tilted slightly over his face, he let his eyes roam the room, taking in every detail.

Only three people sat at the bar. The rest were spread out at the tables. The customers were mostly men, only two of them with women. They looked like tourists who'd lost their way, huddling together while they tried to appear relaxed.

Ethan had a bad feeling about the situation, and he hadn't ordered his first drink yet. Unless the evening crowd changed a lot, bringing Lisa here tonight had all the makings of a colossal disaster. He'd hoped there would be enough of a mixture of people they could blend in, but it looked like that idea was shot to hell.

Damn that woman, anyway. He should have tied her up and locked her in a closet in Tampa until this was over. They'd have to really play the honeymoon couple determined to soak up some local color. He'd never get what he needed in this place with just one visit. All he could do this afternoon was identify his most likely pigeon and how to make a connection tonight. And hope the guy would still be there.

Shit! This would probably turn out to be the clusterfuck of all time.

He turned his attention to the opposite corner of the room by the archway leading to what he assumed were the restrooms. A group of nine men was drinking at two tables pushed together.

The man at the obvious center of activity was thin with a heavy moustache and thick, dark shoulder-length hair. The heavy gold R, encrusted with diamonds and hanging from a chain at his throat, was easy to see even at a distance. R for Rafael. Rafael Cortez. Undisputed leader of the deadly group.

Ethan dredged up what Dino had told him about the group and its leader. Rafael Cortez had seen both his parents killed in a raid on their village by guerillas. At fourteen, he'd found a new family when a member of Las Tormentas discovered him hiding in the mountains. Twenty years later, his obstacles to leadership had been eliminated and he was the undisputed ruler.

The group had a long history of violence, fighting for nothing except to protect their own corner of the world. It was common knowledge they made their living through kidnapping. According to everything Dino had learned, including Charles Mallory's five-year history in the area, this was the group most likely to have taken Jamie. Now he had to pin down some facts. Make sure this didn't turn into a wild goose chase.

"Drink, *senor*?" The waitress smiled at him.

She was a carbon copy of a million others he'd seen. Not too young, maybe late thirties. A tired face brightened by red lipstick, her slightly plump body attractive in the full skirt and peasant blouse. Her smile didn't quite reach her eyes. And a potential source of information.

"Yeah, I'll take a beer. *Gracias*." He pronounced it almost like gracious, concealing the fact he spoke fluent Spanish.

"We don't get too many tourists in here," she remarked.

He motioned for her to bend down to him and dropped his voice. "What's your name, honey?"

"Deloris."

"Well, Deloris, I'm on my honeymoon. My wife's taking a little nap right now, but we're gonna hit a few bars tonight. She's not much for fancy places. It's not like I'm short on pesos or anything. But some of those fancy hotel bars and restaurants charge as much for a drink as I make in a week."

Deloris gave a small laugh "That is true."

"So a buddy of mine said we could find lots of places down here in Cancan Centro. Where the folks who live here go. I'm checkin' 'em out this afternoon." He leaned close again. "Gotta show the little woman a good time, right?"

"*Si, senor*. But this might not be such a good place to take her."

"Oh, I don't know." He glanced at the bar. "Looks like you got a bouncer to keep out the riff raff." He nodded toward the man behind the bar, who he estimated as not more than five foot five. He guessed

126

his weight at no less than four hundred.

"Oh, that's Mama. The owner."

"Mama's a man?" Ethan thought slapping his knee might be carrying the act a little too far. "No kidding? Well, I guess he doesn't get much trouble in here."

"No, *senor*." She moved away from him. "I'll get your beer."

He slouched in his chair with his hat tilted over his forehead and watched Deloris swivel her way across the room. Rafael motioned to her as she stepped up to the bar, and she moved over to him. He said something, and Ethan saw her nod in his direction, then giggle. Rafael smiled, a grimace in a death's head, and stared across the room at Ethan. Then he turned to his men and made some remark, and they all laughed.

Ethan pretended not to notice, but he was sure the remark was crude and disgusting. Good. So much the better. They'd think him harmless.

When Deloris brought his second beer, he slipped a twenty into her hand. "Keep the change, sweetheart."

He nursed his drink for several minutes, watching the actions of the men at the table. There was an obvious pecking order, designated by where they sat in relation to *el jefe*. He focused on one man at the far end of the table. Everyone seemed to ignore him for the most part, until someone wanted something. Then he became the gofer. Not a man with much power, the kind most easily turned. Or bought.

"Those folks over there seem like they're having a good time," he commented to Deloris, making his voice as casual as possible. "They from the neighborhood?"

She shrugged. "Here and there."

"Who's the guy in the middle? Looks interestin'."

He dropped a fifty on the table, and she quickly palmed it. "Just between you and me, *senorita*." He winked.

"That's Rafael Cortez. *El jefe. Mucho hombre*." She wiggled her eyebrows, but the smile on her face didn't get anywhere near her eyes.

"And the little skinny guy? He doesn't look too happy."

"Tonio. The peon. He does *el jefe's* bidding."

"I'd say he's not havin' as good a time as everyone else," Ethan commented in his exaggerated drawl.

"No. I'd say not. He has a wife and child, or I think he might not be here at all." She tucked the money into her pocket with barely any movement. "I talk too much. I must go, *senor*. They will want more drinks."

"Looks like they've had plenty already."

"Oh, no, not yet. When they come in they are here until closing."

Okay. So tonight, the alcohol would have softened his mark a little more. And hopefully made everyone else let down their guard just a tiny bit.

Deloris walked away, hips swaying. Cortez motioned to her again. She said something to him, and the man laughed. He gave Ethan a look of contempt.

Finally, Ethan stood up, making a show of dropping a couple of dollars on the table for Deloris and made his way to the door. He forced himself not to look over his shoulder as he walked slowly along the three blocks to where his car was parked. The middle of his back itched, as if eyes were fastened on him.

He stopped at a tiny neighborhood bakery right near his car, ostensibly to look at the pastries in the window, and slid his eyes to the right. Sure enough, one of the men at Rafael's table was about half a block behind him. When Ethan stopped, the guy leaned against a street light and lit a cigarette.

He'd been right. Strangers attracted too much attention, and Rafael was apparently suspicious of everyone. He wished he had more than one day to do this, time to establish himself as a harmless gringo bum who didn't raise anyone's eyebrows. Well, it couldn't be helped. He was stuck with what he had.

Deciding to play out the role of honeymooner, Ethan stepped into the bakery and bought some wedding pastries for Lisa, a tactic to throw off his shadow. He didn't give a damn if she ate them, although she could certainly afford to indulge. The last time he'd seen a woman that skinny was in a hospital. He was actually surprised that Lisa handled the physical training as well as she did. He'd expected her to collapse before they got to the halfway mark.

The woman was an enigma. She was both tough and fragile, accepting and rejecting. His body had reactions to hers that made being near her hazardous, and the proximity this task demanded made it even more perilous. It wasn't just the physical attraction that frightened him. In her eyes, he saw the same fires of hell that burned in him. A kindred soul. The most dangerous kind. Somehow, he'd have to figure out how to handle her while getting the job done. A daunting task.

He emerged from the bakery carrying his little box of pastries and whistling tunelessly as he made it to the car.

Everything nice and slow, Caine. Remember, you're going back there later. Don't stir the pot.

As he pulled out of his parking space, he glanced in

the rearview mirror and saw the same member of *Las Tormentas* standing in front of the bakery. The man took a final drag on the cigarette and ground it out deliberately under his foot. He watched until the car pulled away and blended into the chaos that was Cancun traffic.

Ethan let out a slow breath, forcing himself to relax. Bringing Lisa with him when he came back here was sheer idiocy, but he'd set himself up for it. He just hoped he didn't get her killed. He didn't think he could handle one more death on his watch.

Chapter Ten

Lisa had studied the map and finished marking the very narrow routes into the jungle within the first half hour after Ethan left. After that, she was reduced to pacing and staring at her watch until she decided that would get her nowhere. Besides, she was tired, exhausted enough from tension and the hard week of workouts that, even on edge, she was sure she could nap a little. Then she'd be alert for whatever Ethan had in store when he returned.

She slipped off her shoes, turned back the spread on the bed, and sipped beneath the covers. Even if she didn't sleep, at least she could try to rest and store up her energy. But the moment her eyes closed Ethan's form danced in her dream.

He was naked, his body just as hard and firm as it had seemed beneath his T-shirt and workout pants. His cock rose proudly from a nest of curls at his groin, the head a dark purple. A tiny bead of fluid rested at the slit. She couldn't tear her eyes away.

His laugh was deep and rough.

"Like what you see? Because I sure do."

His eyes raked over her from head to toe. At first, she'd been hesitant about being naked with him. She hadn't been with a man in a long time, and after Jamie was born, Charles had done little to instill confidence in her as a woman. But the heat and hunger in Ethan's dark eyes made her nipples harden and ache for his touch. The walls of her pussy clenched with need.

He reached out to cup her breasts with his warm hands, his palms rough against her soft skin, but the feeling of abrasion only ramped up her reaction to him. The scent of her musk was so strong she knew he could sense it.

"You have gorgeous breasts." His voice still had that gravely quality to it, but its very timbre only made her hotter.

"I—I'm glad you like them." She forced herself to stand still while he kneaded them with a gentle squeeze of his fingers.

"Oh, I like every part of you. All the parts." There was no mistaking his meaning.

When he lowered his head and pulled one stiff nipple into the wet heat of his mouth, an electric shock raced through her. The graze of his teeth over the surface set all her nerve endings on fire. She closed her eyes and gave herself over to the erotic sensations sweeping through her.

When he had nipped and licked the one nipple for a while, he turned his attention to the other one and did the same things all over. Lisa had to hold onto his shoulders to keep herself from falling backward, and a jumble of hot pleasure cascaded through her. Before she realized what he was doing, he nudged her to the bed where she collapsed on the edge her knees hardly able to hold her any more.

"Lisa," he murmured in that sexy gravel voice. "Beautiful, gorgeous Lisa. I could lick you from head to toe" In the next moment, he dropped to his knees, parted her thighs, and proceeded to stroke each leg with his tongue from ankle to thigh, pausing for a barely-there taste of her throbbing pussy.

Shivers skittered through her, and she sucked in a breath. She wanted to tell him to leave his tongue there. To keep it there. She couldn't remember the last time she'd felt this turned on. This wanton.

She gripped his head and tried to hold it in place, but he just chuckled, the sound vibrating through her core. He teased her everywhere with his tongue, licking and stroking, until she was ready to burst into flames. She almost wept with relief when at last he spread the lips of her sex with his thumb and gave a long, slow swipe of his tongue up the length of her slit. Then he did it again, and punctuated it by nipping her aching clit.

"God!" She gripped the hair on his head even more tightly and rocked into his mouth as shivers of sensation skittered over her.

Then, without warning, he thrust his stiffened tongue into her core, scraping the sensitive inner walls and hitting that special hot spot. That was all it took for her body to explode, her juices pouring onto his tongue, her inner walls spasming.

She was breathless when the orgasm was over, panting, but he gave her no rest. Grabbing a condom from the nightstand, he rolled it on with practiced expertise, lifted her legs, and drove into her with one powerful thrust.

Oh, god!

If she thought his mouth did magic things to her body, it was nothing compared to his hands and his hot, thick cock. He filled every inch of her, scraped every sensitive inner nerve as he thrust into her again and again. Bracing himself with one hand, he slipped the other between them, found her clit, and massaged it with expert thoroughness.

"Now, Lisa," he commanded, as if he knew every nuance of her body. "Come now."

And she did, exploding with him in a cataclysmic orgasm that rocked both of them. The spasms went on and on, his thick shaft throbbing inside her, his breath rasping, although she could barely hear it over the pounding of her heart.

Then he collapsed forward, his breath choppy and warm against her arm, her own heart pounding in a heavy rhythm.

She was totally unprepared for his kiss, startled both by the act of it and by the innate tenderness. The unspoken emotion. His tongue danced lightly with hers before he slid his lips to the right and peppered kisses along the line of her jaw.

She pressed her body up to him, winding her arms around his neck, and—

"Lily? Hey, sugar, open up. It's me."

And just like that, reality slapped her like a cold drink of water. She pushed herself off the bed, did her best to straighten her rumpled clothes and the mussed bedspread.

And to wipe the vestiges of the erotic dream from her brain so she didn't say something stupid.

"Who is it?"

"It's me, Lily. Come to collect my honey." Ethan used his fake honeymoon voice.

As she thought about what his "honey" had been doing, had been dreaming, a hot flush raced over her body. She took in a deep breath and let it out slowly, slapped the wig temporarily on her head and headed for the door.

Wait! What if it wasn't him? What if this was a trick? She swallowed hard and cleared her throat.

"How do I know it's you?"

She heard him curse briefly, then, "Who else would propose to you at Manny's Diner? Come on, sweet thing. Let me in."

His voice was strained, but when she opened the door and he slid in, he nodded approvingly. "Good. You have a brain."

She didn't know whether to laugh hysterically or smack him, so she just ignored the comment. The wig came off again and she raked her fingers through her hair, hoping he'd think her slightly disheveled appearance would be from studying the material he'd left her.

"You know that thing goes back on when we leave here."

"I just needed a little break from it." She wet her lips. "I have the information you wanted. How was your outing?"

"Interesting." Ethan handed her the small box from the bakery.

"What's this?" She frowned.

"A present from your new husband. If you don't like the stuff, you can throw it out. It was a couple doors down from the bar, and I needed a distracting errand. They sent someone to watch me when I left."

She opened the box and looked at its contents. "These look delicious. Thanks."

He tossed his hat onto the small round table and dropped onto the bed, running his hands though his hair. She gave silent thanks he didn't notice the rumpled spread and pillows. Or if he did, he chose to ignore them.

"I wish to hell I could figure out a way to leave you out of it tonight. I'm having serious second thoughts about dragging you along on this."

She frowned. "Why? What's the problem?"

"This place is a little rougher than I'd expected, and they don't get enough *touristas* in to provide cover. I'm hoping tonight will be different. I should never have agreed to let you come along. Fuck. If you get hurt, or worse—"

"Stop." Lisa held up a hand. "Listen to me. There's no way I'd still be home in Tampa chewing nails while you were down here looking for Jamie. So don't go there again. Okay? I don't know the details of the mission that sent you into such a tailspin, but I can believe it wasn't your fault."

"You don't know—"

"I don't have to. Josh said it wasn't your fault, and that's good enough for me. Nothing is going to happen to me, Ethan. You spent all those hours conditioning me, teaching me to defend myself. I have a gun that I know how to handle and won't hesitate to shoot someone if I have to. And you are going to do what you always did, in the Marines, at Guardian, and in…whatever you did after you left them. You're going to watch out for me."

"But—"

"No buts. Now shut up and let's get to it."

He clenched his jaw. "Just so you're prepared, this place we're going to is dangerous. It's risky enough for me, and the last thing I want is for something to happen to you."

"Damn it, Ethan." She curled her hands into fists and forced herself to stay calm. The man pushed every one of her buttons. "Nothing is more dangerous than the years I spent with Charles Mallory. If I hadn't had Jamie to think of, I would have been happy to die just to be free of him. But now my son is all I have, so don't even think about shutting me out of this."

"Doesn't matter anyway." He wiped a hand over his face. "I can't leave you alone here. If someone followed me or sniffed us out you'd be a sitting duck. So. We go as planned. And we're on the alert every single second." He got up, went to the minibar, and took out a bottle of orange juice. He gestured toward her. "Want a drink of something? A snack?"

"A juice if there's another one."

He brought two bottles to the round table by the window and sat down. "Okay. Show me what you marked on the map. After that, we'll eat and pay another visit to La Mama's."

She raised her eyebrows. "La Mama's?"

He actually laughed. "Yeah. Wait until you see Mama." He drank half the juice in two swallows and wiped his mouth with the back of his hand. "Okay. Let's have it."

Lisa unfolded the map on the table and showed each marked route to Ethan. He studied them carefully and nodded his head. "Good. You did a good job."

She hated to admit that his praise warmed her. "Thanks."

"I'm hoping, after tonight, we can zero in on which of these we'll take." He folded the map and stuck it inside his jacket. "Let's go eat."

Lisa set the wig back on her head, fluffing out the curls, and took a moment to make sure her makeup was as thick and exaggerated as when she'd applied it. Then she followed him out of the room. He took them to a small restaurant on a side street running off Cancun's main drag. The small room inside was dark and cool, but Ethan asked for seating on the patio, where several tables with gaily colored umbrellas made an eye-catching scene. He chose one in the farthest corner, next to a gate in the back wall. When the waitress had taken their drink orders, he opened the gate, poked his head out, nodded, and sat down.

"I always like options if I have to leave in a hurry," he explained in answer to her questioning look.

"Do you think that will happen here?"

He shrugged. "You never know, but it's always a possibility. I like to be prepared."

"That's good. Very good." She looked at the menu, but her stomach was so knotted with apprehension she was sure she couldn't digest a bite.

Ethan, however, insisted she get some food into her system, literally forcing the food on her when she simply toyed with it. "You have to have at least one drink in this joint we're going to. You can't drink without food in your stomach."

She tried to protest. "I can order a soft drink of some kind."

He shook his head. "Too conspicuous. Eat up."

He kept his sunglasses on, but behind them, Lisa knew his eyes constantly scanned the area, like a revolving radar.

"Do you see something?"

"No, but that doesn't mean anything. I have an itch

at the back of my neck I don't like. Eat slowly so we look like we have all the time in the world."

Lisa was more than grateful when Ethan's plate was empty at last, and he called for the check.

****

Ethan was right. La Mama's was definitely not on the convention bureau's list of tourist spots.

As soon as her eyes adjusted to the dark, Lisa did a quick visual survey of the room, trying to look like a tourist. The only light in the place came from some tiny wall sconces and candles on the table, a vague attempt at window dressing. She was glad she wasn't seeing it in the daylight. She was sure every bug known to man was crawling around in the corners.

It was immediately obvious they were an unlikely couple for this place. Ethan had been on target about the clientele. The men reminded her of characters in a B movie. A very bad one at that. And the women had a tawdry look about them. Well, with her wig and ten pounds of makeup, she figured she fit right in. Every eye seemed to be on them, and the looks thrown their way as they walked in made her feel as if she were a dot on a microscope slide, but she played her part, hanging onto Ethan's arm and swaying her hips.

When they were seated a table, she glanced around the room and spotted the table with the rough-looking gang. The man she assumed to be the group leader looked as if he'd cut their throats for mild entertainment. But she was trying to take her cue from Ethan and forced herself to appear as relaxed as possible. Only the thought they might get some information about Jamie kept her from bolting.

"The nasty piece of goods over there is Rafael

Cortez." Ethan's mouth barely moved as he whispered to her. "He's the chief badass and the one I think headed up the kidnap."

For the first time since she'd asked Ethan Caine to help her, she realized the full dangerous nature of what they were undertaking. Her whole body tightened.

He had his arm around her, gripping her shoulder. "Look at me. Not over there. Now."

She forced herself to turn her head and smile at him, a smile she was far from feeling. She barely nodded toward the heavy man behind the bar and lowered her voice to the level of Ethan's. "Who's that?"

He chuckled. "That's Mama."

Lisa had to stop herself from reacting. "You're kidding, right?"

"Not a bit. I'll bet he makes sure even the unruliest of patrons behave. Here comes my waitress from this afternoon." He stretched his mouth into an easy grin.

"I see you brought *la senora* tonight." Deloris greeted Ethan with easy familiarity, tipping her head toward Lisa. "I told you, maybe this is not such a good place for her to be. She looks like a classy lady."

Ethan rubbed Lisa's shoulder in an affectionate gesture. "She is, she is. But we been doin' a little cantina hoppin' in the downtown area, and she wanted to see where I'd been this afternoon while she took a little nap." He leaned forward toward Deloris and dropped his voice. "Wore her out last night, ya know."

Lisa blushed in spite of herself. "Oh, Ed," she simpered, nearly making herself gag. She looked at Deloris with what she hoped was a touch of shyness. "He loves to joke around, you know."

Deloris moved her shoulders in an eloquent shrug.

"If you say so."

Ethan nodded toward the table across the room. "I see your friends from this afternoon are still here."

Lisa allowed herself another glance at the men. Rafael's dark gaze made her shudder, and she quickly looked away.

"*Si*, but not for much longer. Tonio will have to leave to go home to his wife and child, so *el jefe* will go, also. No one to fetch and carry for him."

Ethan raised his eyebrows. "Doesn't seem quite fair for the poor little guy to be the only one doin' it all."

Deloris pursed her lips. "Such is life, *senor*. He needs the money badly enough to let *el jefe* use him for a doormat. And now I must get your drinks. I am talking too much. *El jefe* would not be pleased."

Ethan slipped her a folded bill even before he ordered.

"Just for takin' good care of the missus and me." He winked at her.

"Of course, *senor*." She gave Ethan a knowing smile. "What would you like?"

Ethan ordered beer for both of them and tilted the bottle to his mouth as soon as they came. Watching him, Lisa realized he actually drank very little of it. He slouched with his arm around her chair and his hat pulled low, covering part of his face. He was paying careful attention to the group of men at the table across the room while appearing to relax and enjoy himself.

He hitched his chair closer to her and said quietly, "Move over next to me. Act like we're in love."

"What—"

"Jesus, Lisa." He pushed his hat back slightly,

pulled her head close to him, and kissed her full on the mouth.

She opened her mouth to protest, and his tongue slipped inside. The shock to her system nearly paralyzed her. His tongue was like a torch, leaving licks of flame every place it touched in the warm interior of her mouth. At once, her erotic dream of that afternoon popped into her brain, and her long dormant body woke up. Her nipples hardened, and moisture pooled between her thighs, where a heavy pulse throbbed.

Lisa's brain froze, and she forgot where they were and what they were supposed to be doing, so lost in the kiss that nothing else mattered.

When Ethan lifted his mouth, for one brief instant, the pain that was always reflected in his eyes had faded and she saw her own sense of shock mirrored there.

"Jesus," he breathed again.

Her heartbeat sped up and the pulse in her throat hammered so hard she was sure he could see it.

Then his rigid discipline took over again. He moved his head away, and they were two strangers joined in a common plan. The kiss might never have happened at all.

Lisa forced a calmness she didn't feel, focusing on the bottle of beer in front of her.

He put his lips close to her ear. "We're acting, okay? Just think of it as acting."

Acting? Her body wasn't playing let's pretend. She reached way down inside herself to gather her scattered wits.

"Jamie," she whispered. "We have to focus on Jamie."

"That's what we're doing." His mouth was still

close to hers. "This is all part of the plan."

Part of the plan. Right.

But she felt the tension in her body reflected in his, and it wasn't from the danger of the situation. Now what? Had she totally lost her mind? Could the situation possibly get any more complicated? The last thing she'd ever expected was the flare of sexual attraction between her and this unlikeliest of men. But there it was, and she couldn't deny the fact that she craved it.

An overdue reaction. That's all it is.

A delayed response to all the years when sex with Charles had been either brutal, demeaning, or nonexistent.

She picked up her beer and sipped at it, hoping the now lukewarm liquid would, in some measure, cool her heated blood. And what would happen when they returned to the hotel and the room they shared? The room with its one bed?

She didn't have much time to dwell on it, however. Deloris, the buxom waitress determined to earn her tip, brought them two more bottles of beer and did a little harmless flirting with Ethan.

"Ah, but you just have eyes for *la senora*." She laughed. "If only my man would kiss me with such fire." She kissed her fingertips and waved them in the air.

Ethan inclined his head toward Cortez's table. "Think I oughta buy those folks a drink? Show 'em how neighborly I can be?" He smiled at the group and touched the brim of his hat.

Deloris shook her head, just a fraction of a movement. Then she leaned over, showing more cleavage than Lisa thought she'd ever have in a lifetime. "They do not take kindly to strangers. You should take *la senora* someplace else. Cortez, he has been drinking all day and he is eyeing the lady with hunger. Finish your drinks and go."

Ethan nodded and slid another folded bill into her palm. "I thank you kindly. *Gracias*." He stood up. "Can you keep the little lady here company for a minute while I answer the call of nature?"

"*Si, senor*. My pleasure." She didn't sit down, but her posture made it very clear she was engaged in conversation with Lisa, shielding her from Rafael Cortez's avaricious stare.

"Be right back." He leaned over to kiss Lisa on the cheek and whispered, "Whatever you do, try to look relaxed and don't stare at that table over there. Deloris rules the roost here. She'll be sure you're okay." He brushed his mouth over hers. "And by the way, the disguise is perfect. If these guys had a picture of Lisa Mallory, they'd never connect it with you. Good job."

Lisa swallowed a smile and watched him amble off toward the back hallway, trying to tamp down the case of nerves threatening to burst forth. He wouldn't really leave her alone if he thought she was in danger. She had to remember that. Or maybe this was one of those times when she'd be expected to take care of herself.

She turned toward Deloris and pasted on a smile.

****

Ethan had seen Tonio slide from the table and head for the restroom. He had one chance and very few minutes to make this contact and hope it didn't blow up in his face. The itch on the back of his neck was growing stronger.

When he pushed open the door to the men's room, Tonio was just finishing at the urinal and zipping up his jeans. He gave Ethan a quick look, then averted his gaze.

As he moved toward the door, Ethan put out a hand to stop him. "I have some money to spend for a man willing to earn it."

Tonio tried to pull away from him. "Excuse, *senor*."

Ethan didn't budge. "Five hundred dollars American could go a long way to helping your family, Tonio. And maybe I can help get all of you out of here."

At the use of his name, Tonio looked at Ethan, fear flashing in his eyes. "Who are you? Did *el jefe* send you in here to tempt me? Test my loyalty?"

"I'm no friend to Cortez. I'm trying to find a little boy who was kidnapped. Rumor has it *Las Tormentas* did the job. I'm willing to pay whoever can tell me where this boy is now."

Tonio began edging away from him. "*Senor*, I…"

"Five hundred dollars, Tonio. And a chance to escape Cortez. All you have to do is give me the information I need."

"I know nothing. Please."

Ethan narrowed his eyes at the man. "You do want to get out from under this, right? Rumors don't lie?"

Tonio nodded his head.

"Okay. Meet me in two hours." He named a waterfront bar he'd used centuries ago that, according to the phone book, was still in business. "Now you better get back out there. *El jefe* will send someone looking for you in a minute."

Tonio stared at him for a long moment, despair and hope mingling in his eyes. Then he hurried from the restroom as if the devil was on his heels. Ethan waited an appropriate amount of time before going back to his own table.

Deloris was still standing where he'd left her. He gave Lisa high marks for concealing her nervousness and playing her role as well as she did, smiling and chatting with Deloris. Only someone who knew her as well as he had come to would notice her tight grip on the bottle or the nervous movement of her leg.

"Ah, here you are, *senor*. Your bride and I have been having a wonderful conversation." Deloris winked at him. "And now I must get back to work."

"Hi, darlin'." He kissed Lisa's cheek while he skillfully slipped another folded bill into Deloris's hand. "I don't know about you, but I'm ready to head back to the hotel and get back to the best part of the honeymoon."

He winked at Deloris who laughed.

Chapter Eleven

Nodding casually toward the group at Cortez's table and smiling briefly, Ethan led Lisa out of La Mama's with his arm firmly around her waist and his head angled so he could drop a kiss on her cheek. When they reached the sidewalk, he popped the locks on the rental car and settled them inside. He sat for a few minutes, nuzzling Lisa's neck until she was afraid her self-control would shatter. The sensual dream still clung to her brain, her nipples hardening and poking into the soft fabric of her dress. Her sex pounded so hard she had to squeeze her thighs together. In a minute, she might have to rip off both her clothes and his and tell him to take her right there in the car.

Insanity. This is pure madness.

"What are you doing?" She was trying her best to keep her voice even and slow the pulse that was beating like a butterfly on speed.

"Watching to see if we have an audience like I did this afternoon. Sure enough, there he is. No." He gripped Lisa's chin and held it firmly. "Don't turn your head. Don't look. I can see just fine from this angle."

She dug her fingernails into the outside of her purse, willing herself not to react to Ethan's nearness or the feel of his body. "How long do we stay like this?"

"Just a few seconds more." His mouth was at her ear. To the outsider looking in, it would appear he was busy necking with his wife. "Okay. Now he's looking this way again. Make this look good."

He threaded his fingers through her hair, gripping her skull, and melded his lips hard against hers. This time, he didn't wait for her to open her mouth. He thrust his tongue against the seam of her lips and forced them open, the flame of his tongue scorching the insides of that dark wet cavern. His other arm was wrapped around her shoulders, binding her to him so tightly she could feel the buttons on his shirt.

She couldn't help herself, drowning in the kiss as she was. She met his tongue and dueled with it, thrust her fingers through the thick stands of his hair, and pulled his head tighter to hers. She pressed herself as hard to him as she could and forgot their situation and their location. Forgot everything except the assault this man was making on her mouth and the fire that raced through her body because of it. Her pussy ached with need, and she was so damp she was sure he could smell her musk. God, how she wanted him inside her. She hadn't wanted a man this way in so long she was ready to explode.

Not good! Not good!

There was something about Ethan Caine that was so primal, so male, she couldn't tear herself away from it. The tiny functioning part of her brain was shouting I'm in trouble.

When he released her and moved back into his seat, she felt a sudden sense of loss, a chill replacing the heat. She forced her eyes open and saw him reaching for the ignition.

"Sorry about that." His voice was gruff but matter of fact. "I wanted to put on a good show for the guy on the sidewalk."

A good show. Yes. That's all it is, Lisa. Keep that in mind. This is nothing to him.

Her pulse was beating an erratic tattoo, and she wasn't sure if it was the kiss or the threat of imminent danger. She smoothed her skirt, adjusted the top of her dress, and ran her fingers through her hair. Her lips felt swollen, and she wasn't too sure she could form words with them.

She cleared her throat. "No problem. Whatever it takes."

Jamie. Keep thinking of Jamie.

They pulled out onto Kukulcan Boulevard, the main street that ran the length of Cancun, and blended into the traffic.

"Now what?" she asked.

"I'm afraid Ed and Lily Cameron's honeymoon is about to be derailed."

"I don't understand."

Ethan swore softly as he played dodge 'em in the erratic Cancun traffic. When he was clear of a jumble of cars, he answered her. "Sometimes, no matter what part you play, something triggers a reaction you don't want. The guy who came out on the sidewalk looking for us is the same one who followed me out this afternoon. We stuck out like sore thumbs at La Mama's and made Cortez take notice of us."

Lisa's stomach knotted. "So what does that mean?"

"Think. Why else would two unlikely *gringos* be scoping out a place like La Mama's? What's the diciest thing they've done? Kidnap Jamie."

"But…"

"There's more behind this than a band of guerillas.

Normally these groups don't cross over the border for their kidnappings. A lot of times, it's purely the opportunity of the moment. Jamie's was well planned and orchestrated. It means someone a lot smarter with a lot more connections is behind the whole thing, and they're on the lookout for anything suspicious."

"But who?" she burst out, fear gripping her. "With Charles dead, Jamie and I are of no importance to anyone."

"That's what we have to find out. Going back to the hotel is too risky. I don't want to be trapped in a closed room. We'll leave our stuff there in case anyone followed me this afternoon and asked questions about the honeymooners. If they think we're still hanging around and they can find us, that might satisfy them. Or they might simply walk away from it, in which case we'll know they were just nosy about two strangers and haven't connected us to Jamie. Anyway, anything we might need is in the car."

"What are we doing now?"

"We'll do a little bar-hopping just to try and throw people off if they're following. Also to make sure we shake them before we head for the marina area."

"And we're going there because?" she prompted when he didn't continue. God, getting information out of him was like digging a trench in stone.

"Did you see the guy who came out of the men's room before I did? I'm meeting him in two hours."

"Is he the weak link you talked about? The one who could be bought?" She did her best to keep her voice even, but she wanted to scream at him and rip the words out of his throat. "Can he tell us where Jamie is?"

"That's what I'm counting on. Maybe even the name of the person really behind all of this. My end of the bargain is to get him and his family away from where Cortez can get at them. Someplace safe. At the same time, I'll arrange to have some things delivered to me that we'll need. So wherever we stop tonight, just keep up with your act if you can."

"For God's sake, Ethan." She spit the words out. "I'm not going to screw anything up. I'm not an idiot, you know. I'll do whatever I have to if it means we're closer to finding Jamie. That's the most important thing. I'm not going to get myself killed, okay?"

Next to her, every muscle in his body tightened. Then he flexed his hands on the steering wheel. "Fine."

Lisa studied him as he drove, weaving his way through cars and pedestrians. Gone was the man who'd let life consume him. Who ate and drank to excess. Who considered rudeness an admirable trait. All things, by the way, she'd figured out were a disguise to hide the constant pain he lived with. The guilt that he couldn't deal with, even if it was misplaced. In his place was a hardened warrior focused on a mission. Thank the lord, was all she could think. At last, she was able to believe that there was some truth to the myths about him after all.

They worked their way in an aimless pattern to the west side of Cancun one bar at a time, staying just long enough in each one not to look suspicious and for Ethan to check out who came in and went out. In the car, Lisa used all her willpower not to constantly turn her head to look out the rear window.

By the time they reached their destination, her nerves were stretched as far as they could go. She was beginning to get the itch in her back like Ethan, sure someone's bullet was about to hit her any minute. Her eyes took in every face, every pair of eyes, wondering if she was looking at friend or foe. Fear was gripping her again, and it took everything she had to maintain the appearance of a lovesick newlywed.

When they pulled into Juana's on the Beach, Ethan parked at the far end of the parking lot, killed the engine and the lights, and put a hand on Lisa's arm to stop her from opening the door.

"Wait." His voice was so quiet she almost didn't hear him.

"For what?"

"To see who comes into the parking lot next. I wish we'd had time to give Tonio a little test drive, see if he really came through on something, but we don't have any time to spare. So we wait and pray. Besides, I need to touch base with Nick."

He pulled a cell phone out of his pants pocket and pressed the speed dial for Nick Vanetta.

"It's me," he said in his now familiar abrupt way. In concise sentences, be brought Nick up to date. "Just checking now to see if we've been made. If we have, you need to help us figure a Plan B. If not, we're good to go. I'll need help getting my source to safety. I'll touch base with you as soon as I know."

They sat in the car for five minutes, Ethan draping his arm around her shoulders to give the impression they were doing a little more impromptu necking.

Lisa forced her mind to think of unpleasant things, cold things, anything to counteract the heat they generated between them. She took some small measure of satisfaction knowing she wasn't the only one affected by their playacting. Ethan wasn't as immune to the kisses as he tried to pretend. Or to her. He was a disciplined person, so only if she'd been looking for it would she catch the slightly erratic breathing or the tremor in his arms. But it was there. And it wasn't due to their mission.

When had sexual attraction suddenly taken on a life of its own between the two of them? Was it during that almost kiss back at the farmhouse? The caresses at the airport? That first scorcher in La Mama's? Whatever, it lay there now like an elephant between them, taking up far too much space.

How was it possible that, in the midst of her terror and fear for Jamie's life, erotic need was insinuating itself into her existence. Ethan Caine was hardly a person she'd choose to break her long period of abstinence, but God, her traitorous body responded to him without her even directing it.

And that dream today. Her nipples and her core ached with the memory.

It's the danger. The unreal situation. Just remember. We're here to find Jamie, not to have sex. Nothing's going to happen. We're adults. Nothing is going to happen.

Yeah, keep telling yourself that.

"Okay." He slid his arm away from her. "Fluff up that wig a little and wipe off your lipstick. You can put more on when we get inside."

"Excuse me?"

His bad temper edged his words. "You don't want people to think we've been out here discussing world politics, do you?"

"Oh." And please continue to be rude to me so I

can think of a million ways of killing you. That should keep my libido in check.

"Come on." He reached for her hand and led her across the lot to the back door of Juana's.

Inside, music was playing loudly from speakers over the bar and the level of conversation was competing for dominance with the music. The room was wall-to-wall people—sitting at the tiny tables, jammed along the bar, standing in whatever space they could find.

Two bartenders were working at top speed to keep up with the orders hitting them in a steady stream. A couple in one corner attempted to dance on the few inches of floor beneath their feet, although Lisa wasn't sure what they were doing could technically be called dancing.

Ethan steered her to a space at the end of the bar and shoved some money into her hand. "Hang onto your purse and be sure you can get to your gun."

She tensed. "My gun?"

"I don't expect you to need it, but let's not take any chances."

"All right. I'm good, Ethan. I can handle myself. Truly. Do what you need to." She hitched the strap up higher on her shoulder and brought the purse around so she had her hands on it. Be prepared with the gun. Sure. Exactly. Shoot it off in a crowded bar, right? She could do that. For a moment, she had the urge to giggle, which she quickly stifled.

"Order us drinks. Anything. It doesn't matter. We won't be drinking them. And don't be in too big a hurry to do it."

"Where are you going?" And leaving me here in

this mob.

"To see a man about a bathroom." He raised his voice.

****

Ethan spotted Tonio making himself small near the hallway to the restrooms the moment they entered. Leaving Lisa at the bar, he headed in that direction. Two men stood at urinals, and a third was washing his hands, but Tonio wasn't visible. Ethan took the opportunity to relieve himself, and when the last person had left, Tonio slipped out from the single stall.

"We can't talk inside here." He stood beside Ethan at the sink, his hands shaking as he washed them. "Too much traffic in and out."

"Outside. You go first."

Ethan followed him out of the rest room. Lisa was still standing where he'd left her, a fake smile on her face as she watched the bartenders. He yelled at her that he was getting something from the car, then made his way to the back door.

The heat of the tropical night wrapped itself around him, a humid blanket that should have had him dripping in perspiration. But he had that chilled feeling he always got when he was on a mission, the feeling that someone was watching him. He stopped in the shadow of the building and let his gaze travel over the entire area—the other bars and restaurants along this strip, the parking lot, wherever he could see—but nothing jumped out at him.

Tonio was waiting next to a storage shed, away from any illumination.

"If this is a trap," he told Ethan, "go ahead and kill me but leave my family alone."

"No trap. You have my word."

"What do you want with me? And how can you help my family?"

Ethan studied the man. Fear rolled off him in waves, and his eyes shifted constantly. They both knew the kind of revenge men like Cortez extracted for betrayal. But Tonio could be as much danger to Ethan as Ethan could to him. Right at that moment, their eyes assessing each other, the decision would have to be made by both whether to trust or not.

"I hear you have a family, a wife and child, that you're worried about."

Tonio said nothing.

"A wife and child," Ethan repeated. "Wouldn't you like to get them—and you—away from Cortez if the opportunity came up? Get all of you somewhere far away?"

Again, Tonio just stood there, but Ethan could see him processing the words, trying to decide what to do.

"If that's so," the man said at last, "what does it mean to you? You're just a gringo down here for whatever reason. If my family and I are dead tomorrow, your life still goes on."

"I need information," Ethan told him. "I told you that. You give it to me, and I'll have you and your family out of here before daylight."

"You give your word?" Tonio watched Ethan's face.

Ethan nodded. "My word is good. It's not to my advantage to lie to you. Dead bodies don't make people trust you."

"What is it you want to know?"

"Did *Las Tormentas* engineer a kidnapping three

months ago across the border? In Florida?"

He'd be able to tell if Tonio tried to bluff him. He'd cut his losses and walk away. But the frightened man answered him truthfully.

"Yes. To my shame." His face twisted with misery. "You have to believe me that we don't usually take children."

"I'm looking for that boy, Tonio. Eight years old." Ethan watched Tonio carefully. The telltale flicker in the man's eyes told him he was on the right track. "Here's his picture." He held out the photo Lisa had given him. "This is the one you and your people kidnapped in Tampa, Florida, right? And took to some place in the Quintana Roo. His mother is desperate to get him back."

Tonio said nothing, just shifted his feet and stared out at the Gulf of Mexico as if deciding what to say next.

"Tonio." Ethan softened his voice. "You have a child yourself. How would your wife feel if that child was ripped from her arms and taken far away?"

Tonio fidgeted. "If you don't get us out of here, that is liable to happen. Or else Cortez will kill us all, and not in a nice way."

"I told you," Ethan insisted. "It's a done deal. Just give me the information."

At last, the man nodded, just a sharp jerk of his head.

"I will tell you what you want." He blew out a breath. "*Las Tormentas* was hired to kidnap a small boy in Florida. And yes, this is him."

An unexpected thrill of excitement tickled Ethan's nerves. Lisa's son! Now maybe within their reach.

"And?" he prompted.

"Cortez received a million dollars for getting the boy and handing him over to a man who owns a huge *finca*, a plantation, deep in the Quintana Roo"

"Who was the man?" Ethan demanded.

"I don't know his name, but Cortez knew him." Tonio frowned. "I think they do some other business together."

"Drug business?" Ethan probed.

Tonio shrugged.

"Can you give me directions to the *finca*?"

"When we meet I can bring you a map."

Ethan swallowed a smile. This kid wanted to make sure help would really be waiting for him. "All right. Hang on a minute."

He walked a few feet away, pulled out the cell phone again, and speed-dialed Nick. "It's a go."

"You got the information?" Nick asked.

"As much as he could give me. Now I have to get him and his family out of here before they're slaughtered."

"Okay." Nick spoke to someone in the room, then came back to the conversation. "Take him to Sunfish Charters at the end of the pier where you are. They're good people. They've done some black work for Guardian a time or two. And be on time, because they won't be able to hang around."

"Okay. Got it. No problem." Finished with the call, he separated the battery from the phone and put each piece in different pockets. "It's all set," he said to Tonio. "Go home and get your wife and child. Do you know Sunfish Charters? At the very end of the row of marinas?"

Tonio nodded. "*Sí.*"

"Meet me there at five-thirty a.m. That's only a few hours from now."

"And you'll take us away from here?" Tonio had a look in his eyes halfway between fear and pleading.

Ethan nodded. "I have friends who will get you away from Cancun. Take you to the United States. There'll be a job for you and a place for you and your family to live. If you want it, that is."

"What about the immigration people? And green cards? No green card and I can't work."

Ethan tamped down his impatience. "My friends are taking care of all that. And one of them will have a job for you, too. A good paying one, working at the marina." He watched Tonio through narrowed eyes. "Well? Time's running out here."

Tonio seemed about to say something, then nodded his head. "I have no reason to trust you, but I also have no choice. We'll be there."

"And if you can, draw a map of where the plantation is and how to get to it."

Ethan waited until Tonio had trudged off to his car in the parking lot and pulled out onto the street before he went back inside the cantina.

Lisa was in the same place he'd left her, wedged in at one end of the bar, sipping from a glass that was still mostly full. The man on her left was doing his best to engage her in conversation, and Ethan could tell she was holding her own. The more time he spent with her, the more he realized just what a gutsy person she was. How the hell she'd ever gotten mixed up with someone like Charles Mallory still puzzled him.

He stepped up behind her and tapped her shoulder.

"Time to split, honey bun. Too much noise here."

Lisa turned, threw her arms around his neck, and smashed her mouth against his. "I was just telling this…gentleman…here we're on our honeymoon, and you'd be coming right back in for me."

He pulled her tight against him. "That's right. And we're wasting too much of it in public. I think we've had enough night life, don't you?" He leered at her.

A smile teased the corners of her mouth. "Whatever you say, sweetie."

Ethan guided her to the door with his arm wrapped tightly around her. He could feel the eyes of the man at the bar raking over him. A stranger? Someone who'd followed them? In any event, they needed to get out of there *pronto*.

Chapter Twelve

Lisa felt the tension vibrating in Ethan's body as he walked her across the bumpy parking lot to their car. The urge to hurry was in his hard grip on her arm and his deliberate, measured breathing, but he made them stroll as lovers would. She reached for a calm that she was far from feeling. When they got in the car, she turned to ask him a question, but he put his fingers to his lips and shook his head.

When they were five blocks from Juana's, he turned off onto a side street, pulled to the curb, and killed the lights.

"Don't move," he mouthed.

Lisa nodded, trying to hold back the fear that sat like a ball of lead in her stomach.

He unscrewed the overhead light, then in the darkness of the car, he searched every inch with his fingertips, even the column of the steering wheel. When he'd completed the front, he moved to the back. Lisa fought her impatience while he did his thing, wishing he'd get around to telling her what had happened.

At last, he was back in the front seat, starting the engine and pulling away from the curb.

"Okay. Now we talk."

"What were you doing?" she asked.

"Looking for bugs."

"Bugs?" Lisa's eyebrows rose to her hairline.

"Like in the hotel?"

He nodded. "Or a GPS tracker. I wanted to make sure no one zeroed in on us while we were inside Juana's and decided to put listening devices in the car, or track us. So far so good."

"Did he show up? The man from La Mama's? Will he help us?"

"Yes."

She waited for him to say something else. Finally, she said, "And?"

"And he told me what we need to know. I made arrangements to get him and his family out of here, and we have some things to do, too."

"You know where Jamie is." She tried to keep the excitement from her voice.

"In a manner of speaking. He's alive, just as you thought, and—"

"Ohmigod!" She took a deep, sobbing breath. "Thank god. Thank god."

"Yes, well, we have to get him out of there while he still is. Tonio said they turned him over to some man who has him at a huge *finca* in the middle of the Quintana Roo jungle. That man is the one who hired them." He turned to look at her. "Can you think of any man who'd want Jamie badly enough to kidnap him and keep him?"

Lisa felt the edges of fear claiming her again. "I have no idea who would do that."

"Maybe some enemy Charles had?" he pushed.

"Oh, God." The fear was tight in her throat. "Would he… Do you think he's killed Jamie? Whoever he is?"

Ethan shook his head. "If he wanted to kill him, he

wouldn't have paid Cortez half a mil to kidnap him. And if it's an old enemy of Charles's, if he wanted some kind of revenge or to send you a message, he'd have had him shot in front of you."

Her stomach heaved, and the nausea she worked hard to keep at bay threatened to erupt. "What would anyone want with an eight-year-old boy? Besides, Charles has been dead for four years. They got whatever money I could lay my hands on, so what's the point?"

He lifted a shoulder. "Sending a message. Don't fuck with me or your family isn't safe."

"After all this time?"

He shrugged. "It's possible they're having trouble with someone else, and you're just the example they want to set."

"That's why you're getting that man and his family out of here," she guessed. "So they can't go after him."

He nodded. "He's the weak link in that band of guerillas, the only one I could approach. It might not have worked with anyone else. He's the most needy and the most desperate. Lisa, you know there's one more possibility."

She'd had a sense of that possibility the more they got into this. At first, she'd dismissed it as foolish, but now... "You think Charles is alive. That the body wasn't his and he has Jamie."

"Makes sense, doesn't it? He's made a clean getaway, and now he wants his son."

"And the ten million that he cleverly tied up in life insurance with a clause."

Ethan nodded. "Don't fall apart on me, okay?"

She sucked in a breath and let it out slowly. "I

won't. But I might kill the son of a bitch myself."

He chuffed a laugh. "That's my girl."

He pulled into an alley, got out, and put something under the front wheels. Then he got in and drove over whatever it was twice before picking it up and climbing back in the car.

"What are you doing?"

"Destroying a cell phone. I can't make any more calls from it, so I crushed it, just in case." He drove around to the back of a restaurant and pitched the phone into a trash bin. A few blocks later, he repeated the same procedure with the battery.

"So they can't trace it," she guessed.

"Yes. Those things are too easy to triangulate."

She frowned. "But what if we need to make calls again? You said your friends would help us if we needed them."

"All taken care of."

A million questions banged around in her head, but one look at Ethan told her he was in no mood to give answers right now. Anyway, it was time to stop questioning everything he did. There was no longer any doubt in her mind that he knew what he was doing.

He headed back toward the beach and parked in a crowded lot at the far end of the row of marinas, then killed the engine and lights.

"What now?" she asked.

"Now we wait."

"Here?"

He nodded. "I'm in a good spot to see what's happening, and no one can sneak up on us."

The silence stretched between them in the darkness of the car, thicker than cotton stuffing. The tension vibrating in the air came from more than one source.

From the moment they'd entered La Mama's, Lisa had been on edge, just as she sensed Ethan was. The air was thick with the sense of danger, she knew one wrong word, one false step, and they could both be dead. The unexpected was always waiting around a corner.

But as her confidence in him grew, so did her belief that whatever had happened on that last op, he as in no way to blame. With each passing moment, she saw the Marine, the security agent, the black ops specialist come to life again. And it shocked her to realize this was a man she could respect, one who hid behind a persona carefully calculated to turn people off.

There was another reason she moved as close to the door as she could, however, putting as much space between them as the seat allowed. The kisses she and Ethan had exchanged might have been for the benefit of an audience, but there was more than playacting behind them. They both knew it even if neither of them said it out loud. This wasn't something they should be exploring right now.

Maybe never.

She hadn't realized just how vulnerable she was or how afraid she was of a man's touch.

Thank you, Charles Mallory, for screwing up my life in more ways than one.

She closed her eyes and tried to think of anything except the man sitting next to her. Jamie's face kept swimming to the forefront, and she dug her nails into her hands to keep herself from crying. No time for tears now.

Finally, she turned to look at Ethan. "How much

longer do we sit here?"

He spoke without taking his gaze from the windshield and whatever he was watching out there. "Not much. We're waiting for another hour to pass. Then we're going to a marina where, hopefully, my friend will have a boat waiting for Tonio and his family along with some equipment for me. And Tonio will have a map we need." He tapped his fingers on the steering wheel and stared out the windshield. "I hope."

"A map to show us how to get to wherever Jamie is?"

Ethan nodded. "This could still be a trap. I want to make sure Tonio isn't just selling us out to Cortez. That's always a very real possibility in a situation like this. Whoever's behind this—whoever hired this guerilla group to kidnap Jamie—doesn't want us to find him. We have no idea what they might have told Cortez to do to keep people from looking too hard. We just have to operate as if there's a shooter behind every rock."

They lapsed into silence again. Lisa tried to sit as still as possible, but her body was tensed to spring at a moment's notice. It didn't help that the damn wig was like a hot blanket on her head. Every sound, every movement made her jump. She kept her purse open with her hand on her gun, and she noticed Ethan had slid his own weapon from the small of his back and kept it on the seat next to him, hand resting on the grip.

At last, Ethan cranked the engine and slid out of the parking lot, leaving his lights off until they hit the street. He drove at a normal pace to the other end of the row of marinas, checking all his mirrors on the way to be sure once more they weren't being followed. He drove into another parking lot, this one dark and silent, and pulled up to a chain link fence. A sign that proclaimed Sunfish Charters, Keep Out, This Means You in faded black paint on a dingy white background hung on the padlocked gate.

Ethan flashed his lights twice, and they got out of the car.

A man dressed in black jeans and black T-shirt materialized from a tiny shack on the other side of the fence, nodded to Ethan, and unlocked the gate. They shook hands silently, and Ethan urged Lisa into the dock area ahead of him. The man's eyes swept over her in an assessing gaze, but Ethan made no move to introduce them.

"Are we all set?" Ethan kept his voice to a whisper.

"Yes. Everything arrived a half hour ago, and the boat's ready." He looked over Ethan's shoulder, frowning. "Where's your extract?"

"He'll be here any minute. I wanted to get here first." Ethan turned to Lisa. "I want you to wait in the office over there until I come for you. Don't talk to anyone and don't ask questions. Take your purse with your gun in it."

She opened her mouth to say something, but the sudden deadly air surrounding both men made her close it again. She just nodded. This was for Jamie. For him, she could follow orders. And neither Ethan nor this man all in black looked like they wanted to hear anything she had to say.

The so-called office was little more than a tiny room with a battered desk and chair. But along one wall were steel cabinets with heavy locks. Not your average fishing charter equipment.

Two tiny windows gave visual access to the marina and parking lot. Through one of them, she could see the two men walk to the end of the dock. A third man, also in black, climbed out of a boat, and he, too, shook hands with Ethan. Then he reached into the boat and hauled out a large canvas that looked heavy, along with a smaller, lighter one. Ethan carried them back up the dock to the parking lot.

The air these people projected was calmly lethal. Lisa wasn't sure if that made her feel better or worse. No amount of deep breathing would dissolve the knots in her stomach, and she jammed her hands in the pockets of her dress to keep them from trembling. She had no doubt these were men he'd worked with in every facet of his life. He must have been the king of black ops.

Nothing happened for the next few minutes, and Lisa did what had become a habit when she was nervous. She paced. Finally, a car pulled into the lot, and as soon as its headlights went off so did all the lights on the dock. Lisa opened her purse and took out her gun, trying to steady her hands. By straining her eyes, she managed to make out three people getting out of the car—two adults and a small child.

A fourth shape joined them. Ethan. Then the entire black mass moved toward the dock. Lisa could no longer see them, but she heard the creaking of wood as they made their way to the boat at the end. Squinting, she could just see the outlines of Ethan and the man in the boat shaking hands again. Then the craft moved slowly out into the water, barely breaking a ripple on the surface, and two black shapes headed back toward the office.

Lisa put her gun back in her purse, took another deep breath to control her erratic heartbeat, and wiped her hands on her skirt. She was standing by the door when it opened, and Ethan motioned to her.

"Let's go. We're clear so far, but I'm not taking any chances."

He took her hand and pulled her toward the parking lot. The lights were still out so she took care not to stumble or trip. Instead of heading for the car, he pulled a set of keys from his pocket and popped the locks on a black SUV.

"What's this? And why is everything so dark?"

"Our new wheels. Get in. I don't want to hang around here." He was backing out of the space before Lisa even had the door closed. "And it's dark so no one will see us."

"But what about the car? We can't just leave it here."

"Someone will return it to the rental agency tomorrow." He merged quickly into the traffic on the highway. "We had to ditch the car that Cortez's people have seen me in twice. And now we've got a vehicle we can drive into the jungle plus new cell phones."

Her stomach was flip-flopping again, and she did her best to contain the fear that kept rising. This whole evening they'd been skating on the razor's edge of danger. She sensed it in his manner, even though he'd said little. Or perhaps because he'd said little.

She swallowed hard and tried to make her voice calm and even. "So what do we do now, since you said we can't go back to the hotel?"

"Now we're going to get the hell out of Dodge." He shifted in the seat. "Tonio gave me a crude map, but

I want to get as far away from here as possible before stopping to take a look at it. We still don't know who's behind all of this, and they might have someone scoping things out. I haven't seen any sign of it except the guy at La Mama's watching us, but I don't want to take any chance. Don't forget. Someone took a shot at us at Manny's back in Tampa. It has to be connected to this."

"Forget? How could I forget?" She still couldn't get the episode out of her mind. Lisa chewed on her fingernail. She'd already destroyed the one on her thumb and had started on the index finger.

"In case someone senses how close we're getting to the truth about Jamie's disappearance," he pointed out, "we need to move as quickly as we can."

"Okay." She yanked her finger away from her mouth and leaned back in her seat. "So where are we going now?"

"Playa del Carmen." He gave her a quick glance. "You should try to get some sleep on the ride."

"What about you? You must be tired, too."

He gave her a tight smile, lacking in humor. "I've gone a long time without sleep before. I can do it again. Go on. Close your eyes."

As positive as she was that nerves alone would keep her awake, they hadn't gone two miles before tension and exhaustion caught up with Lisa and sleep captured her.

****

"You're so wet."

Ethan's fingers slid into her easily, stroking her inner walls and finding the sweet spot that made every nerve fire. She squeezed her thighs together, trapping his hand, demanding that he stroke harder and faster.

His thumb found her clit, rubbing back and forth against the sensitive flesh and sending heat through her veins. Her nipples ached so much she cupped her breasts and pressed her thumbs against them.

Suddenly, he added a third finger, completely filling her aching core. He increased the pace of his strokes, curling his fingers just enough to scrape that hot trigger spot with every thrust.

She pinched her nipples, hard, just as an orgasm flooded through her. She pressed down on his hand and moaned softly.

"You okay? Lisa?"

She sat up abruptly, sucking in a breath. Holy crap! Had she just dreamed of another orgasm with Ethan Caine? And sitting right beside him in this car? The skin on her face felt hot, and she had to fight to control her breathing. Had he seen her? Did he know what was going on?

"I asked if you're okay," he repeated.

She glanced over at him, but he didn't look as if he had any idea what she'd been dreaming. He was his usual stoic self, his face masking any emotion. At least she hadn't used her own hand to bring herself to orgasm. Had she?

No. She looked down and her clothes were still in place.

"I—I'm fine. Thank you. Sorry. Just dozed off."

And a whole lot more.

"Okay. Just checking." His voice sounded gruff. "I know this has been a strain on you."

You have no idea.

"I'm okay. Really. Thanks for asking."

To distract herself, she gazed out the passenger window. The sky was the pink of early dawn and a faint breeze stirred the leaves of the banyan trees. They were parked once again in a busy lot bordering the beach, the waves of the Caribbean Sea rolling in just beyond.

She stretched and worked her neck back and forth, trying to relieve the kinks. "What is this place?"

"We're between the bus station and the ferry on Avenida Quinta. The busiest place in Playa del Carmen. No one will pay attention to us sitting here or wonder what we're doing."

"And what are we doing?" She looked at the gear on the seat between them with a curious stare.

"Getting ready." He pointed at two black boxes that looked like oversized walkie-talkies. "Satellite radios. They're set on the same frequency as Nick's. That's how we'll communicate." He picked one up and showed her how it worked. "I've set the numbers. This one will connect you to mine. This one dials the number for Nick." He snorted. "Damn fool. I expected him to send a team in, and he's decided to lead it himself."

"Because you're his friend," she said in a soft voice. "And you'd do the same for him. What's the rest of this stuff?" She looked over the back of the seat to the open canvas bag. "Is that camping gear?"

Ethan nodded. "Thermal blankets and tent. Knives for hacking at the underbrush. Some other stuff."

She started to run her fingers through her hair and realized her head was still trapped in the damn wig. "Can I take this thing off now? I sure can't wear it in the jungle."

"Go ahead." He chuckled, a rusty sound. "I think

you've suffered enough with it."

"Thank you," she breathed and began the process of removing it. When the wig was finally free, she tossed it into the back seat and stuck the bobby pins she'd anchored it with into her purse. Then she pulled out a makeup remover wipe and took as much of the goop off her face as she could.

"We're going to make a stop at a big box store," he told her. "You'll be able to wash your face better there."

She couldn't wait. Meanwhile, she ran her hands through her hair, raking it back from her face. Maybe she could also brush the cobwebs out of her brain and think intelligently. "Do we know where we're going?"

"I'm hoping. I've got the map Tonio drew of where the *finca* is. I'm pretty damn sure that's where the boy is."

"Jamie." She breathed his name.

"Yes. Jamie." He pulled out the map she had marked lines on. "Now I need to figure out which of these mud tracks will take us the closest without putting us in their sights."

Lisa's head was filled with questions, but the edge in Ethan's voice said I'm busy and I'll tell you what you need to know when you need to know it. Instead, she took a brush from her purse, ran it through her hair, and pulled out a band to fasten it into a ponytail.

"You'll need different clothes."

His voice startled her. She looked down at her skirt and sandals. "I didn't figure I could go hiking in these. My other stuff is back at the Holiday Inn."

"As soon as I'm finished with this, we'll get something to eat and I'll find that store I mentioned.

We both need clothes and supplies, and again, we can't go back to the hotel. I have jungle food in here, but we need bottled water and some other things."

She raised her eyebrows. "Jungle food?"

"Granola bars, power bars, stuff like that." He indicated everything else spread out on the seat. "I have two backpacks here to carry all this stuff with us when we leave the car. And we'll need water so we don't dehydrate." He looked at his watch. "I'm hoping we can do this in twenty-four hours, but I'll know better when we get where we're going. We have to make sure Jamie's there and then figure out how to snatch him."

"Oh." As she listened to him and watched him, Lisa realized that she'd been right earlier in the evening. The more Ethan got into this operation, the more confident and in control he seemed. The pain in his eyes, while still there, wasn't quite as sharp. And in his demeanor, she could again see the Marine ready for a mission, the agent ready for the special operation.

Not for the first time, she wondered if in saving Jamie, he might in the end save himself. She hoped so, because as the layers he hid behind peeled away, she was startled to realize Ethan Caine was nothing like she'd thought. He was sharp, intelligent, and clever in too many ways to count.

But she'd better not dwell on that. She was already battling shocking and unwanted feelings for him. Neither of them needed any more complications in their lives, and certainly not in this situation.

While Ethan repacked the backpacks, Lisa sat watching people move in and out of the bus station and around the ferry and did her best to keep her nerves under control while her mind raced. None of this made any sense at all. Unless… No. That was too totally farfetched. For a minute, she thought about voicing the weird idea, but she was sure he'd think she was crazy. Wouldn't he? She kept trying to push it out of her mind, but it bounced right back, like a yoyo on a string, each time hitting harder.

They stopped at a modest-looking restaurant a few blocks down Avenida Quinta and bought breakfast tacos, which they ate in the car. Leaving their gear unguarded didn't seem like a smart option.

Then Ethan pulled into the parking lot of a big box store and pulled out one of the new cells.

"I'm touching base with Nick while you're inside." He handed her a list and some money. "I'll wait here with the stuff. Change clothes in the restroom after you pay for everything and get rid of the dress and shoes you're wearing."

"Throw them away? Why?"

Again the exasperated sigh. "Lisa, could you just not keep asking questions, please? You don't need any excess to carry on your back. I'll buy you a damn dress and shoes when we get back to the states."

"Fine, fine, fine," she muttered and pushed open her door. She wanted to smack herself for asking stupid questions. He was right. Why did she care about the dress and shoes when they were on their way to rescue Jamie? No wonder he thought she was an idiot.

Washing her face and brushing her hair gave her more relief than she would have imagined. Thirty minutes later, dressed in jeans, T-shirt, running shoes, and socks, hair pulled back in a ponytail, she handed the sacks of purchases to Ethan.

"We're good to go," she told him.

"All right. Let's do it. Here." He tossed the bags in the back seat and handed her the map Tonio had drawn, along with the one she'd marked. "You'll have to be the navigator. Don't make any mistakes and take us on a wrong turn."

She bit back the smart retort ready to pop out of her mouth and studied the map. She'd prove to him it hadn't been a mistake to bring her along. Eventually they came to the end of what appeared to be the tourist area, the sandy beaches disappeared and jungle took over. But then her impatience got the best of her. She hated flying blind, and Ethan was not into sharing.

"I know it irritates you when I ask questions, and I'm sorry. I just think I can be of more use to you if I know what's going on. Can you tell me what Nick said?"

His hands tightened on the wheel, and for a moment, she was afraid he wouldn't answer her. Then he nodded. "It's hard for me to know what to share with a greenhorn, but I suppose you're right. All arrangements are still in place. He's just waiting for a signal from us."

"What arrangements?"

"Those you'll see when the time comes. Right now, I need you to be my navigator. Concentrate on that."

She looked down at the map. "The road Tonio marked should be coming up in just a little bit. There." She pointed. "Right there. Turn left."

"Anyone who calls this a road is stretching things," he grumbled.

And indeed, he was right. It was little more than a dirt track, worn down by other vehicles that had taken this turn and barely visible through the dense vegetation. They moved deeper into the jungle proper, following dirt roads and evading mud holes and fallen tree limbs. All around them was a thick growth of strange plants and trees that were home to multitudes of climbing animals and birds of every color. Sometimes, she got the feeling they were being swallowed up by a giant green hand.

For the next half hour, Ethan drove and she called out directions. The going was very slow, and Lisa called on every bit of discipline to rein in her impatience. Every so often, they passed a narrower road that veered off to the left.

"Where do those go?" she asked.

"Plantations. People's homes. Whatever."

"I can't imagine people living out here. My God, you're in the middle of nowhere."

"Very few people do. Most of the residential area is on the coast where there's a natural rock seawall. But I would imagine, for people who want total anonymity and privacy, this is as good a place to get it as any." He stopped at a tiny clearing and took Tonio's map from her, smoothing it out on the steering wheel. "Okay. We'll stash the car here."

"This is it?" Lisa looked out the window. "This is where we're stopping?"

"You don't find the Ritz out here." He sounded disgusted. "We're here to rescue your son, not have a vacation. And I don't want to drive too close. That all right with you?"

"Yes," she snapped. "I know that. Okay. And you don't have to keep biting my head off. This is fine. Whatever. And then we hike, right?"

Ethan actually grinned. "And then we hike."

"But…" She held up a hand, palm outward. "I know. No buts. Except I have to ask. We're just leaving the car here? How do we know it'll still be here when we're ready to leave?"

"We don't. If it is, it means we accomplished our mission without much conflict. Otherwise, we'll be leaving by other means." He folded the crude map and stuck it back in his pocket. Then he set the burglar alarm on the SUV, and they climbed out with their gear. In moments, they'd covered the vehicle with vegetation he hacked from the surrounding area and netting he'd pulled from the cargo space. Then he filled a backpack for each of them with bottled water, power bars, a satellite radio, and their weapons.

"I'll take the tent gear." He pulled out a GPS. "Do you know how to use one of these puppies?"

"Yes. Charles showed me how to use one on a trip we took before…before things fell apart."

"Good. Okay. Tonio said the place is at least two miles in from this road, in this direction. I want to camp far enough away so we don't attract attention." He traced a line with his finger, then punched in some coordinates on each of them. "We'll use these to keep track of our direction. Stay right behind me and make as little noise as possible. All right, let's get moving."

A terrible screech, like chalk on a board magnified a thousand times, split the air.

Lisa jumped, barely suppressing her own scream. "What was that? My God, it sounds like someone's being tortured."

Ethan grinned again, and she thought how different he looked when he did.

"Howler monkeys. They're all around us. You'll hear them all the time so get used to them."

She swallowed hard and took deep breaths to calm her racing pulse, convinced she'd never get used to a sound like that.

They walked for more than an hour, shafts of blazing heat from the sun piercing the thick jungle growth. The air was heavy with the rich scent of tropical flowers and the symphony of sounds made by myriads of colorful birds. Now she knew where Ethan had acquired the habit of wearing his disreputable straw hat, and she was glad she'd thought to buy a baseball cap when she got the clothes.

She had no idea how he even found footing for them as they made their way through thick vines and giant roots. When the foliage was too dense, he took the sharp knife hanging from his belt and simply hacked a pathway for them.

At last, he came to a stop in a small clearing. Mopping the sweat from her face with the hem of her T-shirt, she began to understand why he'd taken the time for his week of boot camp. This was a little more than jogging along Bayshore Boulevard.

"I don't want to go any farther," he told her. "We're about a mile from the perimeter of the *finca* so we're far enough away to avoid detection and close enough to get to an observation spot." He took off his backpack and the portable tent, hung binoculars around his neck, and put his hat back on. "And I need to see what's going on. Where's your gun?"

Lisa obligingly removed it from her backpack and checked to make sure there was a round in the chamber.

"All right," he said. "Don't take your hand off it

until I get back. Stay here while I scout things out."

Before she could say a word, he was gone, so silent only the things he left behind assured her he'd even been there. Another skill she was sure made him so valuable. She leaned back against the tree trunk to capture the shade from the leaves and stretched out her legs to relieve her aching muscles. The gun stayed on her lap, her finger on the trigger guard. The hot air surrounded her like thick cloth, and she spent much of her time brushing away the infinite variety of bugs that thought she might make an interesting meal.

Being alone in the jungle, every sound and movement was magnified. She hated sitting here waiting, yet she was smart enough to know she would only have slowed Ethan down. Let him scout the area, do his recon, and bring back the information.

Please, God, let him see Jamie.

She couldn't believe they might actually be this close to him. Close to rescuing him.

Reaching into the pocket of her jeans with her free hand, she pulled out the tiny snapshot of Jamie she'd carried since the day he was taken. It was from his last birthday, and the innocent smile on his face cut into her already bleeding heart.

We're coming, Jamie. Just hold on.

When she'd first thought Charles might be the one who'd taken him, she was afraid she'd lost her mind. But now, with everything Ethan had learned from Tonio, he agreed with her. It was the only logical answer. If Charles was dead, there would be no reason for a revenge kidnapping. If it was for money, they would have released Jamie when the ransom was paid.

Her head was beginning to hurt from thinking, and

she closed her eyes, rubbing her temples.

"Don't go to sleep. You might not wake up."

Lisa jerked at the sound of Ethan's voice. "I didn't hear you come back. My God, you're like a ghost."

"That's good. If you can't hear me, neither can anyone else." He dropped down to the ground beside her.

"So what did you find out?"

"In a minute." He reached into his backpack and removed one of the bottles of water, taking slow sips to conserve the liquid. "You should drink some, too," he ordered. "It's easy to get dehydrated out here, even if you're not doing anything."

Lisa did as he ordered, barely containing her impatience. "Now can you tell me what you found?"

"I found the place, right where Tonio said it would be. I didn't get as close to the house itself as I'd like. I'm still not sure if they have sensors or cameras outside the perimeter, although I have to assume they do. But I did find out the place is surrounded by a concrete wall ten feet high that must have cost a fortune to build."

"And the house? Did you see it?"

"Only from a distance. After it gets dark, we'll get up in the trees and take a better look. But I can tell you this. Whoever lives there must have a shitload of money."

"Charles." She spat the word. "My god, Ethan. He stole my son, got the money, and tried to kill me."

"And again before we even left town," he reminded her.

"At Manny's."

"Yes. People like Charles have a long reach and

can pay people for anything." He stared off into space for a moment "I've seen too many people like him."

"And did you capture them?" She hated the note of anxiety in her voice.

He took a moment before answering. When he turned to look at her, she saw that same haunted look in his eyes but his face was set in lines of determination.

"Let's just say they got exactly what they deserved." He rubbed a hand over his face and let out a breath. "I agree that nothing else makes sense. It's been four years since Charles's so-called death. Enough time for him to get himself established again and plot something like this. It gives him your son and the ten mil."

"But I saw his body," she reminded him. "And they compared dental records."

"When you have as much money as Charles, you can arrange anything."

"Now the shooting at the ransom drop makes sense. He'd want me out of the way."

He nodded. "And the one at Manny's Diner. He probably didn't want you taken out at your house. Too specific. The cops would start digging."

She hitched a breath. "Does that mean he knows about you?"

He was quiet for a minute. "No. Charles would have no way of knowing me or anything about me. If we accept this whole premise, then it was just dumb luck we were together when they tried the hit at Manny's. I'd say whoever the shooters were might have gone back and told Charles about the men you were with, but I don't think they'd be too detailed. If they were stupid enough to miss you, they're too stupid to collect information."

"Let's hope." She wrapped her arms around herself, suddenly chilled. "God. This is like finding out the devil has come back to live with you."

"Lisa." He touched her shoulder. "We're going to take care of this and get Jamie. That's a promise."

She gave him a weak smile. "I hope you're right."

He pulled out a power bar, unwrapped it and bit into it. "But the whole thing makes sense. Remember all those trips to the Yucatan you told me about? Charles picked a location he was familiar with and where he had already established connections. Do you have any idea at all why he traveled here so often?"

"No. He never told me anything. Just said it had to do with his import business."

Ethan snorted. "I'll bet. Dope import. Well, I'd say it's safe to assume he's back in business and manipulating this whole thing."

"Finding out that's where his money came from was one of the biggest shocks in my life." She rubbed her forehead. "He had me so buffaloed, with his smooth manner and impeccable behavior. Until after we had Jamie."

"He wanted a son and heir. Most people like him do." He shifted to a more comfortable position. "Based on what came out after his so-called death, I'd say he was deep into it with narcoguerilla groups like *Las Tormentas*, who mix kidnapping with drug-running with a little political upheaval. Money laundering. Arms dealing. You name it. A smorgasbord of illegal activities and Charles was a kingpin."

Lisa rubbed her face as if scrubbing something away. "I'm angry at Charles for what he did to my life, but I'm angrier at myself for being such an idiot."

"Hey. We all do stupid things. The trick is to get past them and not do them again."

He had taken another bite of the bar, and a tiny piece of it clung to his lip. She had to clench her fists to keep from reaching over and brushing it away. She remembered how his lips felt pressed against hers, the taste of him, the scent of him.

Get a grip here.

She stood abruptly and went to lean against a tree, needing to put distance between them.

"Something wrong?" His knowing eyes looked at her.

"No." She hoped she didn't blush. "I just wanted to stand up for a minute."

"You'd better sit down and get all the rest you can. We'll be doing more walking later."

"So." She stared at Ethan. "Maybe we can get rid of Charles once and for all. That sounds good to me."

"It's your lucky day, because we may have to do just that." Ethan crumpled the wrapper, stuffed it in his backpack, and stood up. "Okay. Let's get the tent pitched while it's still light and get ready for our evening's adventures."

His eyes were still locked on hers, watching her, something hot swirling in those melted chocolate irises.

He knows. And what's worse, he's fighting the same feelings. Oh, God, we are in big trouble.

Chapter Thirteen

They made the tent secure, then sat down to wait for darkness. Nothing could happen before then. Neither of them had anything to say. The howler monkeys continued to screech, and birds of every size and color flew around them, their songs a variegated concerto. Ethan pretended to sleep, and Lisa fought off the continuous invasion of insects, wondering if he was having as much trouble tamping down the sexual tension as she was.

No, wait. He was a Marine. A black ops specialist. A man who operated in the shadows. Superhuman control was a requirement, and sex would be the last thing on his mind right now.

Lord, she certainly had misjudged hm. But that just went to show what a good actor he was, to fool so many people into thinking he was a bum and a slob. But that just showed how good he was at what he did. More and more, she was coming to believe that they'd succeed in this.

By late afternoon, Lisa's nerves were stretched as taut as guy-wires.

"Why don't we talk about something?" she asked, sitting down on a thick broken branch.

"About what?" He was sitting on the ground, leaning against a tree, his hat tipped over his face as usual.

"Something. Anything." She waved her hands in the air. "Tell me about Ethan Caine."

He was silent for a long moment. "Tell you about Ethan Caine. What is it you want to know, Lisa? What I did as a Marine? With Guardian? After that? If I killed people? Were they good or bad? Did it bother me?"

His voice was like an axe chopping wood, and she recoiled from it. "I'm sorry. I don't mean to pry. That was very rude of me. If you wanted to talk about yourself, you would."

Again, the silence stretched before he broke it. "Why don't you tell me why a woman with as much to offer as you have would tie herself up with a loser like Charles Mallory?"

She jerked as if he'd slapped her. "I had my reasons."

"Millions of them, I'd guess."

"It wasn't money," she snapped. "Not at all."

"No? Then why don't you tell me what it was?"

"I don't think that's any of your business."

"Okay. I just thought if we were going to play Twenty Questions, you could offer up something first." He settled his hat more firmly over his face.

More silence.

Lisa chewed on the thumbnail that she'd already bitten to the quick.

"I hadn't dated a lot," she blurted out.

"Excuse me?" The hat shifted, and Ethan turned his gaze on her.

"You heard me. I was the proverbial prodigy. Graduated high school at sixteen, college at nineteen and law school at twenty-two. Social activities didn't seem all that important to me. I was focused on what I wanted and working to get there." She swallowed. "Anyway, most guys were either intimidated by me or turned off. Fighting them off wasn't a problem."

"Josh never said anything about that."

"Josh and I don't discuss each other with people, no matter how close they might be." She brushed a fallen leaf off her leg. "Anyway, he was in the Marines, as you know, and then off doing his own thing. I don't think my sex life would have been a priority topic for him."

"You had hardly started at that law firm before you were being fast-tracked for partnership," he commented.

She nodded. "Aaron Burke took me under his wing. He wanted a tough litigator, and I seemed to come by it naturally."

"So Mallory came in and swept you off your feet, right? He was a charmer from all that I found out about him."

"Yes," she said bitterly. "A charmer." She stood up and began her familiar habit of pacing. "We were married almost two years before the real Charles Mallory showed up."

"You could have left him any time," he pointed out.

"When you're in a prison, it's very hard to break out. The guards don't give you any breathing room. And Charles was a maniac about Jamie. He'd never have let me take him if I left. I think he'd have killed me first."

Ethan was silent for so long it made her itchy.

"What, no sarcastic comments? No digs? Where's that famous arrogant Caine personality?"

He sat up straighter, pushing his hat back off his forehead. "I just hate to see a woman with so much to offer throw it away on someone who could never appreciate her. And look at the mess he left you when he was killed. Just seems a damn shame."

"Well, not all of us have happily ever after." She heard the edge in her own voice. "I don't see you lugging home the pot of gold at the end of the rainbow."

"I'll say this. You came out of it a lot stronger than most women would have. It took guts to stay in that situation to protect your son. And you didn't run around afterwards crying and wringing your hands."

"Oh, good. I'm so glad I have your approval." She couldn't help the acid tone of her voice. This man got under her skin more easily than anyone she'd ever met. "Especially since you seem to have done so well with your own life."

"My life isn't for people with your delicate sensibilities," he told her in a flat voice. "Leave it at that."

"So will I ever get the real story of what happened?"

He looked past her, staring at nothing. "Believe me, you wouldn't want to hear it. It's not a bedtime story."

She raised her eyebrows. "I beg your pardon?"

He tossed down the plant leaf he'd been mangling. "I had ideals once, believe it or not. And a belief in noble causes. Then I learned what so-called civilized people can do to each other." A muscle jumped in his cheek. "Not to mention those who are outright savages. What I had to do to deal with them. And what happens when the people you believe in turn out to be more evil than the bad guys. So, no, I don't think we'll be discussing my life."

She got the picture. Ethan wasn't about to share any details with her. Or anyone.

Finally, he got up and opened his knapsack, motioning for her to do the same. "Supper time. Better eat something. You'll need your energy. Eat a piece of the fruit and one of the power bars."

She sat down on the deadwood again, wiped a peach against her T-shirt, and took a bite of it. By the time they'd eaten and Ethan had wrapped their trash and buried it, the sun had set and the first edges of darkness were creeping over the jungle.

"We'll wait another fifteen minutes before getting started," he told her, checking his watch. "I want as much night as we can get to cover us without waiting too late."

"All right. Just tell me whatever you want me to do."

He cocked an eyebrow at her. "You know, you're not at all what I thought you were. Not a bit."

"Is that good or bad?" She rubbed her hands nervously against the sides of her jeans.

"Good, I guess. You're plenty gutsy, nothing's made you run screaming for shelter yet, and you don't seem afraid of every bug crawling over us here."

"I intellectualize them," she said.

He stared. "Excuse me?"

"I was always scared to death of anything creepy crawly. Then I read a book about intellectualizing things you were afraid of. You know, reducing them down to what they really are and if they can really hurt you. So while I don't like them any better, they don't send me shrieking under the covers anymore."

"I'll be damned. Maybe I could try that with a few things myself."

They both stood at the same time, and when Lisa turned, she bumped into Ethan's hard, muscular chest.

"Oh." She looked up at him and saw that same heat burning she'd seen before.

With no warning, he grabbed her arms, pulled her tight to his body, and gave her the most intense kiss she'd ever had. There was nothing tentative about it. It was hard and passionate and giving and taking, all at the same time. His tongue was a flame scorching the inside if her mouth and igniting her own heat.

When he broke the kiss at last, they just stared at each other.

"This can't happen," he stated in that flat voice. "Just forget about it."

Anger rippled through her. "No, I will not forget about it. If I'm going to die tonight, I want at least one real orgasm before that happens."

Ethan chuffed a laugh. "That's a strange way to put it. I wouldn't have expected that from you."

"The old me wouldn't have said it. This is the new me, who will go to desperate lengths to get what she wants."

His gaze burned into her. "And you want me."

She nodded.

"Fine."

The next kiss might have been lacking in romance but made up for it in erotic flavor and intensity. He scoured the inside of her mouth with his tongue, then dragged his lips away and sprinkled kisses along the line of her chin.

Lisa clutched his shoulders, pressing her body against his and outing every bit of the hunger she was feeling into the kiss. It seemed only seconds before they both had their clothes off, frantically tossing them to the side. Then he lifted her, and carried her into the tent, setting her down on the sleeping bags he had placed there earlier.

"If you think this is a bad idea, now's the time to tell me."

She shook her head. "Not bad, but please no more talking."

She didn't want excuses or promises or anything else about why they shouldn't be doing this and how she should forget about it when it was over. She just wanted to do this with him now.

Lying beneath him, she ran her hands over his hard, muscular back, arching up to him as he took first one nipple then the other in his mouth, teasing them with his lips and his teeth. Heat streaked to her pussy where her inner walls were already fluttering with tiny spasms.

Cupping one breast with his hand, he licked a feathery line down to her navel, swirling his tongue in the indentation before moving even lower. Shivers skated over her skin, and the hunger in her body grew more intense. When she tried to lift her pelvis up to him, his rough chuckle vibrated against her overheated skin.

"Anxious, are you?" He nipped gently at the top of one thigh. "That's good, because I'm about to explode myself."

He nudged her thighs apart, spread the lips of her

sex, and stroked his tongue the length of her slick flesh.

"Oh, god!" She threw her legs over his shoulders, doing her best to climb right up into his hungry mouth, but he held her in place while he teased and tormented with his tongue and teeth.

Shifting to his knees, he nudged her legs farther apart, ran the tips of his fingers along her wet slit before thrusting two of them inside her.

Oh, god!

"Jesus," he swore, "you're hotter than a pistol."

And about ready to fire.

It felt as if her entire body clamped down on his hand, squeezing as he worked his fingers in and out in a smooth rhythm. Little moans bubbled up from her throat as she arched up, her body demanding that orgasm that hovered just out of reach.

When he slipped his fingers from her grasp, she shook her head. "No, no, no. More."

That rusty laugh was an erotic sound, rumbling through her.

"Just hold on." He reached to the side for his pack he'd tossed down, unzipped a pocket, and pulled out a condom.

His lips turned up in a small grin when her eyes popped at what he held in his hand.

"Condoms make the best coverings for gun barrels, believe it or not. Keeps out moisture and dust." His eyes held hers. "I didn't plan to use them for this, Lisa, but I'm damn glad I have them."

When he rolled the latex onto his cock, she paused a second to admire his length and thickness, worried for a moment it might not fit.

"It'll work," he assured her, kneeling between her

thighs again and draping them over his legs.

He wrapped his fingers around his shaft as he leaned forward and nudged her opening with the head. Little by little, he eased it into her slick passage. He rubbed her clit with his other hand, the abrading movement sending licks of flame through her core.

As much as he'd hurried before, he did not rush this time, slowly easing his way into her body until he was fully seated. He studied her face as if seeking some kind of signal. Then, taking a deep breath, he rocked into her, again and again, each time pulling back a little farther and thrusting deeper, until at last he was pounding into her again and again.

Without warning an orgasm rose from within her, and he rode her through it. He let her rest, sprinkling kisses on her warm flesh before patiently arousing her again, as if he innately knew how her body needed coaxing. Not only after the length of time she'd been abstinent but also because of the abuse she'd suffered from Charles. He roused her time and again, always with the same slow but passionate seduction.

Lisa wrapped her legs around him and locked her ankles into the small of his back, pulling him to her as tight as she could. Her surroundings fell away so nothing existed but this man, the feel of him on her and inside her, his cock filling every inch of her as he rode her harder and deeper.

This time, when the orgasm broke, it gripped her body, spasms shaking her as her inner walls flexed against his thick shaft. And this time, he went with her. She had no idea how long it went on, only that at last they were both spent, their limbs relaxed even as his shaft still rested inside her.

The kiss he gave her was totally unexpected, both in the fact that he did it and that it was tender rather than demanding. Then he eased from her clasp with a slow glide, fingers pinching the condom until he rose and dropped it into some scrap paper from his pack. Then he lay down beside her, pulling her close to him, stroking her cheek with unexpected tenderness.

"Close your eyes," his whispered. "We've got a long night ahead of us. I'll wake you when it's time to get ready."

Okay, so they weren't going to discuss what happened. Fine by her. When this was over, she'd probably never see him again. So why did that make her heart hurt?

Chapter Fourteen

The touch of a hand on her shoulder woke Lisa at once. She blinked at the sight of Ethan, already dressed. He was back to his other self, behaving as if nothing at all had happened between them.

"Okay. You've been very good about following orders so far, so let's see if you can follow a few more."

She wanted to ask him if he felt anything about their situation, but she knew better. He was all business now, and that was the way it had to be. Anything else would have to wait until later. If it happened at all. "Just tell me what to do."

He reached into her backpack and took out a strange device that looked like something an alien would wear. "Night vision goggles. NVGs. We obviously can't use flashlights, and we need to be able to see."

Lisa stood still while he fastened hers on and adjusted them to fit. "Weird."

"Yes. But it lights everything up. Just remember, if we do run into a patch of light, yank them off right away or you'll be momentarily blinded. We don't want to give away any advantage."

"I hear you."

He took her gun, tucked it into the small of her back, and tightened her belt. "You need to be able to get to it if necessary. Just don't shoot yourself in the ass."

"Believe me," she snorted, "I'll do my very best."

"Let's go." Ethan adjusted his own NVGs and set off on the path he'd followed earlier.

The night sounds of the jungle echoed all around them—the calling of wild animals, the cries of some birds as they settled down, the beating of wings as others flew overhead. Lisa did her best to ignore them. After the first minute or so, her eyes completely adjusted to the NVGs. It made seeing Ethan ahead of her a lot easier.

He stopped every few minutes to check the GPS, then started off again. They'd covered nearly two miles by her estimation when he came to a complete stop and motioned with his hand for her to do the same and be silent. He pointed, and through the dense foliage, she could just make out the top of the concrete wall he'd mentioned earlier.

Ethan touched a thick tree with his hand and pointed up with his finger.

Lisa swallowed, nodded, and began to climb the tree. She thanked God for the training on the rock wall back at his farmhouse. She'd never been fond of heights of any kind, but at least the training had given her some confidence in what she was doing.

When she reached the place where a thick limb formed a crotch with the trunk, she felt Ethan's hand on her calf. Forcing herself to look down, pushing away the dizziness that any height usually caused, she saw him motion for her to stop and sit. Gingerly, she edged herself around until she could sit in the spot and waited for him to follow her.

He climbed past her until he was just a little higher

and settled himself in place.

Now she dared to look straight ahead. The concrete wall was just as Ethan had said, thick and surrounding the entire perimeter. It ran off in two directions into the jungle until she couldn't see it anymore. Inside the wall was a carpet of low-growing jungle vegetation split by walkways of crushed shells.

The estate house, at the end of a driveway also made of crushed shells, rose majestically in Spanish splendor. The driveway curved in front of the door, and between it and the wall, water sprayed constantly from a huge fountain formed by figures of angels. Three steps led up to a wide terrace that ran across the front of the house, centered by carved wood double doors.

A man in khaki pants and shirt, a rifle slung over his shoulder, leaned against the fountain smoking a cigarette. Another stood by the front door.

Ethan tapped Lisa on the shoulder. "We need to watch the guards, see if there's a pattern," he mouthed. "If they stay there until someone relieves them. Or do they patrol? However they do it."

She nodded.

"And keep your eyes out for two things—Jamie and anyone familiar to you. Like Charles."

The waiting was the hardest part. Lisa marveled at how Ethan seemed to become part of the tree, as still as the bark, not even the faint movement of a leaf. He stayed in one position as if he'd been poured there from a mound of clay and left to harden.

Bugs and other tiny creatures seemed to know enough to avoid him, although Lisa could feel them crawling over her. She brushed them off with as little movement as possible when they became too bad to bear. Her muscles began to cramp after a while, and rather than try to shift position, she massaged them as best she could, afraid even the slightest movement would betray their presence.

Ethan had mentioned there would most likely be perimeter cameras or sensors. She had to trust he knew what he was doing, that he had figured out a safe path for them to the house. It was more and more obvious he really had years of doing this behind him. She wondered if she'd ever find out the real truth about Ethan Caine.

They sat in the tree for what to Lisa seemed an eternity, the only sounds those of the jungle night. Whatever words the guards exchanged didn't carry to them. The pattern of their routine seldom varied. Mostly they stood around, smoking cigarettes and talking, once in a while taking a turn around the grounds. Apparently, out here in the middle of the jungle, they didn't expect unplanned visitors.

After a while, her eyes became gritty with strain, watching for any sign at all of Jamie. Anything that would confirm his presence. They only had the word of a guerilla gang member that he was even here. What if the information was wrong? What if Tonio lied just to get safe passage for himself and his family? What if everything Ethan had uncovered on his trip meant nothing and Jamie was actually half a world away right now?

No! She wouldn't let herself fall into that trap. He was here. She could feel it. Sense it. Somewhere behind that wall, her child was a captive.

Were they feeding him well? Taking care of him? Abusing him in any way? Was he sick? Did he miss her? Did he think she'd abandoned him?

Stop it! Jamie's fine. And soon I'll have him back.

She finally had to move one leg, shifting it very gingerly so as not to dislodge any debris. Ethan glanced over at her, but she shook her head and made the okay sign with one hand.

How did people do this for a living? Sit for hours with almost nothing happening. How did Ethan stay so calm? She worked hard to conceal how terrified she was that they'd be discovered. Captured. Killed.

She was startled when he reached down and touched the bare skin of her arm. He pointed at her, then down. She nodded and maneuvered her body around to descend from the tree with a minimum of fuss and noise. When her feet touched the ground, her legs wobbled a little. Not too sure they'd support her, she leaned against the tree until she felt steady.

Ethan dropped down beside her, and she saw him study her carefully, raising his eyebrows in silent question. When she motioned that she was fine, he nodded and set off back the way they'd come, Lisa following behind him.

Neither of them uttered a word until they reached the tent, removed their NVGs and guns, and took off their backpacks. Lisa bent to stretch and touch her toes, the release of tension in her muscles a relief after all those hours in one position.

Ethan unzipped the tent, sat down on the thermal sheet he'd spread out on the bottom, and motioned for her to join him. She hesitated, remembering what had happened the last time they were in the tent together. She thought about the fact they'd be sleeping here again and pushed it out of her mind. She'd worry about it later.

He slid over to make room for her. "Let's talk."

"Good." She sat cross-legged. "What did we find out tonight? We don't even know for sure if Jamie's in that house."

He patted his shirt pocket, then made a disgusted sound. "Why did I have to pick this particular time to stop smoking? Okay." He stretched out his legs and leaned back on his elbows. "Nothing, you say? Did you notice any of the shadows in the upstairs windows? No? Well, in one room there was a shadow considerably shorter than either of the other silhouettes I saw. Unless they have a dwarf living there, I'd say it's a safe bet there's a child in that house."

"I… No, I… No." Let's hear it for the blithering idiot. And how did I miss seeing that?

"Next. The guards changed at least six times while we were in that tree, and we never saw the same face twice. That means a minimum of twelve armed men. And we don't know if there are more in the house."

Lisa's shoulders slumped. "You're describing a hopeless situation. If Jamie's really there and it's Charles who has him, I can't imagine how we'll ever get him out."

Ever since Ethan had agreed to help her, she'd clung to the hope that he could do the impossible—find her son and safely rescue him. Now, realizing the odds they faced, with Charles a wild card in the mix, she was beginning to doubt the possibility of their success. To come so close and fail…

She crossed her arms over her knees and leaned her head on them, forcing back the tears that threatened to leak from her eyes.

She jumped when she felt Ethan's hand on her shoulder, gently massaging the muscle.

"I didn't picture you as a quitter." His voice was deep and unusually soft. "What happened to the woman who told me she'd do anything—anything—to get her son back? Who said her son means the world to her?"

She drew in an erratic breath. "She didn't realize how close she'd come and maybe fail."

"I don't fail, Lisa. And what we saw tonight doesn't mean failure. It only gave us information we need to put an effective plan together."

"I guess this all seemed so unreal to me, so far away when we talked about it."

"We've only just gotten started here. And one night doesn't give us everything we need."

She jerked her head up. "You mean we have to do this again?"

"Uh huh. And I'd like to see what goes on during the day. I also need to scout this area better so we'll know how we're getting out of here when we have Jamie with us. When, Lisa. Not if."

His hand never stopped massaging her shoulder as he shifted so his legs bracketed her. Now both hands eased the tension in her body. The feel of his fingers kneading her muscles was so soothing, like a narcotic, easing the tautness that had her strung tight as a bow.

His touch brought back their moment in the tent earlier, and the incredible sex. Was he thinking of it, too? He was the most masculine man she'd ever met, and the secrets in his life only made him hotter and sexier.

Be careful, Lisa. Trouble here.

He slid closer to her, his cock pressing up against

her ass. How was she supposed to handle this? Was the man an ice cube that he could just put all the electric desire in the air aside?

"I agree our task isn't an easy one, but we're not alone. Nick has people ready, and he's waiting for a signal from me, waiting for me to put a plan together. We'll get him out. I promise. And I don't make promises lightly."

She closed her eyes, soothed by the movement of his hands, the cadence of his voice. It wasn't just the last few months that she'd been carrying around like a satchel full of bricks weighing her down. Charles Mallory was in there, too, and the years of hell with him she'd somehow survived. Taking the punishment. Living like a prisoner. Suffering the abuse. Anything to keep Jamie with her. And safe.

"Lisa?" His voice was so close his breath was a warm breeze against her ear.

"Mmm?"

She turned her head, and instant desire struck her, like a visceral blow. The same heat glittered in Ethan's eyes. So he wasn't as stoic as he claimed. As able to just pack all that away on command. All that heat and desire from earlier floated in him just as it did in her.

Their gazes locked for the space of a heartbeat. And then, somehow, she was leaning backward, his arms were around her and his mouth was seducing hers. Seducing. That was the word for it. And any protest she might have made disappeared like a wisp of smoke.

Chapter Fifteen

The sounds of the jungle were all around them, and a tiny breeze carried the lush scents of the tropical underbrush. The edge of danger they'd been living on and the bewitching nature of the tropics combined to heighten the moment, pushing the real world away and enclosing them in a magical embrace.

Ethan's mouth moved over hers softly, gently, sensuously. He somehow managed to make the rest of the world disappear for her. His teeth took tiny nibbles at her bottom lip then soothed it, the tip of his tongue tracing over the bite marks. He licked the inside of her bottom lip, then turned his attention to the upper one.

Lisa felt as if she'd fallen down a well and was floating in the water. His tongue was like a feather drifting across the surface of her mouth, bringing each nerve to jolting life. Sensations she hadn't even known she had came to life in every secret corner of her body. She opened her mouth on a soft moan, and his tongue slipped inside as if it belonged there.

He tasted of fruit and power bars and the jungle, and it was the most exhilarating taste she'd ever experienced. She wanted to roll it around in her mouth, swallow it, absorb it into her system. It was headier than the finest wine or the most expensive brandy.

She danced her tongue with his, a slow waltz to imagined music. Together. Retreat. Together. Retreat.

His tongue slid across the surface of hers, teasing at it. Tantalizing. She couldn't imagine ever kissing anyone else after this.

She tried to press her mouth harder against his, but he held her head captive, keeping the pressure of his mouth and tongue as light at the touch of a butterfly's wings. The sense of him permeated her body.

She had no idea how long he played with her mouth. When he lifted his head, a tremendous sense of loss swept over her. She opened her eyes and saw his black bottomless ones burning into hers.

"I can't make promises to you, except where Jamie's concerned." His voice was taut with emotion.

"I didn't ask for any." She heard the tremor in her own voice.

"Trust me, Lisa. I have very little to give to anyone anymore, and what I do have, you don't want. Nobody would. We're just two people seduced by the jungle, hiding for a little while from what's really happening."

She swallowed hard and nodded. "Right."

"Okay then."

He lowered his mouth to hers again, just brushing his lips over hers. He dusted her face with the softest of kisses—her forehead, her eyelids, her nose, her cheeks. Even her chin. Each touch was like a hot wire igniting her skin.

It barely registered when his warm hand closed over one breast, massaging it gently through the fabric of her T-shirt and bra. A gentle glide, just like his kisses. Somewhere in the back of her mind, she realized she'd expected Ethan Caine to be an aggressive lover, harsh, demanding. But it seemed the seduction was as important to him as the act itself.

She moaned again, trying to thrust herself into his palm. One of her hands snaked around his neck, and she tugged the leather thong holding back his hair. It fell loose around his shoulders. She raked her fingers through it, letting it sift against her skin like fine silk.

When his mouth closed over one nipple, sucking at it through the fabric covering it, she closed her eyes and let the feeling of warmth wash over her. Her nipples hardened as he pulled on them with a gentle tug of his teeth, and she wanted more. More. She wanted her clothing gone and nothing between them.

She was trembling in his arms as her body responded to him. Sensations Charles had never roused in her swept over her like waves of electricity, every nerve so sensitized it felt as if their protective coverings had dissolved. Her heart was beating so loudly she wondered how Ethan could miss hearing it. But then she felt the hard thump of his through the wall of chest muscle and it somehow grounded her.

The warmth of his hand as it slid under her shirt and moved over her bare skin heated her from her breasts to the apex of her thighs where her panties were surely soaked. A fluttering started deep inside her and called up responses she'd long ago buried.

He stroked her midriff, the roughened pads of his fingers creating a pleasant friction on her skin. With quick, deft movements, he had the clasp of her bra open and shoved it and her T-shirt up around her neck. When his warm, wet mouth closed over a nipple, shards of lightening sparked throughout her body. Her hips began to move against him, and tiny little mewling cries escaped her lips.

She slid her hands under his shirt to find the thick

matted hair of his chest, twisting her fingers in the curls. The skin beneath the soft pelt was warm and hard, and she couldn't stop touching it everywhere.

He reached for the zipper on her jeans, and she lifted her hips to accommodate him, willingly allowing him to roll them with her panties down her legs and over her feet. Then his mouth moved over her, leaving a wet trail that his breath wafted over like a hot breeze.

A soft nudge on her inner thighs and she opened her legs for him, wanting his touch, his heat, every part of him.

"Don't move." His voice was hoarse and uneven. "Stay just like that."

He rose, and she watched through half-opened eyes as he stripped off his clothing and tossed it to the side with hers. She realized again that, in the bare flesh, Ethan was a magnificent animal. Every wonderful inch of him. She could see what he'd been before his fall from grace and what his conditioning campaign had brought him back to.

He knelt to unzip the large canvas bag he'd brought into the tent with them and reached in for something.

Another condom.

Then he was beside her again, on top of her, sheathed, poised. In one smooth motion, he slid inside her, filling her, and a strange feeling of homecoming washed over her.

This time was slower than before, as if he didn't want to be rushed, wanted to savor every moment, every friction, every touch. His cock filled her so full, but even then, she arched toward him, wanting more.

He set up a slow rhythm, his gaze locked with hers, the hunger in his eyes hot as fire as he watched her carefully for signs of her response. She couldn't believe she was ready so easily, that her orgasm was already reaching for the peak. When her breathing quickened and she pushed hard against him, he picked up the pace. Without warning, the orgasm crested and broke over both of them, his cock pulsing inside her as she milked him with her hot sheath.

On and on it went, until Lisa was sure she had nothing left to give. Then they were still, and Ethan collapsed forward on his forearms, his erratic breath a warm breeze on her face.

Just like before, he didn't say a word, just took care of business before dropping back onto the thermal sheet beside her. But he did pull her body against his, cradling her against him, whisking a light kiss over her cheek before settling into sleep.

****

When they rose in the morning, Lisa wondered if they would feel awkward with each other, but Ethan was so matter-of-fact she wasn't even sure the night before had actually happened. He simply went about whatever he was doing as if nothing had changed. And maybe in his mind it hadn't. A dozen times, she had to stop herself from saying anything.

They had bottled water, more fruit, and another power bar for breakfast, took care of personal business, and washed with moist towelettes.

Finally, she couldn't stand it anymore. "Ethan."

He looked at her, his expression plainly telling her he knew what was on her mind. "Forget it. Whatever you were about to say."

"But—

"Don't make something out of nothing. We're

under a lot of tension here. I've been there before. A little recreational sex is better than tranquilizers."

A little recreational sex? She recoiled as if he'd struck her. He'd been such a considerate and attentive lover, yet now he turned away and went back to what he was doing. Conversation over.

Okay. I can be just as cool about it as he can. He said no strings, and that's fine with me.

But no matter how much he tried to deny it, she knew inside where it counted that last night had been a lot more than what he tried to make it be. They'd connected on a plane far greater than the physical one, and she was sure it was scaring the shit out of him.

Fine. Plenty of time to talk when this is all over.

Ethan sat cross-legged in the tent field-stripping and checking their guns. About midmorning, he turned on one of the satellite radios and punched in a number.

"Me," he said. "I'll recon the surrounding area today and check the *finca* again tonight. We don't have near enough information yet to make a move."

He listened, nodding to himself.

"We'll have to make a decision after tonight," he said at last. "We can't hang around here too long or someone will find us for sure. Here's the GPS coordinates of our location in case we get caught and you have to bring in the troops. I'll do regular check-ins. More later."

He shut down the phone and returned it to his backpack.

"Was that Nick?"

"Yes." Short, sharp, and to the point.

Lisa cleared her throat, the feeling of dread coiling in the pit of her stomach again. "Did you say something about us getting caught?"

His hard gaze pinned her, and that same spike of agony flashed against the dark irises. "On any mission, there's always the possibility you'll get caught. That the whole thing will be blown. Always. You have to set your mind for that eventuality and then do everything you can to avoid it."

She rubbed her hands against her thighs. "Do you think they know we're here?"

"No. Not yet, but we're still scanning the area."

"I heard you say we're going back there today. Do you think it's wise to go in the daylight?"

He busied himself repacking his backpack. "I said I was. Not you."

"But—"

"No buts, remember?" He stood up and shouldered the pack. "I can do this part better by myself. It's second nature to me."

"You just want me to wait here until you either get back or get shot?"

He actually grinned. "Preferably the first one. But, yes, that's what I want you to do. Get out your sat radio."

She pulled it from her pack and showed it to him.

"You remember how to use this?"

She nodded.

"Fine. Here's your assignment. Once every hour, on the hour, press this button." He pointed. "When someone answers on the other end, just tell him we're still clear. Can you do that?"

"Of course." She huffed with impatience. "Do you think I'm some kind of moron?"

"No." His voice softened. "I think you're a very

brave, very smart, very courageous woman who's been shortchanged by life. Watch my back, darlin'.'"

While she stood there stunned by his words and his term of affection, he leaned down and kissed her with all the passion he'd shown the night before. When he lifted his head, he winked at her.

"See you later."

****

The day dragged interminably. Every time the minute hand hit twelve on her watch, she punched the number on the sat radio. To the disembodied voice that answered, she said, "Still clear."

The voice answered, "Okay," and disconnected.

She wondered if that was Nick Vanetta on the other end, or did he have someone else monitoring this until it was time to move? And exactly where was he? Back in San Antonio? Here in Mexico? In Cancun? Waiting at the edge of the Quintana Roo? Her questions were giving her a headache.

In between calls, she tried to pass the time with exercise, keeping her muscles loose and stretching them. Shortly after noon, she treated herself to a small lunch, then went back to her stretching routine. It kept her from falling asleep.

Her ears strained constantly for sounds of Ethan, but all she heard were the howler monkeys screeching in the trees, the cacophony of the birds overhead, the beating of their wings in the trees, and occasional sounds of some animal crashing through the undergrowth. She kept her gun ready at all times to shoot anything that wandered into their clearing.

For a while, she battered her brain, trying to dissect every moment of the previous night. A kaleidoscope of feelings ran uncontrolled through her body—satisfaction, the need for more, fear that they'd crossed an invisible line and couldn't go back, amazement that a man she'd despised for so long could call up such a strong response.

Josh and Nick were right. Ethan was a lot more than what he allowed people to see. He had been a wonderful lover, despite the fact that each time, afterwards, he'd tried to act as if it was a mere nothing. She wondered how dark his secrets were that he had to divorce himself emotionally this way.

She'd laughed once at the seemingly inexhaustible supply of condoms. He'd just told her he was always prepared for anything.

He'd shown an unexpected tenderness, not with words but with actions, as well as respect for her. Not once had he made her feel cheap or embarrassed by what happened. Then this morning, he'd thrown her into a tizzy by ignoring what happened altogether and then giving her that heated kiss.

What would happen when this was all over and they were back in Florida, back to their normal lives?

Lisa laughed to herself. Normal lives? What was normal anymore?

Would they see each other again? Make love? Something more than that? Would he just crawl back into his cave, leaving her with nothing but memories?

When her head began to ache, trying to think through all the possibilities, she shut off her brain by doing multiplication tables, a trick she'd learned to distance herself from Charles's humiliating treatment of her both in bed and out.

By the time several hours had passed, her nerves

were getting the better of her again. She kept sending the "still clear", hoping she was right but expecting armed men to burst from the jungle at any minute.

Then he was back, moving as silently as he had the day before. He was soaked with sweat, and his hat looked even more battered. She couldn't tell by his expression if he had good news or bad. He took his time settling his pack, pulling off his T-shirt, mopping his face and body, drinking water in long gulps.

"Well?" she asked, her patience finally at an end.

He settled himself against a tree trunk before answering her. "I have good news and bad news. Which do you want first?"

"Good news," she almost shouted. "I could use some."

"All right, but don't go crazy. Sound carries out here."

"I promise. Give."

"I saw Jamie."

She would have shouted with joy if she hadn't remembered Ethan's warning in time. "Where? How is he? Does he look hurt? Is he…"

He held up his hand. "Whoa. Let me give you the details, okay?"

She blew out a breath. "Yes. Of course. I'm sorry. It's just that…"

"I know." He drank down two more swallows of water. "He looks fine. At least physically. He was riding a bike up and down the driveway with one of the guards watching him at all times. He's wearing clean clothes, and he doesn't look like he's been abused in any way."

"I'm sensing there's a but."

Ethan nodded. "I don't remember the last time I saw a child look so unhappy."

"Damn!" Lisa smacked her fist against the tree trunk then shook it to relieve the sting of the pain. "He misses me. I know it. He can't be happy cooped up with a houseful of strangers."

"Two pieces of bad news. One, I couldn't get a glimpse of who the owner of the place is. He never came out in the yard. I guess because he was having a busy day."

Lisa frowned. "What do you mean?"

"Cars arrived and departed all day long. Sometimes one man, sometimes two. A guard would take them inside for maybe an hour, then the next crew would arrive. Whatever business this guy is conducting he's doing it from home."

"What's the other bad news?"

"I used a nifty little piece of equipment Nick included with all this stuff to check out the perimeter. I spotted cameras in some of the trees, but worse, the ground outside the wall is loaded with sensors. My guess is they're hooked up to an alarm system."

She resumed her nervous pacing. "So how will we ever get inside? How will we get to Jamie? How will we even know where he is?"

"Lisa, stop." Ethan reached out a hand and grabbed her arm. "This isn't the first time I've done something like this. We're going to check out the routine once more tonight, then we'll be able to make a plan. And have the right equipment to help us. That's why I needed to do a reconnaissance."

She yanked off her hair tie, raked her hands through her hair, and pulled it back into a ponytail.

"Can we do this ourselves?"

"No. When we've got the plan put together, I'm signaling Nick. He's on standby in Cancun with a team."

So that answered her question. "In Cancun," she repeated.

Ethan nodded. "So he'd be instantly available when I was ready for him, and his crew. When I called him yesterday morning in Texas, he and Reno put it all together and left shortly after that." He gave a short chuckle. "I think Nick's been itching for some action. He was ready to leave almost before I called."

She rubbed her hands up and down her arms, suddenly cold in the jungle heat. "I'm afraid, Ethan. I don't want to be, but I am."

He pulled her down to sit facing him. "Only a fool isn't afraid, Lisa. Those who operate without fear are courting death. Fear keeps you on your toes and your senses sharpened."

She picked up a little twig and drew a circle in the dirt with it. "I just want to be able to get Jamie out of there and bring him home safely."

"And we will. That's what this is all about." He took the twig from her hand and wrapped his arms around her, a gesture way out of character for him.

After a moment, she looked up at him. "Ethan…

As if he knew what she was about to say, he shook his head. "Not now. We have a job to do. I know you want to talk, and that will take longer than five minutes. I also don't want to distract us from what we're here to do. Time enough when we're all back in Tampa."

Would that be a good talk or a bad one? She was almost afraid to find out.

Chapter Sixteen

They said very little to each other after that, eating their simple evening meal, then waiting until enough darkness had fallen to give them protection. Ethan checked their guns one more time and made sure every other piece of equipment he stuffed in his backpack was in working order. Finally, he strapped on their NVGs and they were off.

The going tonight was a little easier since Ethan had been here during the daylight hours and Lisa remembered some of it from the night before. They climbed the same tree, took up the same positions, and began again to wait.

The night was incredibly still, and the humidity lay on them like a blanket. The insects seemed to be worse than ever, and she was glad he had rubbed both of them down with repellent. Tonight, knowing what lay ahead, she managed to arrange herself in a more comfortable position. Her eyes were totally focused on the compound, trying to register every tiny detail.

They'd been there a little more than an hour when they heard shouting from the house, the front door opened and a pajama-clad boy ran out into the front yard. He was screaming something at the top of his lungs and waving his arms wildly.

"Jamie." Lisa whispered the name to herself, digging her nails into her palms to keep herself from shouting it out. "Oh, Jamie, what are they doing to you?"

Then she heard a man's voice swearing in both English and Spanish. When he came striding through the open door, cursing the child, she thought her heart would stop beating. Every bit of blood drained from her face, and she began to shake. She'd fallen into a nightmare.

When it was just an idea, it seemed so abstract. Now she was seeing the devil in the flesh and all the terror came creeping back.

Ethan hadn't moved as the tableau unfolded before them. She reached up and touched his leg.

"Charles," she mouthed at him. "My God, it's Charles. He's alive, just like I thought."

Ethan didn't answer, just touched her fingers to let her know he'd heard.

It was a different Charles than the one she'd known, at least physically—longer hair, deeper tan, a moustache. Despite that, she'd know him anywhere. You never forgot your tormenter. Or your jailer.

Now he was in an obvious rage, grabbing Jamie by the arms.

"Your mother is dead, do you hear me?" he shouted. "You will never see her again."

"She's not." Tears ran down Jamie's face. "She was in the restaurant. She thinks I've run away. I told you and told you. Let me go." His body thrashed wildly. "I want to go home to my mother."

"Jamie, listen to me." Charles tried to hold the boy still.

"No. I won't." He beat his fists against his father's chest. "I hate you. You're mean. And you were mean to

Mommy. I don't want to live with you. And I don't want to stay in this place anymore."

Lisa bit her lip so hard she tasted blood. Oh God, oh God, oh God.

"I am your father. You will obey me. Do you understand?"

The guards watched, as if unsure of what their role should be.

"No, I won't." Jamie began kicking.

"You need to learn some discipline, young man." He set Jamie down on the ground and slapped his face in one quick motion.

"No!" The cry escaped her mouth before she could stop herself.

Charles's head snapped up, and he looked around. The guards held their rifles at the ready.

"What was that?" He looked at both of them. "Did you hear that?"

The guards spoke too softly to hear what was said, even as Lisa strained to listen. She was afraid to look up at Ethan, knowing the censure she'd see on his face. And well deserved. She'd done a stupid, foolish thing and endangered both of them.

"Go out and look around," Charles shouted, holding a kicking Jamie firmly under one arm. "I'll take the boy inside. Find whoever is out there and bring them to me."

Lisa's heart beat so rapidly she was sure it would burst from her chest. As hot as the night was, the sweat trickling down her spine was like ice water. The guards would find them, and this would be over. Their efforts would have all been for nothing. And Ethan might be killed because of her stupidity.

She didn't know where she found the courage to do what she did next. She pulled off her NVGs and her backpack and stuffed them in the crotch of two branches, looked up at Ethan, and whispered, "It's up to you now."

Before he could stop her, she dropped down out of the tree.

She could feel Ethan's anger vibrating in the air even at this distance, but she had no choice. She pretended to be thrashing in the underbrush when the guards found her. They stared at her, stunned to find a woman alone in the jungle outside the *finca*.

"*Se habla español?*" one of them asked as he grabbed her arm roughly.

Lisa tried to jerk away from him, but his grip was too tight. She shook her head at his words. "English. I speak English."

"And what's a *gringa* like you doing running around in the Quintana Roo? Tourists never come this deep." He looked behind and around her. "Who else is with you?"

"No one." Her throat was so dry she had to force the words. "No one," she repeated. "I'm alone."

"A *gringa* alone, wandering in the jungle at night? I don't think so." He motioned to his partner. "Esteban. Look around. See what you can find."

Esteban moved off into the foliage, slashing back and forth with the barrel of his rifle. Lisa held her breath, praying he wouldn't look up. Praying that Ethan was well concealed.

"If its money you want, I have friends who will pay you," Lisa said. "Just don't…hurt me. If you hurt me, no one will pay."

The guard laughed. "You think we do this for money? Ah, *senorita*, if we do not bring you back to the hacienda, we will not live to spend even one peso."

"Then what do you want? I'm not hurting you." She peered toward the *finca*. "If your boss knew you were doing this, he'd punish you."

The man's eyes glittered as he looked at her, his fingers tightened even more on her arm. "You will be lucky if he does not kill you himself. He does not take kindly to strangers on his territory."

At that moment, Esteban came back to where they stood. "Nada, Ramon. No trace of anyone."

Lisa allowed herself a sigh of relief. Get away, Ethan. You're our only hope.

Esteban raked his eyes over her. "She's *muy linda*, Ramon. Perhaps we could enjoy her charm before taking her back to *el patron*."

"Are you a fool? He'd kill us both. Come on. Let's go."

"Wait." Lisa tried to drag her feet. "Where are you taking me? I'm just out here collecting plant specimens. Your boss can't complain about that." It was the first thing that came to her mind.

Both men laughed.

"Oh yes?" Esteban raised an eyebrow. "Where is your specimen bag? Your tools? A flashlight to see at night?"

Lisa just stood there, saying nothing.

"Tell that to *el patron*," Ramon said. "He'll get a good laugh out of it."

They maintained a bruising grip, one on each arm, as they half walked half dragged her through the jungle growth up to the perimeter wall, through a gate, and up to the house. Her heart was pounding so loud she was sure they'd hear it. Her stomach heaved at the thought of facing Charles again, but maybe being in the house would give her a chance to get to Jamie.

Help us, Ethan. I trust you. I know you can do this.

Then they were dragging her through the door and Charles Mallory, not one bit dead, stood before her, his face a mask of rage.

****

Sitting rigid in the tree while the guards manhandled Lisa was one of the hardest things Ethan had ever done. One minute he wanted to kill her, the next jump down and save her. She'd done a foolish, foolish thing, but he knew the minute she did it that it was the only choice she had. If they were both discovered, Jamie Mallory would never leave Mexico and neither would they. She'd left everything in his hands, trusting him to find a way to get both her and her son to safety.

But a cold rage gripped him. He could only imagine what she'd face at Charles Mallory's hands.

Mallory! With the confirmation he was alive, every answer fell into place. The man had been smart enough to fake his own death to get out from under the drug dealers and the IRS and give himself a fresh start. The kidnapping allowed him to get his hands on the ten million dollars. And he had his son without the inconvenience of the mother.

No wonder he'd tried twice to have Lisa killed. She was the one stumbling block he needed to rid himself of. With her gone, no one would ever look for Jamie or the money. Or him. And to his way of thinking, Josh was just a minor stumbling block to be eliminated. He'd be home free.

If he only knew.

Ethan ground his teeth as he sat in the tree in total stillness, waiting for the guards to leave with Lisa. Everything had changed now. He'd need a new plan, and he'd need it damn quick.

From his vantage point, he saw Lisa dragged up to the open doors of the *finca*, and Charles confronting her before the front doors closed. Ethan was sick at the images that flashed through his mind of what might happen to her, but he couldn't afford that kind of self-indulgence. Lisa had done what she had so he'd be free to save them all.

He'd better get to it.

He gave himself another hour surveilling the *finca* and surroundings before finally climbing down from the tree and making his way back to the campsite. He dropped into the open tent where he and Lisa had made such incredible love the night before. And that was truly the only word for it. Even as he cursed himself for the insanity of it, he'd lost himself in her loving body, her kisses and caresses more healing to his damaged soul than all the alcohol or pills in the world.

Ethan had had many women in his life. Almost too many to count. But none had had the sweetness or goodness of Lisa Mallory. None had given of themselves with such unrestrained fervor, holding nothing back. He could still smell her scent of vanilla and jasmine, still feel the satin warmth of her skin, still feel the heat of her body clench around him like a wet fist.

As he fought to pull himself together, he was shocked to discover his emotions had broken out of the cell he kept them contained in. And he had no idea what to do with them. For the first time in his life, this was more than just an op to him. More than an assignment. But Lisa was a forever kind of woman and that wasn't even in his wheelhouse, so what in the ever-loving fucking hell was going on with him? Yet, if ever a woman could reach his black soul, she could do it. But he had no right to ask it. To expect it. Even to want it. He had nothing left to offer a woman like her except a ruined life

Giving himself a mental shake, he used all his discipline to shut down those thoughts. Time was fleeting and he could do this one last thing for her. He could save her and her son.

****

Charles sat in a high-backed leather chair, his eyes taking in every inch of Lisa as she stood before him. The two men who had dragged her in still held her firmly by the arms.

"You can leave us," he told them. "She won't run away. She has no place to go. And besides, I have what she wants. Oh, and Esteban? Call Cortez and tell him to get his mangy ass down here. We may have use of his talents tonight. I don't know who else is out there in the jungle, but you can be damn sure she's not here alone."

"*Si, patron.*"

She rubbed her arms when the men released her, but she kept her back straight and her eyes firmly locked with Charles's. She would never again give him the satisfaction of seeing her cower.

"So you're alive," she said, the sight of him making her ill.

"Of course, my dear." His demeanor was arrogant.

"I was far from ready to leave the mortal world. I just needed to rid myself of some…difficulties."

"I want my son," she told him defiantly.

"He's my son, too." Charles's voice was like ice. "Believe me, if I could have gotten rid of you in time and taken him with me I would have."

"But why?" she cried. "What for? What place can he possibly have in this life you live?"

"Because he's my son," he told her in a mild voice. "I knew the minute I met you that you and I would produce an exceptional child. An heir to carry my name. After that, I had no use for you."

"Then why didn't you let me go?"

He laughed, a sound so unpleasant it made her mouth go dry. "Too many reasons, my dear. You would have fought for custody of Jamie, and I couldn't have that. And then you'd have hired a shark lawyer and cost me a great deal of money."

"Money you owed to a lot of not so very nice people," she pointed out. "Not to mention the IRS."

"Yes, well, things got a little dicey there at the end. That's why I had to bow out, so to speak."

Lisa's legs threatened to give out on her, but she refused to show any sign of weakness. "It certainly took you a long time to make your move."

"There were many reasons for that. I had to wait for the media circus to die down from my supposed death. Make sure I was far enough removed from all the events that some stupid cop didn't get a bee in his bonnet and decide to take a closer look at the remains. Or the situation. And I needed time to prepare for my future."

"You staged the kidnapping so you could get the

ten million dollars."

His smile held no warmth. "Of course. It was, after all, my money to begin with. And I needed it."

She stared at him, trying to comprehend that the man she'd been married to had been, on top of everything else, a killer. "You killed another man so you could get away. Just…killed him."

Charles shrugged. "A pitiful bum. People like that are disposable." He leaned forward in his chair. "I'm curious. How did you find me? I spent a lot of time and money covering my tracks. People better than you haven't been able to discover where I am."

But Ethan's smarter than all of them.

"I wasn't looking for you. Just Jamie. I… Someone I hired discovered this was where he'd been taken. I didn't know you were the one who had him until tonight."

"Amazing." He rubbed his moustache as his eyes raked her from top to bottom. "I wouldn't have believed you had it in you."

"I want to see Jamie."

His eyes widened. "I beg your pardon?"

"I want to see my son. Right now."

He shook his head. "First of all, you're in no position to make demands. Secondly, he won't want to see you."

Lisa gripped her hands together and forced herself to breathe evenly. "Because you told him I'm dead? He doesn't believe you."

"Ah. So you heard us."

"I saw how you treated him. I want to see him right this minute."

"Why don't you tell me who else was out there

prowling the jungle with you? Maybe then, I'll give you a few minutes with your son. There's no way you're in this by yourself."

"No one." Please let him believe me.

"Surely, you don't think I'm gullible enough to believe you could manage all this by yourself. A name, Lisa. I want to know who came here with you. You want to see Jamie, don't you?"

Even for the chance to see her son, she couldn't betray Ethan. He was the only salvation for all of them.

"I told you. I'm alone."

Charles stood up so fast Lisa didn't even see him move. The blow he struck against her face rattled her brain, and blood trickled onto her chin where her lip had split.

"Do you take me for a fool? Give me his name."

Lisa clenched her hands into fists and tightened her body against what she knew was sure to come. "There's no one."

Smack! His hand cracked against her cheek again. And again. Forward then back. Her vision blurred, and tears ran down her face. She held onto the image of Ethan's face to give her strength.

Charles drew in a deep breath. "Whoever he is, he won't get away. I'll have my men out covering the entire area. They'll find whoever is out there. Then I can take care of you all at the same time." He picked up the phone on the table next to the chair where he'd been sitting. "Come take this piece of trash out of my living room. Put her in one of the rooms upstairs. And do not let her anywhere near the boy."

Shaking her head to clear her vision, Lisa saw Charles hang up the phone and turn to her. "Perhaps you need time to consider your situation, my dear. I'll be up to see you in a little while."

Lisa choked back the nausea rising in her throat. She would almost prefer a beating to what she was sure Charles had in mind.

Hurry, Ethan. Please.

Chapter Seventeen

Ethan had spent a good deal of his life sitting and waiting. Part of the job. And he'd trained himself to do it patiently, not to lose focus, to always be alert. This time he'd stupidly let what was left of his emotions get involved, and his patience was wearing very thin.

How the fuck had he let Lisa Mallory slide in under the concrete wall around what was left of his heart? He had nothing left to give her, or anyone else, but definitely her. If he believed in love, that would describe what he felt for her. Fuck. He needed to save her, then get her away from him as fast as he could before he did more damage to her. Because forever was a word not in his future, and that's what he saw with Lisa.

He'd been sitting with the phone in his hand for two hours now and not handling it very well. But when Mallory's headbangers grabbed Lisa, he realized he was running out of time. He punched a number into the sat phone that connected to Nick.

"Mallory's alive," Ethan said in a voice so quiet it was barely a whisper. "She was right."

"Why am I not shocked?" Nick said. "It's the only thing that makes sense."

"But I fucked up, Nick. I let Lisa fall into his hands."

"I'm guessing you didn't let anything happen,"

Nick corrected. "Lisa was her usual stubborn self and did something to protect you and Jamie."

"Stupid woman," Ethan grumbled.

"Brave woman," Nick corrected.

"I never should have let her talk me into bringing her along. Except—"

"Except you knew she'd try to do it on her own. Right?"

"Yes. And my ego is so big I thought I could control the whole situation." If he could manage it, he'd kick himself in the ass. With both feet.

Damn, damn, damn.

"Okay. It sounds like it's time for us to move."

"It is. Let me know when you're on the way."

He was still missing one piece of the puzzle, however. He chewed it over in his mind while he waited for Nick to call back. Mallory had to have some kind of help setting everything up, and right now, he had no idea who or what that could be.

As he was considering the wisdom of taking another look at the man's compound the sat phone beeped.

"All set?" he asked.

"We're in the air," Nick told him. "Hogan's driving the helicopter, and two other Guardian agents plus two of Dino's men make up the rest of the team. We've got enough firepower with us to hold off the entire *federales* if they happen to show up."

"How are we doing this so we don't alert Mallory? He's sure to hear the 'copter cruising overhead."

"I checked the area. There's an ecotours company that does night flights over the jungle. A friend cranked out a magnetic sign in his little shop, and we slapped it on the ship. We only need to hover long enough for the drop. When he comes back for the pickup, he won't care who hears him."

Ethan looked at his watch. "What's your ETA?"

"Ten mikes. I figured we'd better wait until we were almost there to call you. Otherwise, you'd be bugging us every other minute."

"You've got the coordinates?"

Nick chuckled. "Do you even need to ask? See you in a few."

Ethan clicked off the phone and began to make his own preparations.

****

There was a bathroom adjoining the bedroom Lisa was locked in, and she took advantage of it to clean up as best she could. Her lip was badly split from Charles's blow and already puffy. One eye was closing, and the other one didn't look too good.

After washing her face and hands, she took one of the towels, soaked it in cold water and held it to her face. Then she sat down on the bed and tried to figure out what her next move was. Charles would be showing up any minute, determined to extract information from her. And she also knew how he would do it.

In the last few years of their marriage, sex had not been like it was in the early years. It had become something Charles used to punish her with. Humiliate her. Debase her. Just remembering the things he did to her brought back the nausea, and she had to swallow hard to fight it.

If she could just make him let her see Jamie, maybe she could come up with a plan to get the two of them out of there. She could do anything for Jamie. She had to keep remembering that.

As she was wetting the cloth again, a key turned and the door to the bedroom opened. When she looked in the mirror, she saw Charles come up behind her. He dropped his hands to her shoulders and a shudder ran through her.

"I don't like hurting you, Lisa," he smirked, "but I can't have you ruining all my plans. Not when I've worked so hard and so long to put them in place."

"And what exactly are your plans? What do you do here, anyway?"

"I barter. I trade. Not unlike what I did in my other life."

She frowned. "You're a stockbroker? You manage finances?"

He laughed. "Only my own. No, my dear. It's a new world today, and it requires new business plans. There are groups all over the world eager for weapons, for whatever their cause is. Others are just as eager for drugs. I trade one for the other and make money from both parties."

She forced herself to control the feeling of revulsion that swept over her. "I see."

"Do you?" He ran his hands up and down her arms. "What is it you see? A criminal or a businessman? A lover or…a man you hate?"

She whirled to face him, slipping away from his touch. "What if I said I'd stay here with you? You and Jamie? We could be a family again."

His eyes glittered with hatred. "I think not. I know exactly how you feel about me. Not unlike my feelings for you. And I will never, ever let you near Jamie again. I've waited too long to get him back. He's mine and

I'm keeping him. Now." He dropped his hands to her breast, pinching the nipples so painfully she cried out. "Let's talk about who's in this with you. I'll find out eventually. You know that. You can save yourself a great deal of pain by telling me now."

Lisa closed her eyes and prayed for the courage to get through this.

****

As attuned as his ears were, listening for sounds, Ethan still never heard them approach. The *whap! whap! whap!* of the helicopter blades had sliced the night air ten minutes earlier, the machine hovering for brief seconds before taking off. He hoped not long enough to pique anyone's interest, but you never knew. Since then, his eyes and ears had been waiting for the sight and sound of his friends.

And then they were there, emerging silently from the jungle foliage, three figures all in black, hoods ready to pull over their heads.

Nick was in the lead. He and Ethan shook hands wordlessly, then the others moved forward.

"We'll have to find your previous position," Nick reminded him, "and take a fix from there. We brought two Thermal Vision MilCam Recons. These babies are tops for hand-held long-range reconnaissance. I didn't know how close your observation post was to the compound, and I wanted to be prepared."

Angel Rodriguez, a longtime Guardian agent who Ethan had worked with before, opened a smaller bag and took out two items that looked like cameras locked into metal frames. "PTZ-35x140. You get great situational awareness with them without sacrificing a wide field of vision. We figured between the two types of units we could catch everything."

"They'll read through any surface or material," Marsh told him. "This way we'll get an accurate picture of how many people are in the house and where they are."

"Weapons?" Ethan asked.

Octavio Marsh, the third agent, dropped a canvas bag in front of him. "HK MP5s. Fires semi-automatic, three-round bursts or full auto. You can set it for whatever you want. And they're fitted with suppressors." He pulled one from the bag, clicked a magazine in place, and showed Ethan the settings.

"A little fancier than what we used to use," he said.

"The better to do the job with," Marsh grinned.

"Enough chatter," Nick told them. "Let's pinpoint where we need to be and get going."

Ethan wondered how he'd ever be able to thank these friends who, at a moment's notice, had disrupted their lives to help him.

"Nick, I..."

"We know," Nick said, as if reading his mind. "And you'd do the same for us."

Ethan swallowed the unfamiliar lump in his throat. "One last thing. Is Hogan set to extract us? I've got the SUV hidden in the bushes here, but I don't think we'll get much chance to drive out of here."

"Not to worry," Angel assured him. He held up a small unit that looked like a miniature walkie-talkie. "Two clicks on this, and Hogan will be hovering right at this spot. All we have to do is get here."

Ethan drew in a deep breath and let it out. "All right, then. Let's do it."

They spent the next few minutes rigging their gear

and outfitting themselves. Each man had the HK MP5 slung over his shoulder and an HK 9mm tucked into the waistband of his pants. They strapped on NVGs, distributed the thermal imagers, and each man buckled to his thigh a leather sheath holding a seven-inch Tanto Recon knife, razor sharp. Finally, Nick handed Ethan a throat mic like he and the others were wearing. They checked to make sure the comm links were working and ran over their hand signals, so familiar from past journeys like this one.

Ready at last, they headed out toward Charles Mallory's *finca*. Ethan could only pray they were in time.

****

Lisa blinked hard to clear the tears. Her right eye felt even more swollen, her lip throbbed, and Charles was exerting relentless pressure on her nipples. She knew he'd kill her in a minute, as soon as she told him what she knew, and that would leave Jamie alone with him. She'd have to withstand the torture long enough for Ethan to rescue them.

Hurry, Ethan.

Just as Charles opened his mouth to say something, the door to the bedroom opened again.

"Charles, Esteban said you were in here with some woman they'd found…" A man's voice trailed off as he took in the scene.

If Lisa felt faint before, now she was positively dizzy. Standing in the doorway, looking completely at home, was her former boss, Aaron Burke. She wasn't sure which of them was more shocked.

"Lisa?" His face paled. "My God, Charles, how the hell did she find you? And this place?"

"Aaron?" Lisa tried to process the appearance of her former mentor here in the middle of the jungle. With her supposedly dead husband. "What do you have to do with this?"

Charles snickered. "Who do you think has been helping me all these years?"

"The ransom." Suddenly, it clicked into place. "The two of you set up the trust the way you did so it would be easy to get the money. No questions asked."

"And there wouldn't be any now," Aaron pointed out to her, "if the people we hired had shot better and you ended up dead instead of just wounded."

"Yes," Charles added. "That was a little disappointing. You are a pesky little thing, you know. You've managed to survive far more than most women would. I suppose I should admire you for that." He sighed. "Lisa, Lisa, Lisa. If only you had mourned the loss of your son and gotten on with your life."

"Aaron." She couldn't drag her eyes away from her former boss. His participation in all this was just too far-fetched. "I can't believe what I'm hearing. Was the introduction to Charles also a setup?"

"No, that was an unexpected bonus for your husband. At least for a couple of years. He was instantly attracted to you."

"For a while," Charles said, "I thought, with your fine legal mind, I wouldn't need Aaron anymore. That we could be a team."

"A team?" She gaped at him.

"Unfortunately, my dear, you turned out to be an uptight prude who began to bore and irritate me."

Lisa was sure she'd fallen down a rabbit hole and ended up in Wonderland. None of this made any sense to her. But then again, when she thought about it, it made all the sense in the world. The senior partner in one of the most prestigious law firms in the South, practicing international law, would have every contact Charles needed. And was no doubt well paid for his troubles.

"You know she's not alone," Aaron said. "Someone's helping her. And not that techno geek brother of hers. He couldn't find his way to the bathroom."

A lot you know. But at least they didn't know about Josh's connection to Ethan.

Hurry, Ethan. Come now.

"I was just on the verge of finding out when you barged in," Charles answered. "Go on back downstairs and make sure I'm not disturbed."

"But…"

"Just get the hell out of here and let me take care of business, Aaron. Now."

"Don't fuck this up, Charles. We've worked too hard and too long to get where we are to let someone bring us down now."

"Worked hard selling drugs?" Lisa spat out. "And arms to terrorists?"

Charles backhanded her, and she thought she felt her brains rattle. But it was worth it to see the look on Aaron Burke's face. Apparently, he was all right with everything as long as he didn't have to face what they were really doing.

"How does she know that?" Aaron asked, his tone sharp.

"It doesn't matter. She won't be telling anyone. Now get out of here and let me finish what I started."

Aaron backed out of the room, closing the door behind him.

Charles stared down at Lisa with eyes colder than anything she'd ever seen. "And now, my dear, it's time to get down to business. Surely, you don't think you can come in here, with whoever you brought, and ruin everything I've worked so hard to build up again?" He grabbed the neckline of her T-shirt and ripped it down the front. Her bra followed.

"Last chance, Lisa. I really don't want to do this."

"Yes, you do." She bit off the words. "You always liked hurting me. You just hid it well the first couple of years. Go ahead, Charles. I have nothing to tell you so you might as well kill me and get it over with."

"Oh, no. That would be too easy. But let's soften you up a little more."

She never saw the blow coming until it landed along the side of her head.

"Had enough yet? No? All right, then." His hands gripped her bare breasts and squeezed as hard as he could. She gritted her teeth against the pain and felt momentary relief when he removed his hands. But then he clenched one hand into a fist and she had no time to evade it before he punched the side of her head with great force.

Lisa closed her eyes and fainted.

Chapter Eighteen

"We're here," Ethan whispered into his mic. He stopped and reached out his hand, pointing. "This is the tree where we did our spotting."

They'd crept silently through the jungle, each man a stealth machine as they'd been trained to be years before. Killing machines who moved undetected at will. Tonight, they would definitely need all the skills they'd acquired.

"All right." Nick said. "You already know the setup. Let Marsh and Angel get up there and take a look. Then we'll pull out the thermal imagers."

Ethan and Nick stood with their guns held ready while the other two men silently climbed the tree. In less than two minutes, they were down.

"He's got a sweet setup," Angel said, "but nothing we can't handle." He pulled a tiny object from his pocket that looked like a toy remote.

"What's that?" Ethan asked.

"This, my good man, will tell us where the sensors are so we can avoid them while getting closer."

"All right. We need to go over things one more time. The closer we get, the less we should chance talking. Even over a closed comm circuit."

In silent whispers, they reviewed the plan with all its alternatives. Then, with Angel in the lead, they began to move slowly forward. Each time Angel's little unit found a sensor, it glowed green, and the men maneuvered left or right to avoid it. Aware of the cameras Ethan had spotted, they moved in a crouch to escape detection by them.

The going was slow as they zigzagged to evade the traps Mallory had laid out to protect his compound. Each sound of the night, each stirring of leaf or animal was magnified as they proceeded in their stealthy approach. They were halfway to the wall when Angel held up his hand to stop. He clicked his mic twice. Enemy approaching.

And not too silently, Ethan thought, as footsteps crashed through the dense foliage. The men separated, each taking cover, as they waited for the steps to get closer. In a moment, they heard cursing in fluent Spanish.

"There's no one here. Esteban and I looked pretty good. We just—"

His speech was cut off abruptly by Angel's arm around his neck. He scarcely felt the razor-sharp Tanto Recon knife as it severed his carotid artery with one quick slice.

"Ramon?" One of the men raised his voice. "What happened? Where did you—"

Marsh wasted no time taking care of him just as Angel had done with Ramon. They lifted the bodies and carried them into the underbrush, relieving them of their rifles.

"Hey! *Mi hombres*! Where the hell are you?" The third man sounded a little frantic.

Ethan materialized in front of him. "Waiting for you to join them, *pendejo*." Asshole.

He placed the dead guard with the other two, wiped

his knife on his pant leg, and sheathed the weapon.

Nick touched his arm and raised his eyebrows in a silent question. More coming?

Ethan shrugged, then shook his head. Don't know but don't think so, he mouthed. These guys were expected to do their job.

Angel clicked his mic once. Let's go.

They had reached the perimeter wall and could see the two guards on the doorway. They pulled out the thermal imagers and began looking for heat signatures.

Nick nudged Ethan. "Ten live bodies in the house."

"Where's Jamie?" Ethan was just as silent.

Nick turned to Angel who pointed to an upstairs window. A small figure too tiny to be an adult was crouched in a window seat, bent over as if crying.

Anger rose up in Ethan.

Using their prearranged hand signals, they identified who would take out each person. Ethan would look for Lisa.

As they were preparing to breach the wall, a scream of such human agony split the night that Ethan's blood turned ice cold.

****

Lisa had come back to consciousness to find herself stretched out on the bed, naked from the waist up, her hands tied above her to the headboard. Charles was staring down at her. She looked at his eyes, and a fear greater than she'd ever known crept through her.

Drugs! He was using his own merchandise. Again. Or maybe still. Cocaine. She always knew when he started using before. The signs were the same. The cruelty increased. The erratic behavior. The light of insanity in his eyes. That's when she'd begun to dread sex.

"I see the expression on your face, Lisa. Do you think I'm going to play one of our kinky games with you?" His laugh sounded like ice breaking. "Perhaps if you'd been into that, our sex life might not have been so pathetically boring. I might not have tired of you so easily."

"Then what are you going to do?" She knew the answers, but asking the questions might buy her a little more time. She tried to keep the fear out of her voice. Her terror had always incited Charles to further cruelty.

"I need answers. As I said, I can't afford any loose ends that could destroy everything it's taken me four years to rebuild. And I don't have that much time to waste. I need information now. Who's with you? Who else knows about me? About this place?"

She clamped her jaw shut, a signal to Charles that she'd say nothing.

He held up a thin, sharp knife. "Fine. Don't say I didn't give you plenty of opportunity to avoid this." He pinched one nipple between thumb and forefinger and very lightly drew the edge of the blade across it.

Lisa opened her mouth and a scream louder than a siren ripped from her throat.

****

"Jesus Christ," Nick breathed. "What the hell was that?"

"That was Lisa." Ethan leaped to the top of the perimeter wall. "I'm going in."

He lifted his rifle to sight along the barrel, but before he could pull the trigger, he heard two quick puffs next to him. The two guards fell where they stood, and Angel was over the wall beside him. He didn't hear

Nick and Marsh, but then they were there, all four of them running in a crouching position toward the house, Ethan well out in front.

Nick caught up with him and pulled on his arm. "Be careful. Use your brain."

Ethan pulled away and kept moving forward.

No one had heard the silenced shots so no one had come to check on the guards. When they reached the heavy carved doors, Ethan and Nick hit them together. Another guard was standing in the hallway, talking to a tall man in slacks and polo shirt.

"Hey!" the tall man shouted. "What the hell—

His words were bitten off by the pressure of Nick's arm on his throat.

Ethan had the guard in a hard grip, the point of his knife pricking the skin under his chin. "Where is she?"

The guard stared at him in dread, no sound coming from his throat.

Ethan moved the knife in a line, making a thin cut along the underside of the man's jaw. "Once more, *pendejo*. Where is the woman?"

Before the man could say anything, a second scream echoed through the house from above.

"Go," Nick hollered. He'd knocked out the tall man and had him immobilized with two sets of flex cuffs.

Ethan ran his knife into the guard's throat, wiped it on his pants and took the stairs two at a time. Every door on the second floor was open except one. When he tried it, he discovered it was locked and wouldn't budge. He yanked out his 9mm, shot the lock, and kicked open the door.

In all his life, he hoped never to see another sight

like the one that greeted him. Lisa, stripped to the waist, tied to the bed, with a rivulet of blood running from one bare breast down her rib cage onto the sheets beneath her. Her face was rigid with terror. Her last scream still echoed in the air.

Standing over her, knife in hand, was Charles Mallory. He paused with one hand on her other breast, the knife poised over it. At the sound of Ethan's entrance, he spun around to face him.

Ethan might have aged since his black ops days, but his reflexes were still sharp. Without pausing, he pointed the 9mm at Mallory and squeezed off three shots. The first one was the kill shot, dead center in his forehead, but he added the other two for insurance.

Shoving the gun in the waistband of his pants, he pulled out the Tancro and sliced through Lisa's bonds. Her face was so white he was afraid she was going to faint and she was shaking so badly he thought her bones would break. He pulled her off the bed and cradled her in his arms.

"Shh, darlin'. It's all right. Everything's all right now."

She tried to push away from him. "Jamie. We have to find Jamie."

"We've got the boy." Marsh appeared in the doorway. "Ethan, we have to get the hell out of here. One of the guards said *Las Tormentas* are on their way. We got everyone we could, but there's more in the bunkhouse and they heard the commotion."

"We're set," Ethan told him." He ripped a pillowcase into strips and used them to bind Lisa's wounds. Then he pulled off the shirt he'd thrown on over his T-shirt, slid her arms into it, and buttoned two buttons. "I'll take better care of you when we get back to camp. Okay?"

She nodded.

Ethan heaved her over his shoulder and took off down the stairs. He heard the rapid staccato bursts of MP5s firing, guessing that Nick and Angel were backing around the side of the house. There were two bodies in the front hall, and two more on the wide porch. Ethan detoured around them and kept running.

The roar of gunfire followed. The resident guards didn't have suppressors on their weapons, and the sounds were magnified in the still night of the jungle.

"Go, go, go," Marsh yelled at him, running with Jamie over his shoulder. The child was flopping against his back, screaming for help.

Ethan covered the distance to the perimeter wall in seconds and heaved Lisa to the top. She rolled off and was waiting for Ethan when he climbed over.

Even in the danger of the moment, he had to admire her guts and strength. She'd been terrified and tortured yet she hadn't collapsed. She stood waiting for Marsh and her frightened child.

"It's all right," she yelled when she saw Marsh breech the wall. "I can take him."

He landed beside them, and Jamie held out his arms when he saw her.

"Mommy! You came. I knew you weren't dead."

"You and Mommy can have a reunion later," Marsh said. "Ethan, we've got to get the hell out of here. Nick and Angel are laying down cover fire, but Cortez and his men just pulled up so the game's changed. Those guys skin people alive just because they're bored. Mallory's guards are like pussycats compared to them."

"Can you run?" Ethan asked Lisa.

"I can do whatever I have to."

"All right. Come on." He grabbed her hand, and they took off running, Marsh right behind them with Jamie.

Lisa ran, heedless of the pain the jarring steps caused to her bleeding breasts. The sound of men crashing through the foliage behind them was too heavy for just their small band, and she had no intention of being caught by any of Charles's people.

Before they even reached their clearing, they heard the helicopter overhead.

"Ethan?" she yelled.

"Keep going. Don't stop." He tossed a look at Marsh as they ran.

"Nick called him in when we hit the house," Marsh said as if reading his thoughts. He should be here right about—" He looked up. "—now."

They'd reached the clearing, and sure enough, the helo was hovering. A ladder dangled from the open door, and a man crouched by it, ready to help.

"Who's that?" Ethan asked.

"Angel's brother. He was visiting and decided he'd like a little excitement."

"He got that all right." Ethan boosted Lisa up to reach the ladder. "Can you grab the rung? Start climbing and don't look down. Diego will help you at the top."

"I can do it," she told him between clenched teeth.

"Good girl. Go on, now."

As soon as Lisa reached the top, Marsh began the climb, holding tightly to Jamie. Ethan heard the firing of rifles and the soft answering sounds of the MP5s moving closer. In a moment, Nick and Angel backed into the clearing.

"Get the hell up that ladder," Nick yelled at him. "Then you can cover us."

Ethan scrambled up the ladder with more agility than he thought he still possessed. As soon as he tumbled into the cabin of the helo, he positioned himself at the door and began firing his own weapon. First Nick and then Angel made the climb. As each man reached the top, he, too, knelt and fired at the gathering mob below. Angel flinched as one of the bullets hit his leg, but he kept on coming.

The minute he threw himself on the floor, Nick yelled, "Go, go, go ".

Hogan pulled back on the collective, and they were airborne.

Chapter Nineteen

Despite the intense pain in her breasts, Lisa cradled Jamie to her as tightly as she could. He was crying against her shoulder, and her own tears ran down her cheeks onto his tousled hair. His tiny hands clutched her shirt as if he'd never let her go. She felt the same way.

She glanced behind her where Nick attended to Angel's wound.

"Is it bad?" she asked.

"Nah." Angel forced a grin. "Don't worry, pretty lady. I've had much worse."

"I'm so sorry you got hurt." She tried to smile.

"He's a tough nut," Nick told her. "Anyway, it just scraped him. I've hurt myself worse reeling in a marlin."

Lisa hiccupped a laugh. "I don't know how to thank you. All of you. You don't even know me."

Nick gave Ethan a long look. "No, but we know this big jerk sitting next to you. Guardian owes him a lot. We thought it was time to pay it back."

She felt Ethan's arm around her, his breath warm against her neck, and she wondered if it was just for show.

"We ought to take a look at those knife wounds," he told her softly.

Lisa shook her head. "I don't want Jamie to see. I

can wait."

"You've been running and climbing with two open wounds, and the front of this shirt is soaked with blood. I need to put something tighter around you"

"A—all right."

Ethan pulled thick rolls of bandages from a first aid kit, but when he tried to move Jamie a little to tend to her, the little boy just hung on tighter to his mother.

"Don't let go," he wailed.

"It's all right, sweetheart," she soothed. "Mr. Caine just has to wrap something around Mommy. I'm right here."

Ethan tied the wrapping in back as tightly as he dared. "I'm getting you to a doctor as soon as we land." He shook out two tablets from a container and handed them to her with a bottle of water. "Swallow these. You'll need them."

"Where are we going, anyway?" She tightened her arms around Jamie again, biting her lip against the pain from the pressure. She bent her head so Ethan wouldn't see, but he reached a hand under her chin and tipped up her face.

"I know you don't want Jamie to know you're hurt," he said in a low, soft voice. "But we will get you taken care of when we land."

"We're heading for Sailfish Key," Nick told her in answer to her question. "Guardian has…contacts there. Then we can go anywhere by car or boat."

He introduced the others who smiled at her in an easy manner, then went back to what they were doing.

Jamie had fallen asleep on her chest, exhausted from his ordeal, and she shifted him slightly to give herself some relief. Ethan sat with his back against the wall of the copter, his legs bracketing her as they'd done the night before. There was a warm sense of comfort in their position, a feeling of security. Which was idiotic, of course. As soon as they were back in Tampa, he'd be hiding out in his farmhouse again and she'd probably never see him.

Why did she care, anyway? He was a man with his own isolationist policy. This morning she'd wanted to talk to him about what happened between them, but now she realized the futility of that. Despite the fact that she was sure in her heart something real had clicked between the two of them, he would never acknowledge it. She needed to concentrate on getting her life and Jamie's back on track.

She was sure her son would need counseling. The last few months had to have been a nightmare for him. Being snatched away, finding out his father was alive. Held as a virtual prisoner miles away from anyone. She couldn't afford to indulge her own emotional needs when her son's were so much greater.

Anyway, in her heart of hearts, she had the feeling she'd forfeited the right to a happily ever after. She'd made so many unforgivable mistakes. If she could just get herself and Jamie through the next few years and he turned out to be a normal human being that would be enough for her. She hoped.

"What about Aaron Burke?" she asked, pushing her hair out of her face. "God, that was the shock of all time."

Ethan grunted. "I left him trussed up like a pig in the hallway. Cortez may just hack him to bits to pass the time of day."

"I can't say I'm sorry about whatever happens to

him. He was part of this all along."

"I like to think people get what they deserve," Ethan said in a quiet voice.

Lisa leaned back against him, Jamie cradled in her arms. She wasn't aware she'd dozed off until something startled her awake, and she realized it was the absence of noise and motion

Ethan bent his head to her ear. "We're here. Let Angel take Jamie while you climb out."

Jamie put up a mild protest, but they all managed to debark without problems. Lisa climbed down onto the tarmac and looked around. To her left were two enormous hangars, to her right a row of SUVs.

"Is there a regulation you all have to drive these?" she asked Nick.

He grinned. "Yes, ma'am. Part of the uniform."

"They're good anywhere," Angel explained. "Sometimes the places we need to go don't exactly have roads."

She decided that was as much as she needed to know.

Ethan led her to one of the vehicles, Marsh behind her carrying Jamie. In what seemed like seconds, they were all buckled in and Ethan was pulling away from the airfield.

"I don't think I thanked them properly," she told him. "What they did... They could all have been killed. You, too."

He shrugged. "Goes with the territory. They know I'd do the same for them."

"So where to now? I'm so exhausted I think I could sleep for a year."

"There's a doctor on the Key here that we've used

before." He paused. "That I've used before."

"Okay." She really didn't care where it was as long as they could give her something for the pain.

"He's got a little two-room hospital-type setup at his clinic," Ethan explained. "I want him to check both of you out."

"Oh, Ethan, I really want to go home."

He nodded. "And you will. But not until I'm sure you're both okay."

She was just too tired to fight with him. She leaned her head back and closed her eyes, vaguely aware of Ethan drawing Jamie into a conversation. The soothing sounds of their voices lulled her to sleep.

****

Josh arrived on Sailfish Key within hours of Nick's call. He'd been in a murderous rage when he learned the details of what happened.

"It's a damn good thing that bastard's dead," he ground out between clenched teeth. "Otherwise, I'd be down there letting him know what it feels like when someone takes a knife to him."

"We're safe now," Lisa soothed. "Please. I just want to try and get past this."

Since then, he'd been dividing his time between her and Jamie. She had been sleeping and recovering in one of the two airy patient bedrooms in the clinic where Ethan had taken her. Now she lay propped up on several pillows, the soft island breeze stirring the curtains at the window, the ceiling fan turning lazily overhead. Applications of ice had taken down the swelling in her eyes and cream had helped the bruises and the split lip. The danger of concussion had passed, and the doctor Nick had sent her to assured her she was mending well. Except for the pain where her knife wounds were healing, and the bruises on her face, the hellish escape from Quintana Roo was beginning to seem like a bad dream.

Dr. Keith Wardlow, tall and lanky with a thick shock of red hair, was possessed of a natural bedside manner. From the instant Ethan delivered her to his office, his demeanor was soothing and comforting. The only time she'd seen a change of expression was when Ethan told him how she'd been hurt. His jaw tightened, a muscle jumping in his cheek, and his eyes darkened with fury.

Right now, he was changing her dressings again.

"I've been here for three days," she pointed out. "I'm doing much better. Don't you think it's time for me to leave?"

"You're healing nicely," he told her as he spread more antibiotic cream on her wounds. He'd loaded her with antibiotics the minute he examined her and kept her wounds medicated with the cream.

"The pain isn't quite as bad as it was," she told him.

"That's always a good sign. Of course, I've been keeping you pretty well sedated, too."

"So," she prompted, "back to my question. When can I leave? I can't stay in bed forever, you know. And where's my son today?"

"I believe Ethan and your brother took him fishing."

Lisa jerked up in bed. "Fishing? Ethan is still here? And he took a child fishing?" She shook her head. "It's funny. I would have thought he'd have been out of here as soon as Josh arrived."

Keith laughed. "I know what you mean about Ethan. I've never seen him as someone particularly fond of kids." He shook his head. "Strange."

She had to agree. Ethan, the last person in the world she would have expected to relate to kids, had formed some kind of bond with Jamie. She'd been more than amazed that her son had allowed himself to be sidetracked while she was tended to and expected a real emotional crisis. But Ethan and Josh had managed to keep him occupied and distracted.

Keith cleared his throat. "I just wanted to say I'm happy Ethan was able to get you out before any worse damage was done. To either you or your son."

She shifted her eyes to the window, staring out at nothing. "Yes, I owe him a lot."

"I've known Ethan a good many years. He's given up a lot of his life to help others, and it's scarred him. But I think the right person could help him heal."

A brief flash of some deep emotion racked her. "That's a noble thought, Keith, but I'm probably not that person. I know Ethan would agree with me."

"Yes. Well. We're not always the best judge of our own lives, are we?"

"Not to be rude, but I think Ethan's business and mine is concluded. Lord." She leaned back on her pillows. "I'm sure he'll be glad to wash his hands of us once and for all. So. What about it?" she pushed. "Can I leave?"

He sighed. "I'd like you to stay at least two more days, but I know you're anxious to get back to your life. I told Ethan and your brother they could probably spring you loose tomorrow. I guess Hogan's flying you all up in the helo."

She grinned. "Jamie will love that. It's all he's talked about since we landed. But I'm glad. At least it took his mind off everything else."

"Yes. Well." He turned toward the door. "I'll tell Ethan when he gets back to make the final arrangements."

And then what?

She'd hardly seen him since the night they'd arrived. Helping Josh with Jamie gave him a perfect excuse to avoid her except for the most perfunctory of visits. Twice a day, he stopped in to check on her, then made himself scarce. At night, he seemed to disappear altogether. His actions made it plain he was pulling away from her. She forced herself not to show her disappointment or to ask where he was.

Ethan Caine was the last man she'd ever expected to form a bond with, yet there he was, sitting in a corner of her heart. And her soul. What the hell was she supposed to do?

****

Ethan drove them home from the private airfield where they landed outside of Tampa. Lisa had seldom been so glad to see any place as she was her house. She continued to be amazed at the way Jamie seemed to adjust in such a short time. Keith had told her he was a very resilient young boy, but it also had a lot to do with the way Ethan and Josh handled him during the days she was in bed and healing.

Ethan again.

He didn't get out of the car in her driveway, just waited until they'd all piled out. Josh took Jamie inside, but when Lisa realized Ethan was still sitting in the SUV, she walked back over to the driver's side window.

"Won't you come in for a while? Have a celebration drink with us?"

He shook his head. "No, you need to be by yourselves. As a family. I'll just head on home."

"We wouldn't still be a family if it weren't for you," she protested.

"I'm just glad everything turned out okay. I've still got all the stuff from your purse at the house. I'll send it along to Josh." He took his battered hat off his head and handed it to her. "Give this to Jamie, will you? He begged for it the whole time at Sailfish Key."

"Give it to him yourself,"

"No. Better if it comes from you. He can keep it as a souvenir of his great adventure."

Lisa snorted. "Yeah. Great adventure. I hope he never has another one like that. Ethan, I'll never be able to thank you enough. We owe you so much."

He shook his head. "You don't owe me anything. I told you. Josh is my friend."

"I hope I'm your friend, too." Lisa looked down at her feet. "Or maybe even a little bit more."

She wanted to find out if what happened between them meant anything, but of course, she couldn't voice her words.

Ethan was silent for so long she finally raised her eyes to his face, wondering what she'd see. Something undecipherable flashed in his deep black eyes.

"Ethan, I—"

"You don't want what's left of me, Lisa. Believe me. Finding Jamie and bringing him home helped me put some demons to rest, but there are still too many fighting for my soul."

"Maybe I could help you battle them." She searched for something, anything, but she couldn't seem to find the right words to make him stay.

"I don't think so." He looked at her for a long time as if memorizing every inch of her before he put the car in reverse. "Have a good life, Lisa. You deserve it."

And then he was gone, leaving her standing in the driveway feeling as if part of her had disappeared.

"Is Ethan gone?" Josh asked as she entered the house.

"Yes. I asked him to come in, but he said no." She turned away, afraid of what Josh would see on her face.

But he was busy getting out a celebratory bottle of wine and filling two goblets. "Damn. I just wish... He'll go back to the farmhouse and hole up again. I was hoping something about this trip would nudge him out of hiding. Make him understand that what happened on his last mission was in no way his fault. I think Nick wants to talk to him about being active at Guardian again, but he has to deal with this other issue first."

"I think Ethan's made sure his life has no room for anyone else."

Something about her tone made Josh lift his head. "Did the two of you have problems on this trip? I know Ethan can be a pain in the ass sometimes..."

"No. Nothing. He was beyond wonderful." She picked up her wine and forced a smile. "To happy endings."

"Happy endings," Josh agreed, and they clinked glasses.

This was far from the ending she wanted. She sipped at her wine, but it did nothing to ease the sharp ache in her heart.

In the days that followed, Lisa ruthlessly disciplined herself to forget about Ethan Caine and get her life back in order. The first thing she did was meet with her two law partners who'd been handling the entire case load while she tried to keep her life from disintegrating. She was more grateful than she could express for their support through her entire ordeal.

"You do so much for everyone else," Joe Giamato told her. "We were glad to be able to do something for you."

"Yes," Sally Atkins agreed. "And don't think you have to plunge right back into a full schedule." She squeezed Lisa's hand. "Take some time with Jamie. And for yourself. You've earned it."

When she left the office, she had tears of thankfulness in her eyes, grateful to have such good friends.

She held her breath waiting for news out of Quintana Roo, but as the days went by with no word of any kind, she began to relax. She was surprised no one seemed to be looking for Aaron, but maybe he'd set himself up to be out of pocket.

Maybe the bodies would rot before anyone found them, and by that time, no one would connect her with Charles again. The story of the kidnapping had long ago disappeared from news coverage so there was no notice of the fact that Jamie was safely at home again, for which she thanked God. They were finally able to exist in relative anonymity.

Lisa still battled nightmares, waking up in a cold sweat, shaking, seeing Charles standing over her and feeling the sharp edge of the knife. Her wounds had healed physically, but the mental and emotional ones would take a long time to disappear.

She insisted that Jamie have some kind of counseling. He was adjusting to life at home again, his three months of terror fading. But it was important for him to talk everything out and deal with it if he were ever to go back to being the normal happy boy he'd been. One of the therapists her law practice used was a woman with many years experience in treating traumatized children. Jamie's sessions with her seemed to be going well.

Josh was a constant presence in their lives, providing the solid grounding they needed, and she thought she was almost ready to rejoin her law partners. But there was one glaring absence she couldn't ignore. No matter how many times she stared at the telephone, Ethan didn't call.

Not that she expected him to. He'd avoided her as much as possible at Sailfish Key and told her how it was in straight talk when he drove her home. Now that everyone was back safe in Tampa, he'd crawled back into the hole she'd pulled him out of and blocked out everyone and everything. Josh said Nick was working on him, but Lisa didn't have much hope. Whatever had happened to him must have been soul searing.

But damn it! Those kisses they'd shared and—what did he call it?—recreational sex… She was convinced they meant something, if only he would let go. He could deny it all he wanted to, but she knew he felt it as much as she did. And it scared him, just like it scared her.

So she just kept hoping. And waiting.

"How's Ethan doing?" she asked Josh one night when they were having dinner together.

Josh looked at her with a strange expression. "About the same as always, I'd say. Ethan is Ethan. Although…"

He hesitated.

"Although what?" she prodded.

"I don't know." He put down his fork and looked at her. "Something. I can't put my finger on it. He just seems very…sad."

"Sad?" She cocked her head. "What do you mean?"

"I've known him a long time and seen him in a lot of moods, but never like this." He frowned. "I thought things had gone to hell when that op got fucked up. But this is, I don't know, like he's given up life. And living."

A pain stabbed her heart. "Oh, Josh."

"He hasn't even fallen into the bottle as I expected. Instead, he spends most of his time working out as if he's training for a triathlon. Or working the devil out of his system. I can't figure out which. Nick's doing his best to reach him, but I don't know if he can, either."

Lisa chewed over what Josh had said and despite her misgivings, gathered her courage, and made one desperate effort to see Ethan that turned out badly. After calling and leaving several messages on his answering machine, none of which he answered, she drove out to the farmhouse early one afternoon. Luckily, he was sitting on the porch and couldn't escape without being outright rude, although she didn't think that would bother him one bit.

She could see what Josh meant about working out. The body clad in an old T-shirt and workout shorts was even more toned than when they'd been in Mexico. His hair was still long, pulled back in a tail, but he was clean-shaven. It allowed her to see the deep grooves sorrow had carved on his face.

She climbed up onto the porch, sat down in the rocking chair next to him, and just stared at him.

"Do I have a bug on my face?" he asked at last.

"No. I was just searching for some clue as to how you could walk away from me the way you did."

He took a long swallow from the bottle of beer he was holding. "I didn't walk away, Lisa. The job was finished. We were finished. End of story."

"Tell me what we shared in Mexico was nothing more than relieving tension. Go ahead."

He tilted his head back. "What we shared in Mexico was nothing more than tension-relieving sex. Don't mistake it for some big romance."

"Liar," she rapped out. "I'm not the most experienced person in the world, but I know when something is more than just sex."

Ethan sighed. "Lisa, you have a life. Go back to it. I'm nothing but a ruined hulk of a man with a soul so damaged there's nothing to repair it. I'd only be poison for you."

"Jamie wears your hat all the time," she said, changing the subject. "It's miles too big for him, but he won't let go of it. Josh finally stuffed the headband so it wouldn't fall off."

"Good. I'm glad. I couldn't think of anyone I'd rather give it to."

They rocked in silence for another moment.

"Damn it, Ethan, I won't let you do this." She slammed her fist on the arm of the rocker.

"Do what? I'm not doing anything."

"That's the trouble." Anger rose inside her. "You'll just ignore what happened, not even give us a chance to see if we have something together. For the future. You can tell me it wasn't more than hot sex all you want, but we both know that's not the truth."

He turned his bottomless black eyes toward her. "You have a future. I don't. I just have one day after another." He finished his beer and stood up. "Go home. And stay there."

He walked into the house, leaving her behind with nothing but an empty feeling.

****

"But why can't you come and see us, Ethan?"

Ethan had come out of the house as soon as he heard the car pull into the driveway. Jamie was out of it almost before the engine stopped, running to Ethan and throwing himself at him. Ethan had little choice but to hug the boy.

Shit!

He crouched down so he was eye level with the boy.

"Our adventure is over, Jamie. I was real glad to be able to help you and your mom, but now I have to get back to my real life."

Jamie frowned at him. "What's that? And why does it mean you can't see us anymore?"

"Maybe you should ask your mom."

"She said I should ask you. And she's sad all the time," Jamie went on. "She's real unhappy."

"I think she's probably still recovering from everything that happened," Ethan pointed out, "Remember, for a long time she didn't know where you were or if you were alive."

"Nuh uh." Jamie shook his head. "Then she'd be happy, right? And I miss you, too. I thought you said we were pals?"

Ethan looked over the boy's head at Josh, sending a silent plea.

"Jamie? Come on, kiddo. I think Ethan has some place he needs to be. We'll try again when he has some free time."

"But he doesn't look busy," Jamie protested.

"I do have some place to go," Ethan siad, glad Josh had mentioned it. His heart ached at the expression on Jamie's face. If only—

Cut that out. All that has passed you by.

"Why don't you hop back in the car, kiddo," Josh suggested, "while I have a last word with Ethan. Then we'll stop for ice cream on the way home."

"O-kay."

It killed Ethan to watch this, but what could he do? He was the last person either Jamie or Lisa needed in their lives. Jamie might need a father, but he was far from the ideal candidate. He knew spending all that time with the boy at Sailfish Key was a mistake but damn! He'd just hated to let go of the little bit of pleasure in his life.

See what being selfish does for you?

"You need to forgive yourself," Josh told him in a very low voice. "You've done penance enough for ten people and none of it was your fault. Get that through your thick skull. I never thought I'd say this, but you could be the best thing ever to happen to Lisa and Jamie. Get your head out of your ass, why don't you, and start living life again. Put that in your thick head."

Ethan watched the car back out of the driveway,

Jamie's sad little face peering at him through the window. The pain in his heart was so sharp it stole his breath.

But what the hell was he supposed to do? Being noble just fucking sucked.

Chapter Twenty

If Lisa thought she was done with her fifteen minutes of fame, she was very much mistaken. It had just been the calm before the storm. Reality landed with a bang when Josh showed up on her doorstep at six-thirty in the morning waving a copy of The Tampa Bay Times.

"God, Josh." She pushed her hair out of her face and rubbed her eyes. "Don't you know some people are asleep at this hour?"

"Yeah? Well, they better wake up before the circus starts."

"What are you talking about?"

He brushed past her and headed for her kitchen. He took two mugs from the cupboard, dropped a pod into the single serving coffee maker, and pressed Start. When one mug was filled, he repeated the process with the other.

She planted herself next to him, hands on hips, eyes blazing. "Joshua Taylor, are you going to tell me just what in the hell is going on?"

He handed her one of the mugs then leaned against the counter, one leg crossed over the other. Tension lined his face.

"Aaron Burke's body's been found."

Lisa's eyes widened, and she gripped her mug so hard her knuckles were white. "His body? He was alive when we left him."

"Yeah, well, I guess not for much longer after that. Some eco-nuts wandering around in the jungle got lost and stumbled on Charles's compound. Thinking they could get directions and maybe some water, they were greeted by a site not usually included in tour books."

She drew in a quick breath. "But it's been months since we left there. Why has it taken this long for someone to find the bodies?"

"Word has it that some of Charles's business associates visited the house, but they certainly aren't the type to go running to the law."

Lisa tried to wipe from her mind the image of the bloodbath they'd left behind. "I thought maybe one of the surviving guards might have reported what happened."

"Are you kidding? They hightailed it out of there along with *Las Tormentas*. I'm sure none them wanted to risk a run-in with the *federales*. So the bodies just lay there rotting until the poor dumb tourists found them."

She sipped her coffee. "And what about Aaron?"

"According to the reports he'd been tortured before he died. Badly."

She closed her eyes and fought back the nausea clawing its way up her throat. She could just imagine what Cortez and his men had done, in an effort to get information about the disaster that greeted them.

"What else?"

"Well." Josh took a swallow of coffee. "After that, it seems every law and alphabet agency in the world landed on the *finca*. They had more people than animals crawling around the Quintana Roo for quite a while. Big jurisdictional dispute over who got what papers and records." Josh laughed. "No one seems too interested in who did the killing, though."

Lisa cupped her hands around the mug as if seeking warmth. "Do—do they know anything about Jamie? Or me?"

"Not Jamie. Charles kept him hidden so no one ever saw him except the guards, who aren't talking. Cortez and his thugs have disappeared from view. Unfortunately, though, you're number one on everybody's hit parade right now."

"Why?" She gripped the mug harder to keep her hands from shaking. "I can't tell them anything."

"Doesn't matter." Josh had finished his coffee and got up to refill his mug. "The Tampa cops are re-opening the file on Charles's death. And the shit on Aaron Burke's involvement is fodder for all kinds of speculation. You're Charles's widow. Twice. And you worked with Aaron Burke. The connection's too juicy to pass up."

He opened the newspaper he'd brought in with him and slid it over in front of her.

Her heart stumbled, and her stomach lurched as she caught the picture on the front page—Aaron, Charles, and herself. The headline was the worst. Was Lisa Mallory part of an unholy triangle? And beneath it, how deep was the so-called widow into guns and drugs?

"Oh, God. God, God, God." She closed her eyes, hoping when she opened them, she'd find out she'd been imagining things. Would this nightmare never end?

She closed her eyes and leaned back in the chair, sure she was about to faint. Then she felt Josh taking the mug out of her hands and pressing a cold cloth to her face.

"Breathe, sis. Deep breaths." He shoved her head down between her knees.

She kept it there until the spots disappeared from in front of her eyes. When she sat up again, she held the cloth to her cheeks.

"God, Josh. Where do they get their ideas?"

"Speculation. You know that. Whatever sells papers."

Her eyes filled with tears for the first time in weeks. "I'm just beginning to get my life back together."

"Aaron Burke was a larger-than-life person in this town. For him to be mixed up in something this bizarre will be front page news for a long time, and the reporters will dig for every angle."

"Mommy?"

Lisa jerked upright as Jamie's voice floated into the kitchen. Then she heard his thumping steps as he did his leaping descent to the front hall. She reached over and flipped the paper closed, then grabbed Josh's hand, her nails digging into his skin.

"I can't let this touch him," she whispered. "What am I going to do?"

"I'll take care of it. Just keep taking deep breaths."

"Hi, Mommy." Jamie leaped into her arms and squeezed her in a hug. "Why are you up so early? And why is Uncle Josh here?"

"I decided to come for a cup of coffee, sport," Josh said.

Jamie bounced into his uncle's lap. "Can we go get ice cream today?"

Josh laughed in spite of the situation. "He seems to

be recovering without any ill effects."

"Yes, and I'd like to keep it that way."

Josh set Jamie on his feet. "Ice cream, huh? I'll do better than that. I have to do some work from home for a few days. How would you like to come and be my assistant?"

Jamie's eyes widened. "Oh, wow! Yeah!" Then his face fell. He turned to Lisa. "What about school? Can I miss a couple of days, Mom? Please? Uncle Josh teaches me stuff."

Even Lisa had to laugh at that. "I can imagine what he teaches you. But I think we can break a few rules. Good boys deserve special treats."

"Thanks, Mommy." He gave her a hug and a sloppy kiss.

"Go upstairs and get dressed. Brush your teeth. I'll come help you pack in a minute." She was more than grateful to Josh for his temporary solution.

He also insisted on getting her a top-notch attorney.

"You know the cops will come calling," he pointed out. "Don't talk to anyone until you have representation. I'll get you the best person."

"A lawyer?" She was stunned. "What for?"

"Because they'll zero in on you and your involvement, so to speak, with both men."

She threw up her hands. "But that's absurd."

"I know, but it is what it is."

Josh was right. She'd barely finished her first cup of coffee before her phone began ringing off the hook and people were at her door, knocking and ringing the bell.

"Call your office and tell them you're not coming back yet," Josh told her, switching off both the telephone and the answering machine. "Explain the situation and don't answer your phone. You got a new cell, right? Text me the number. I'll call that if I want you."

Lisa almost cried to see Jamie walking away from her just when she'd found him, but she knew it would be impossible to keep him safe and sheltered at home.

For the next few days, she felt like she was under siege, as the assault continued. Her partners were, once again, more understanding than she had a right to expect. And when they began to be bombarded with calls from the police, the media, and Burke, Rivas and Doyle, they brought in a hired gun to monitor calls and chase unwelcome pests away.

Josh continued to keep Jamie at his house and both stayed away from Lisa, unwilling to put himself or the boy on the media's radar. When reporters somehow obtained Lisa's cell phone number, he bought her a new one under his name. She used it to stay in touch with people she needed to talk to.

True to his word, Josh hired Bart D'Amico, a top criminal attorney who took charge at once. His control of the situation gave Lisa her first sense of security since the news broke. She was only too willing to follow his instructions to the letter. He was like a pit bull, growling through every interview with the police. He also met with the remaining partners at Burke, Rivas and Doyle. No one knew what was said, but after that, the phone calls stopped.

But she felt like a prisoner in her own home. All the stories from Charles's death and the shocking aftermath, the coverage of Jamie's kidnapping, were recycled and became instant fodder for a scandal-hungry public. The media camped out in the street in front of her house twenty-four/seven, gathering like sharks smelling blood in the water.

"What if they find out about Ethan and me?" she asked Josh, her voice thick with desperation. "Our trip to Mexico? And the details of the kidnapping?"

"Not to worry. Ethan's buried the details so deep even someone who knows about it can't find them."

But she did worry, every minute of every day.

Reporters and photographers dogged her whenever she had to leave the house to answer a summons from the frustrated police or some mysterious agency. Bart managed to get a restraining order against the media, ordering them to stay at least fifty feet away from her at all times. But she saw it as a hollow victory because they didn't actually leave. They simply backed away and lay in wait, monitoring her in shifts.

She stopped going to the grocery store, relying on Bart to get food to her. She couldn't stand to watch television, and nothing she did helped to distract her. She was sure she was slowly going mad.

"I can't do this anymore," she told Josh on the phone. "My life is not my own. I hardly sleep, and when I do, I have terrible nightmares. Will it ever end?"

"I've been thinking," he told her. "You need to get out of there. Bart can handle the cops. They've squeezed every drop of blood out of you they can anyway. And the media will give up if they can't get even a sniff of you."

"How can I possibly get away without the vultures all over me?" she cried. "And where would I go? I can't invade someone else's life. Or subject anyone to this…this absurd spectacle."

"I have an idea. Let me get back to you."

Two hours later, he called back. "Leave the back door unlocked tonight and all the lights out in the house," he told her. "Let the media think you've gone to bed. I've got someone who'll sneak you out of there and pulverize anyone who gets in the way if necessary. But if we do this as slick as I think we can, no one will even know you're gone."

"What? Who? What's happening?" Her brain was trying to absorb what he was saying.

"Do you trust me?" he asked.

"Yes. Of course."

"Then just put on something dark and easy to move in. Pack nothing. You can buy whatever you need."

"Where am I going?" She was pacing, the old habit having returned. "And won't the police think I've skipped town?"

"You let Bart handle that. Just be ready sometime after ten o'clock. That's all you need to know right now."

In the early evening, Lisa showered and dressed in black jeans and a long sleeved black shirt. She pulled her hair into a ponytail and found an old black baseball cap Josh had left one time. She choked down part of a sandwich, cleaned up the kitchen, turned out all the lights, and sat down to wait. The only light in the house came in the windows obliquely from the street lamp just outside.

Time dragged until she thought she'd go crazy. At least a dozen times, she picked up the cell phone to call Josh, then put it down again. He'd said to trust him. He'd taken care of her thus far. She couldn't start questioning him now.

The LED on the microwave clock read five after ten when she heard the faint click of the latch at the back door and the creak it made when it opened. She sat frozen at the kitchen table, wondering who in the hell Josh had sent to spirit her away.

A tall, lean figure, outlined by the filtered street light, filled her doorway, and her heart turned over.

"I understand you need a little help getting out of here." Ethan's warm, deep voice wrapped itself around her like a comforter.

Without thinking, she leaped up from the chair and threw herself into his arms.

Chapter Twenty-One

Lisa had never been so glad to see another human being in her life. The tears she hadn't allowed herself to shed through the entire nasty business poured from her eyes and ran down her face. She leaned into Ethan's chest, soaking his shirt, her shoulders heaving, her body shaking with the release of tension. His arms held her to his body, his big hands rubbing her back in a soothing motion.

At last, she lifted her head and gave him a watery smile. "Just what you were waiting for, right? A weepy woman blubbering all over you."

His mouth crooked up in a faint grin. "Saves me from washing the shirt. Here." He pulled a folded white handkerchief from his pocket and handed it to her.

She took it and mopped her face with it, then blew her nose. "I'll wash it for you before I give it back," she promised in a tremulous voice.

"Don't worry about it."

"Oh, Ethan. Everything's such a mess. My life is a nightmare, and I feel like I'm going crazy."

"I know." He put his hands on her shoulders and moved her a step away from him, his eyes studying her face. "You look like hell."

She gave a shaky laugh. "You sure know how to flatter a girl."

He pulled her back into his arms, holding her as if

he'd never let her go. "Lisa, Lisa, Lisa. What am I going to do? No matter what I did, I couldn't get you out of my mind."

Her heart skipped. Coming from Ethan that was quite an admission. "I've thought about you, too."

He looked down at her face. "We have to talk, but not until I get you out of here. This garbage you're going through is just so much bullshit. Got your purse?"

She nodded.

"Come on, then."

Dressed in black as they both were, it was easy for them to blend into the night. With Bart's restraining order in place, they were able to move through her backyard and her neighbor's until they reached the street in the next block. Ethan pulled her against his side, and they walked with his arm tightly around her, two lovers out for an evening stroll. In the middle of the block, away from streetlights, a familiar black SUV sat waiting, and in seconds, they were pulling away from the curb.

Lisa leaned back against the seat and let out a breath of relief. "You don't know how glad I am to see you. When Josh told me someone was coming to get me, you were the last person I expected to show up."

"Yeah, well, a week ago I would have said the same thing." He reached over and took her hand. "Your brother doesn't mince words when he has something to say."

She gave a weak laugh. "Don't I know it."

"And of course, Nick had to add his twenty-five cents worth."

"So what did they say that got you here tonight?"

"Later. After we get where we're going."

They drove in silence through the quiet streets of North Tampa. Lisa studied him, noticing that he was cleanly shaven once again, his hair was pulled back in a neat ponytail, and what she could see of his black shirt actually looked clean. Her heart tripped. Were these all signs of something? Did the fact he'd come for her himself mean he'd changed his mind about them? She hardly dared to let herself hope.

A hundred thoughts rattled through her brain. She had so many questions she wanted to ask, but for now, she was just grateful to be free from the prison her house had become and sitting close to Ethan. And at least they were together. Maybe for as long as this lasted, she could figure out a way to make him take a different look at the way things were between them. The truth was, she missed him like crazy and so did Jamie.

They took Interstate 275 through downtown Tampa and crossed Tampa Bay on the Howard Frankland Bridge, passing through St. Petersburg to the beach area. Ethan held her hand throughout the entire ride.

A sign. Please let it be a sign.

Eventually, they pulled into a marina not unlike the one in Cancun.

A man—another of Ethan's silent guardians, she guessed—met them at the gate and the two shook hands.

"You're all set," he told them.

Ethan nodded and led her along the pier to a berth where a sleek cabin cruiser rode gently on the water. He jumped onto the deck, then reached out to help her come aboard.

"Something from another friend?" she asked.

He shook his head. "Mine, as a matter of fact. I keep it for when I can't stand being on land." He moved forward to the bridge and motioned for her to join him. "Come sit up here with me until we get where we're going. Then we'll talk. Okay?"

She nodded.

The man had followed them and now cast off the ropes holding the cruiser in place. Ethan turned on the engines and the running lights, and they moved slowly out into the Gulf of Mexico. She watched him silently, drinking in the sight of him, storing up images in case this was only temporary.

They'd been chugging along on the calm waters for about half an hour when he pulled into a quiet cove, killed the engines, and dropped the anchor. When the boat was secured, he pulled her into his arms with a hug she was sure would break her ribs. His kiss was just as ferocious, devouring her mouth, invading it, his tongue like a live wire scorching the sensitive insides of her lips.

Lisa clung to him like a drowning person, pressing herself against him as hard as she could. She wanted his heat, his strength, his…everything. She wanted to beg him never to leave her. But Ethan had the lead now. She'd wait to hear what he had to say.

At length, the kiss broke and he cradled her against him, the feel of his hard body like a sanctuary. The familiar touch of his hands wiped away the fear and anxiety she'd been living with every day. If she never moved from this place, this position, she'd be happy.

"Lisa." His voice was gentle but firm.

Her stomach knotted. Would she hate what he had to say? Surely, he wouldn't go through this elaborate scheme just to give her another farewell speech.

He led her to the bench on one side of the bow. When he picked her up and cuddled her in his lap, she began to breathe a little easier.

He cleared his throat. "This is hard for me to get out, so just let me say it all before you interrupt, okay?"

She nodded and pressed her head against his shoulder.

"I've lived alone a long time. By choice. My life hasn't been full of what you'd call sunshine and blue skies. Far from it. I did and saw things that made me want to run away from the world." He sighed. "But I was a solid Marine and the same for Guardian. I thought things were the same when I got tapped for the black ops group, but I forgot about politics. They'll kill you faster than anything else."

She wound her fingers through his. "Tell me."

He let out a long sigh. "We were on a mission in Africa. There was a man on the staff of this particular general who was feeding us information so we knew when bloodshed was about to happen. Our job was to extract him as efficiently as possible."

"So what happened?"

"Many areas of Africa are rich in resources that, if used properly, could put these countries on solid footings. Of course, the despotic rulers can't have that so they manipulate events so thing impinge on their power. They depend on the false information they feed the United States to provide help for them." He let out a slow breath. "And one senator, who was privy to our mission, was getting his share for feeding information to those despots to keep them in power. He found out about the mission and had a trap set. The man we were supposed to extract was killed, along with several people on his staff and almost everyone on my team."

"Oh, my god," she whispered. "But Ethan, there was nothing you could have done. You were betrayed."

"Try telling yourself that when everyone around you is being killed."

She pressed herself against his body and reached up to cup his cheek. "It wasn't your fault. I want you to keep telling yourself that."

"I think I'll keep seeing those bodies for the rest of my life." He shook his head. "Anyway, I crawled back into my hole and pulled it in with me. If not for Jamie, I might still be there. There's no expiration date on bad dreams or the solid grip they have on you."

"Don't you think I know that?" she challenged. "You have no idea how many nights I closed my eyes and all I'd see is Charles Mallory. The things he'd done to me—"

She shuddered, and he hugged her a little tighter, rubbing her back with his big palm. "I know that. So I know you understand what I go through. But I really didn't think you needed someone else's nightmares blended with your own."

"Shouldn't that be my decision as well?" A spark of anger rippled through her.

"Maybe so," he went on. "But you've had all these years of hell, and you deserve a good man, the best man available. Someone who can bring light and sunshine into your life after all the darkness you've lived through. I wasn't sure I could do that. I've lived so long in darkness myself, and I didn't want to suck you down into it with me." He shifted her slightly so he could look into her face. "Then Josh and Nick came out and talked to me for a long time. One thing they convinced me of. If I spend the rest of my life hiding away from everyone and everything, I won't be honoring the sacrifice those people made to get things done."

"That is very true."

He cupped her cheek and tilted her face up to him. "And if I'm going to have to rejoin the human race a little at a time, I don't think I can do it without you and Jamie. They made me see there was something between us. Said they were tired of sitting by while the two of us ruined our lives for no good reason. Told me I owed you the right to make that choice for yourself. I guess they're about the only people who could look me in the eye and see what's going on in my head. What I really feel."

"And how do you feel?" She looked down at her hands, almost afraid to hear the answer.

"That's a question it took me a long time to answer." He absently stroked her hair. "Remember when you asked me why I agreed to help you find Jamie and bring him home? I ducked the answer then because it sounded so self-serving."

Lisa started to say something but thought better of it.

"I had some convoluted notion that, if I could save your child, I could save myself, redeem the soul I thought I'd lost. Maybe find some of those dead ideals." He shifted her on his lap so his lips were against her forehead, and he feathered light kisses across her skin.

"I know," she began, doing her best to ignore the hard thickness of his cock pressing into her bottom.

Ethan pressed a finger to her lips. "But it did make

a difference. Helping you, rescuing him—that gave me the first good feeling I've had since we lost all those agents."

"What you did, Ethan…" She struggled for words "Saving Jamie—and me—had to balance out a lot of the nightmares for you. Maybe there were people you couldn't save before, but this time you did. That counts for a lot."

"Since that night in the tent, since we've been back, I've done nothing but fight the way I feel about you. You were right when you said it was more than a physical exercise. Still, I didn't think I had the right to bring anyone into the mess that was my life."

"I'll tell you again, that isn't only your choice."

"Your brother and Nick made me see that, too. They could sense what was going on with me. Josh has always been able to dig out my secrets better than anyone else. He told me I finally had a chance to catch the brass ring, and I was a damn fool to throw something away without even talking to you about it first." He smiled down at her. "But someone else made a better argument."

"Someone else?" Lisa frowned. "Who?"

"A young man who told me he and his mother really need someone to look after them. They seem to keep getting into trouble on their own."

Lisa's jaw dropped. "Jamie? Where did you see Jamie?"

One corner of his mouth turned up in a grin. "Josh has been bringing him out to the farmhouse a lot while you've been hiding from the media. At first, I was, shall we say, less than hospitable. But damn. It's hard to be cranky with that kid around. That son of yours is a very bright young man."

She laughed. "I think so, but then I'm his mother."

"Besides, I didn't know how else to get my hat back." Ethan's faced sobered. "Josh told me he's also been asking if there's any way to change his name from Mallory. Said he didn't want to be related to anyone who was so bad to him and his mother. Serious, adult thoughts for someone so young."

Lisa's throat closed and tears choked her. "I didn't realize…God. Charles must have really done a number on him. What did you tell him?"

"I told him I had a solution, and if he agreed with it, I'd talk it over with you."

"And what's that?"

Ethan turned her face so his eyes held hers, keeping nothing from her, seeking answers to unspoken questions. "I still wonder if I have the right to ask you this, but I swear, if you say yes, I'll spend the rest of my life doing my very best to make you happy. Marry me, Lisa. Let me adopt Jamie." His voice was stiff with tension, his body tense, as if braced for her rejection. "I love you, you know. I'm such a damn fool. I was willing to throw it away to save you." He shook his head. "But whatever I've got to give is yours. If you're willing to take a chance on me."

She was so stunned she couldn't find her voice.

"Hey, if I'm rushing things just let me know." Ethan sounded unsure of himself, a strange condition for him. "I can—"

The tears broke loose again and ran down her face, and she swiped at them with the back of her hand. She looked into his eyes and saw years of pain branded there. But she also saw something else. Hope. Hope for a new start to a new life. With her and Jamie.

"Oh, Ethan." Her voice was none too steady. "I'll take whatever you can give me. I love you, and I want to be with you. I'm no prize package, either. I still have my own nightmares that won't seem to leave me. But we can help each other, can't we?"

He kissed her, just a soft touch of his lips to hers, and she could feel the heavy beat of his heart thumping against her.

"So is that a yes?" His voice still held a touch of uncertainty.

Lisa threw her arms around his neck and hugged him tightly. "Yes. Yes, yes, yes."

He let out a huge sigh of relief. "All right then. Josh is bringing Jamie here tomorrow. I thought we'd cruise around for a few days to interesting places. Let Bart handle things in Tampa until the media circus dies down. Get married along the way. What do you think?"

"I think that's the best idea I've heard in a long time."

The kiss he gave her then was one full of passion and promise. "That's tomorrow. Right now I've got other things on my mind."

"Oh, you do? I'll bet I can guess what they are."

He put his mouth to her ear, his breath warm against the skin. "I have a great big king-sized bed on this boat. I thought maybe we could start our celebration down there."

"That's the best idea you've had yet," she told him.

"All right, then." He lifted her in his arms. "Let's go start the rest of our lives right now."

Desiree Holt

About the Author

Known as the oldest living author of erotic romance, Desiree Holt has produced more than two hundred titles in nearly every subgenre of romance fiction. Her stories are enriched by her personal experiences, her characters by the people she meets.

After fifteen ears in the great state of Texas, she relocated back to Florida to be closer to members of her family and a large collection of friends. Her favorite pastimes are watching football, reading, and researching her stories. She lives with her three cats, who love to sit with her when she writes.

Desiree loves to hear from readers.
www.facebook.com/desireeholtauthor
www.facebook.com/desiree01holt
Twitter @desireeholt
Pinterest: desiree02holt
Google: https://g.co/kgs/6vgLUu
www.desireeholt.com
www.desiremeonly.com

~*~

To chat with Desiree Holt and other Wild Rose Press authors of erotic romance, join us at
www.groups.yahoo.com/group/thewilderroses.

Also Available
from The Wild Rose Press, Inc.
and major retailers.

Moving Target
Guardian Security Book One
By Desiree Holt

They're trying to kill her, and she doesn't know why...

Kathryn Burke knows only that she has to get far away as fast as she can. In a frantic, cross-country odyssey, she transforms from pliable Kathryn to feisty, determined Kate Griffin, staying one step ahead of the killers on her trail. Then Fate delivers her into the hands of a dark knight with a tortured past. The safety he offers is as tempting as he is.

After having his perfect life ripped apart, recluse Quinn sees protecting Kate as his chance for redemption. He never plans on wanting the guarded beauty, never mind falling for her. Denying the explosive chemistry between them is useless, and as danger closes in, he must fight to expose the killer or risk history repeating itself.

This book was previously published under the title Target but has been heavily revised.

Silencing Memories

Guardian Security Book Two

By Desiree Holt

Just when architect Lindsey Ferrell thinks she's gotten her life back on track, the terrible nightmares return, and out of nowhere, a stalker sends a note to her office. Photos follow, then emails, and she can't dismiss the threat any longer. Hiring security seems the logical answer, but there's nothing logical about her body's reaction to the sinfully sexy expert bent on keeping her safe.

Guardian Security partner Nick Vanetta believes there's more behind the situation than a simple fixation, and he wonders if the answer is buried somewhere in her past. As they dig deeper into her family history, the sizzling attraction between them burns hotter and the job becomes much more than playing bodyguard to this headstrong woman. To protect the woman he loves, he must find the stalker…before it's too late.

Killing Lies

Guardian Security Book Three

By Desiree Holt

After her husband was killed and she lost her unborn child, Sarah Madison believed she'd never find love and happiness again. Instead, she has channeled all her energy into her job as assistant to the sexy CEO of Guardian Security. When he proposes a marriage of convenience, the chance to become a mother is tempting, and so is her new prospective husband. His only flaw—the distance he keeps between himself and his sweet little daughter.

Reno Sullivan's life is a mess. His first marriage was based on a lie, and the fiery death of his wife left him to raise a baby—a constant reminder of his wife's deceit. He desperately needs someone to mother the child and take charge of his personal life, and his no-nonsense assistant is perfect for the job. Unfortunately, the alluring woman in the bedroom next to his chips away at his determination to maintain the hands-off clause in their agreement and the ice around his heart.

A near-tragedy and Reno's fear of love could kill Sarah's hopes of turning their fake marriage into happily ever after…

Also Available
from The Wild Rose Press, Inc.
and major retailers.

Running Scared
Guardian Security Book Four
By Desiree Holt

When computer program designer Zoraya "Zoe" Lombardo wakes up next to her business partner's dead body with a gun in her hand and no memory of what happened, the first thing she does is run. Next, she calls the one person she trusts to help her—the man she walked away from two years ago. He's not as bossy as she remembers, but he's sexier than ever. She made a mistake not listening to his warnings, and she's more than willing to kiss and make up...if she can just stay alive long enough.

Zak Delaney, partner in Guardian Security, never expected to hear from his ex-fiancée again. After Zoe left, it took him a long time to put himself back together. Now, he must cast aside his hurt and anger in order to protect her. He'll have to rely on his resources at Guardian to clear her name and use every ounce of his self-control not to fall for her charms again. But as danger closes in, he will have to learn to trust Zoe as much as she trusts him or face losing her again...and this time for good.